PRAISE FOR *THE BLEEDING*

SHORTLISTED for the CWA International Dagger

'A gripping story of murder and black magic ...Gustawsson slowly weaves together three seemingly disparate strands of her narrative with a skill that shows why she is such an admired crime writer in her native France' *The Times* BOOK OF THE MONTH

'Bewitching and wonderfully Gothic'
Sunday Express Book of the Year

'A wonderfully dark and intricately woven historical thriller spanning three generations, *The Bleeding* will have you hooked from the very first page' B.A. Paris

'This novel is a whirlpool that draws you irresistibly into levels of darkness so much deeper than you can possibly be ready for' Ambrose Parry

'Wonderfully dark and creepy, with a superb twist in its tail!' James Oswald

'Begins with a truly macabre and ritualistic crime that leads back to mysteries in Belle Époque Paris and 1949 Post-War Quebec. Intriguingly dark and vivid, and so cleverly told through three different time frames' Essie Fox

'I was hooked from the first page – a stunning and beautifully written gothic thriller full of atmosphere, intrigue and delight' Alexandra Benedict

'A dark world of elegance and grotesque ... mesmeric' Matt Wesolowski

'What a brilliant, brilliant book ... the last chapters knocked me sideways, and it's a long time since that's happened' Lisa Hall

'Harrowing, compelling, haunting, vivid, twisty and shocking!' Noelle Holten

PRAISE FOR JOHANA GUSTAWSSON

LONGLISTED for the CWA International Dagger
WINNER of the Balai de la Découverte
WINNER of the Nouvelle Plume d'Argent Awards

'A satisfying, full-fat mystery' *The Times*

'Assured telling of a complex story' *Sunday Times*

'Dark, oppressive and bloody, but it's also thought-provoking, compelling and very moving' *Metro*

'A bold and intelligent read' *Guardian*

'Utterly compelling' *Woman's Own*

'A must-read' *Daily Express*

'A real page-turner, I loved it' Martina Cole

'Gustawsson's writing is so vivid, it's electrifying. Utterly compelling' Peter James

'Cleverly plotted, simply excellent' Ragnar Jónasson

'Bold and audacious' R.J. Ellory

'Gritty, bone-chilling and harrowing – it's not for the faint of heart, and not to be missed' Crime by the Book

'A relentless heart-stopping masterpiece, filled with nightmarish situations that will keep you awake long into the dark nights of winter' *New York Journal of Books*

THE BLEEDING

ABOUT THE AUTHOR

Born in Marseille, France, and with a degree in Political Science, Johana Gustawsson has worked as a journalist for the French and Spanish press and television. Her critically acclaimed Roy & Castells series, including *Block 46, Keeper* and *Blood Song*, has won the Plume d'Argent, Balai de la découverte, Balai d'Or and Prix Marseillais du Polar awards, and is now published in nineteen countries. A TV adaptation is currently under way in a French, Swedish and UK co-production. *The Bleeding* was a number-one bestseller in France and is the first in a new series. Johana lives in Sweden with her Swedish husband and their three sons. Follow her on Twitter @JoGustawsson and Facebook, www. facebook.com/johana.gustawsson.

ABOUT THE TRANSLATOR

David Warriner grew up in deepest Yorkshire, has lived in France and Quebec, and now calls British Columbia home. He translated Johanna Gustawsson's *Blood Song* for Orenda Books, and his translation of Roxanne Bouchard's *We Were the Salt of the Sea* was runner-up for the 2019 Scott Moncrieff Prize for French-English translation. Follow David on Twitter @givemeawave and on his website: wtranslation.ca.

Also by Johana Gustawsson and available from Orenda Books

Block 46
Keeper
Blood Song

THE BLEEDING

JOHANA GUSTAWSSON

Translated by David Warriner

**ORENDA
BOOKS**

Orenda Books
16 Carson Road
West Dulwich
London SE21 8HU
www.orendabooks.co.uk

This paperback edition first published in the United Kingdom
by Orenda Books, 2023
First published in the United Kingdom by Orenda Books, 2022
Originally published in French as *Te tenir la main pendant que tout brûle*
by Calmann-Lévy, 2021
Copyright © Calmann-Lévy, 2021
English translation © David Warriner, 2022

A catalogue record for this book is available from the British Library.

Hardback ISBN 978-1-914585-26-5
Paperback ISBN 978-1-914585-27-2
eISBN 978-1-914585-28-9

Typeset in Garamond by typesetter.org.uk
Hand illustration vector created by rawpixel.com – www.freepik.com
Printed and bound by CPI Group (UK) Ltd, Croydon CR0 4YY

For sales and distribution, please contact info@orendabooks.co.uk

For Eva,
my Catalan angel

'I've wrapped my arms around you
And I love you so, I quiver'
—Louis Aragon
(Translated by David Warriner)

Author's Note

While the story Maxine, Lina and Lucienne tell in these pages is straight out of my imagination, the facts and anecdotes that inspired the appearance of several women and men of renown in the story, the likes of Catherine de Médici, Victor Hugo, Arthur Conan Doyle, Goya, Rembrandt, Eusapia Palladino and Émile-Jules Grillot de Givry, are borrowed from the great and only too real book of history.

1
Maxine
2002

My car skips off the paved road and sways like a boat set afloat. I'm navigating the potholes one stomp on the accelerator at a time. *Bloody hell.* The tires are screeching, biting into the gravel and its coating of frost. Spitting crud onto the verge, then crunching back on track.

The Caron place is at the end of this bumpy driveway, cut as straight as a matchstick through the heart of a wood as thick as a fleece. Nestled in a blanket of snow at the centre of a clearing, it looks like the pupil of a lifeless eye: still, dark, ringed in white.

I lift my foot off the pedal to slide over a patch of black ice without losing control of the car again. I think about Hugo. I've had to leave him in his pram. I asked Charlotte to take him out, like I always do after his mid-morning nap. She looked at me as if I was out of my mind. I wonder what happened to my kind, gentle, tender Charlotte.

A hot flush makes me regret keeping my parka on for the drive. Jumping into the car earlier, Marceau barking orders into the phone with her usual charm, I didn't have time to take it off. I wipe a droplet of sweat from my upper lip. I think about the indelible rings in the folds of my grey sweater, the beads of perspiration running between my breasts that suggest I have a baby due for a feed. The greasy, greying roots I'm hiding under my woolly toque.

It had to be me they called. *Me.*

A marked Sûreté du Québec patrol car is parked right in front of the entrance with the arrogance a police badge often grants. Two uniforms are bending over the porch steps, as if they're mooning at me.

They straighten up and turn around at the sound of my involuntary skid, and wave madly as if to stop me. I feel like I should remind these imbeciles I'm not completely blind. Another two bright sparks, here to serve and protect.

I park off to the side, zip my parka up to the chin and release a heavy breath as I open the driver's door. The air feels like a freezer on my face. With a grimace I tug the hat down over my ears and hunker my way over, head down against the wind.

'Lieutenant Grant!' I announce, having to yell to make myself heard.

I flash my badge, but they don't even bother to look at it.

'She's refusing to move, lieutenant,' the uniform on the right says. She sounds apologetic.

I take a step closer and Mrs Caron's face comes into view, in profile. The old schoolteacher is sitting on the porch, head turned to my car, shoulders cloaked in a survival blanket.

'She won't even put anything on her feet. She's been screaming,' the uniform tells me. 'You should have heard her.' She rolls her gaze skyward as I eye the black socks resting on the snow-covered step.

Mrs Caron's face is spotted and streaked with brownish spatters that span her wrinkles and bridge the cracks in her blue, chilled lips. Stray strands of her pale bob lie matted at her temples and ears like greasy breadsticks. A veil of dried blood stretches over her skin like a mask.

'We've managed to wrap her fingers like you asked, ma'am, but that's all,' the uniform continues.

Wrap her fingers. What *have* these country plods been watching?

I crouch down beside the woman who taught generations of children in Lac-Clarence to read and write.

'Mrs Caron? It's Maxine Grant. I'm here. I'm here now. What's happened, Mrs Caron?'

2
Maxine
2002

'Mrs Caron?'

The schoolteacher won't take her eyes off my car. She runs her tongue over her lips, erasing some of the brown splotches. She doesn't react to the taste of her husband's blood. One of the uniforms pulls the blanket back over her shoulders, and she doesn't push away his hand. I'm not there; no one else is there. And neither is she, really.

I get to my feet; my right knee creaks, my left nearly gives way under me.

'Shall I walk you through, ma'am?'

'Lieutenant Grant.'

'Yes, sorry ma'am. Lieutenant Grant.'

I nod, repressing the urge to slap some sense into her. Probably not the best thing for me to do to mark my return from mat leave. And slowly, I climb the porch steps, taking care not to step in the bloody prints Mrs Caron has left.

'Right there, ma'a ... Lieutenant,' says the muppet as soon as we're inside.

Her posture makes it clear to me she has no intention of going any further. She's pointing to the only room with a light on, to our right, eyes sweeping over the scarlet footprints bleeding into the pink carpet that rolls like a tongue towards the French doors of the lounge.

I pull on the pair of gloves I grabbed before I left, and press myself against the wall as I creep down the hallway. The sweetish, ferrous stench turns my stomach. Nine months away from any encounters with death, that's all it's taken for me to forget the smell of it. Nine months nose to nose with a newborn life, which, for the record, is nowhere near as angelic as the sales pitch promises. Ugh, the nappies overflowing with unspeakable filth and the sickening spit-ups.

I know what's waiting for me in this room and still I freeze at the door. My eyes sweep across the light pine floor to the stone chimney breast, up the pale-yellow walls to the decorative ceiling and its mouldings, over the corduroy velvet sofas, the tasselled cushions, the flowery curtains, the plush oriental rug, the glass coffee table, the side tables. Smears of blood, droplets and spurts sully, criss-cross and disfigure the room.

Pauline Caron's husband, whose torso is now nothing more than a heap of grotesque strips of flesh, is lying in a pool of blood muddled by hand and footprints. The blood is soaking into the rug and it's licking at the chimney breast and the legs of the sofas. The footprints are telling. Mrs Caron has walked out of the room where her husband has just died.

Oh, God.

I swallow back the bile, the acid rising in my throat, and suck in a breath of foul air. Nausea has me in its grasp. I tilt my head back, hoping gravity will help me avoid throwing up like a rookie. After twenty years on the force, that would be hard to explain.

'Ah, there you are, Sweet Maxine, love of my life!'

Startled, I turn around, unable to muster a smile or find that laugh my partner always squeezes out of me.

'Hey, Chickadee,' I reply to the man who stands a good four inches taller than my five-eleven.

'You're glowing,' he says with a wink.

'Give me a break, Jules.'

'No, seriously, Grant, motherhood at the peak of a midlife crisis really suits you. Don't mind if I don't give you a proper kiss hello here, it's kind of off-putting, eh?' he says, pulling me into his arms, his full beard cushioning my cheek, before planting a kiss on the top of my toque.

He pulls away from me with a grimace. 'Bloody hell...'

'You can say that again.'

Four soft-footed crime-scene technicians approach us, zipped up in their white coveralls. They raise a hand to me. My name ricochets between them. I respond with a nod of the head and a circumstantial smile.

'Have you seen Marceau?' Jules continues.

'Not yet. But I've had her barking at me down the phone.'

'Oh, lucky you.'

Jules swallows audibly. 'I saw the wife on my way in. She's in shock. Did you manage to get a word out of her?'

I shake my head.

'Right, back to it, then?' he carries on.

'Oh, so you're giving the orders now, are you?' I say, in jest.

'No two ways about it, you're like a deer in the headlights. Makes a change from nappies, eh?'

The nausea's swelling inside me. 'Almost makes me miss them, you know.'

'Are we off then, or should we stick around like a couple of spare parts? We can come back and take a closer look when they're done, right?'

'You really want to get out of here, don't you, Chickadee?' I say, forcing a smile.

'You have no idea.'

3
Maxine
2002

We walk out of the lounge to find Cécilia Lopez, our medical examiner, fighting her way into her crime-scene coveralls in the hallway.

'Grant?' Her made-up eyes look at me in surprise, as she continues her struggle with the suit. 'I thought you were coming back next week? How's that little cherub of yours? What a cutie pie,' she smiles, with a shake of her head. 'When are you going to let me take him off your hands for a while?'

'Don't tell me your six grandkids aren't enough for you?' I reply, suddenly lulled by the scent of Hugo, recalling the joy of nestling my nose in the crook of his little neck.

The withdrawal clutches me by the bosom.

'They're at the age when they only come to see me when they want something. They'll scarf down a slice of cake and leave crumbs everywhere except on their plate, chug a can of pop, give me a quick hug or an air-kiss on the cheek, all in the hopes that I'll pull out a banknote for them, then they go back to their video games. You get the picture.' She pauses to yank at her zip. 'Honestly, I don't know what the hell they think they're playing at with these suits. This one's a medium and look at me, I'm stuffed into it like a great big sausage. Like I need to display any more rolls of fat.'

She straightens up and pulls the hood over her tomboy cut

streaked with grey. 'The young guns out front said it's a hot mess in there, right?'

'More like cold cuts at the deli counter.' Jules wrinkles his nose. 'Apparently, his better half really stuck it to him.'

'Apparently,' I insist, thinking about the schoolteacher still sitting out on her frozen front steps.

'I managed to persuade her to get into the ambulance,' Cécilia tells me, as if she can read my mind. 'Any longer out there in the cold and she'd be losing toes.'

'How did you do it?' Jules asks. 'No one else could get her to move a muscle.'

'I did the same thing I do with teenagers: I didn't ask her anything, that way she couldn't say no. I just took her by the arm and walked her to the ambulance. End of story. She went along without a word. Have you had a chance to question her? Do you know what happened?'

I shake my head. 'She hasn't opened her mouth, Céci, not a syllable. She's not even responding to questions. No reaction at all. She's completely catatonic.'

'I noticed the cuts on her hands and the blood smears on her clothes, so chances are, it was her who tore her nearest and dearest to shreds. But don't quote me on that until I hear what he has to say for himself,' she says, with a tip of the chin towards Philippe Caron's corpse. 'This is Caron the Montreal university professor, isn't it? The famous historian, author, and what have you?'

I nod and can't help but gulp.

'You're not used to the smell anymore,' Céci smiles. 'Right, I'll get started. You know where to find me.'

She turns on her heels and walks away, her hushed steps accompanied by the swish-swish of her coveralls.

'Want to come over for dinner with us tonight?' Jules offers as we pull off our gloves and he removes his shoe covers. 'You can bring the little guy if you like, or would that mess up his bedtime routine? Marius can't wait to mollycoddle him. And see you too, of course. I imagine Charlotte's too caught up in being a teenager.'

I open my mouth to reply, not knowing how to refuse his invitation.

'Grant!' My name sounds like a primal growl.

Reluctantly I go and stand in the doorway, where my gaze plunges into the pool of blood surrounding Philippe Caron's body.

'Yes, Simon. I'm here. What's up?'

'Get suited up, you two, and come have a look at this,' the crime-scene technician says.

He's leaning over an ebony table in the shape of a hexagon. The table top is a tray and it's now sitting on the floor. Céci gets up and goes over to join him.

'Oh, shit,' says Jules through gritted teeth.

We each grab some coveralls from the box the crime-scene team has left by the front door and pull them on – more easily than Céci did.

'What have you found, Simon?' I ask, stepping around the body.

'I ... I'm not sure. I was collecting a blood smear from the edge of the table and I nearly tipped the top over when I pressed against it. I had no idea the thing came off. I didn't realise it was a tray, I mean. When I went to put it back in place, I noticed there was something inside ... something inside the table, or the chest, whatever you want to call it.'

Making our way over, we lean over the table in a slow, coordinated movement, the way you peer into the crib of a baby who's fallen asleep at last. Internally, I wince.

'What the hell is it?' Jules says.

'It looks like a glass dome,' I reply, eyes glued to the object.

'No, the thing inside the glass?'

His question hangs, suspended, between us.

'Have you taken photos? Can we take it out?' I ask Simon.

'It's all right. Go ahead.'

I reach my latex-gloved hands around the sides of the glass dome and touch the bottom of the table. My fingers curl around something that feels as dense as wood. It must be a plinth, a base of some sort. The dome is attached to it. I bend my knees to steady myself and delicately extract the thing.

'What the hell…?'

Jules doesn't finish what he's saying. None of us have any desire to put what we can see into words. We stare at the thing as if we've just reached into a cradle and pulled out a monster.

'It's a hand,' Céci replies. 'A hand,' she repeats, in a whisper.

4
Lina
1949

I knew I was playing with fire. But if I had kept turning the other cheek, as that imbecile Father Dion suggested at confession, those two witches would have kept getting nastier. I had to spend the whole lunch hour kneeling on sacks of rice, but honestly it was worth every grain that dug into my skin.

But now, of course, I won't be laughing so much.

'For God's sake!' I cry, trying to extricate my boots from another drift of snow.

What was I thinking, taking a shortcut through the woods? I'm sinking up to my knees. My toes are frozen and I'm shivering to the tip of my hat. I passed that garden house thing a while back. I can't be far away now.

Mother is right: sometimes I can't see further than the end of my nose, which is a block of ice right now.

When she was called in to see Mrs Morin, Mother went mad. And didn't I know it. She flew into her familiar refrain: my father must be seething with rage up there, seeing his only daughter behave that way. I'm not showing myself to be worthy of him, his legacy, or the hero he was. Now and then, I hear different things about my father, but that's another story. Mother decided that from now on, after school, I shall be going to meet her at her work. The only thing is, she works at the madhouse. 'Your mum cleans up crazy people's crap,' the witches tease, the ignorant bitches.

At last, I can see the side of the grand old building. The former manor house of the Lelanger family, I'm told. What an idea, to turn it into an asylum for degenerates. 'A rest home,' Mother would correct me. A forced-rest home, if you ask me, because they're not exactly right in the head anymore.

I arrive on the driveway, walk up the steps and realise I can't feel my toes.

A bearded man whose belly is threatening to burst through his uniform opens the gate for me. His lips are buried beneath an avalanche of black hair. He's not from around here, otherwise I'd know who he was. Lac-Clarence is the kind of place where we all know each other, and everything about everyone.

'You're Lisette's girl, are you?' he asks me, his face rigid, like a ventriloquist's.

I nod, turning my tongue seven times inside my mouth to resist the urge to tell him it would have been smarter just to ask my name. But then, in a madhouse I suppose they have to keep closer tabs on people going out, not coming in.

'Bloody hell. What have you gone and done now?' Mother's voice is lecturing me before I've even laid eyes on her. I haven't even had the chance to unbutton my overcoat. She's standing at the turn of the corridor.

'Just look at your legs, you're soaked through. Lina, I don't know how you do it. How do you manage to always make a hash of everything? Come on, follow me. And take off those boots and socks, will you? I'll dry them for you, otherwise you'll catch your death.'

'Where are we going?'

'I'm going to set you up in the rest area so you can do your homework.'

A rest area in a rest home. I lower my eyes and bite my lip so I won't laugh out loud. Mother is a master of surprising me at the precise moment I have sinned.

'Do you have your English exercise book?' She peers into my satchel.

I nod.

'Liliiiii! Liliiii!'

We turn around at the same time, Mother and I. A little old lady with a back as rounded as a walnut shell is waving her hand as if she's holding a bell.

'Yes, Solange, what is it?' My mother's tone is not so much empathetic as exasperated.

'I can't find Léonard. He's been missing an hour or more. I'm really starting to fret. He's only four years old, you see, Lili.'

'Yes, I know, Solange.' There's the same note of impatience in her voice.

'He might drown in the pond, or burn himself on the stove in the kitchen, or...'

'Are you sure Anne-Marie hasn't taken him for a bath?'

'No, he had a bath on Sunday.'

'Have you had a good look in your wardrobe?'

They put kids in wardrobes, here?

'Ah, no.'

The old lady's face lights up, only to darken again. 'I'm afraid to open the wardrobe.'

My mother sighs. 'All right, Solange, I'll come with you. I'll be back,' she tells me. 'Wait there in that room for me.' She points to some French doors on our right.

'Charming kind of place,' I mutter under my breath.

'I heard you!' my mother warns me, without turning around, hand in hand with this Solange, whose fingers are clutching hers.

The dying sun hits me full in the face the second I open the doors. I blink and step into the room, shading my eyes with one hand.

It looks like a small drawing room, with two armchairs facing a tall window stripped of its handle. There's a pedestal table to the side.

I sit in the chair on the left, then take off my boots and soaking-wet woollen socks. I wipe my feet on the floor to rid them of the damp, tuck them beneath my buttocks, hoping to warm them up, and lean forwards to grab my satchel. I'm just about to pull out my book when the door opens.

'Here we are...' I recognise Anne-Marie's voice. It's deep and nasal, and carries like a man's.

'Oh, Lina ... hello,' she says, stopping the chair she's pushing.

Her surprise soon gives way to a look brimming with rebuke. This I prefer a thousand times to the lecture lurking behind it. Her eyes linger on me for a second, then drift down to my dripping socks draped over my boots.

The old lady in the wheelchair has a long grey braid curling over her shoulder, running down to her thigh like a rope. She catches sight of me reaching into my bag, and I feel as if I've somehow been caught red-handed..

She gives me a knowing smile. I pull my hand out again.

'Does your mother know you're here?' Anne-Marie asks me, pushing the wheelchair over to the window.

'Yes,' I mumble.

The old lady puts a notebook on the pedestal table beside her. Her grey wisps of hair turn blonde in the setting sun.

'She went off with a woman named ... Sonia. No, Solange.'

Anne-Marie shakes her head with a sigh. 'Right.' She turns on her heels and walks out of the room, leaving the door open.

The old lady turns her back to me, which I don't mind in the slightest because for one, I don't feel like making conversation with her; plus I don't feel like listening to her ramble; also I'm planning to read English, not revise it; and finally, the bright sun would claw at my eyes if she wasn't in the way.

I wait a few seconds before digging my hand into my satchel again.

'I won't say a word,' the old lady says without moving.

I flinch. 'Sorry?'

'I'm sure you'll learn many more things from your book.'

I don't know what to reply. Someone else who's got eyes in the back of her head.

'I know how to keep secrets, and it's not because my memory's failing me that...'

'No, I...'

She starts to laugh. A young laugh that doesn't go with her grey mane, or her wrinkled face.

'Read your forbidden book. Just lift your eyes once or twice to watch the sun die. It's surely the only thing that looks good when it's dying.'

5
Maxine
2002

Jules and I duck into the ambulance, having exchanged a few words with one of the emergency medics. According to him, Mrs Caron is suffering from only mild hypothermia, which could in no way be responsible for her current clouding of mind. He would not qualify her state as 'catatonic' either, given that she had allowed herself to be examined without resistance. She seems more in a state of shock, he thinks.

Using her grey matter for once, the rookie has the sense to make room for me to sit beside Mrs Caron. My former schoolteacher is lying on the stretcher, drilling holes into the roof liner with her eyes. She's wrapped up to her chin in a heavy throw to keep her warm. The shiny edges of a space blanket are sticking out by her feet.

I shift to the edge of my seat; it squeaks unpleasantly.

'Mrs Caron? It's Maxine Grant. You have to tell me what happened with Philippe. With your husband.'

'Plus, you were the one who asked for Lieutenant Grant,' the rookie chimes in. 'So it's important to speak up, madam, isn't it?'

I send her a murderous glare that nails her trap shut. Her cheeks flush purple, as if I'd given her the slap she deserves. Interrupting an interview. Where *do* they train their young recruits these days?

Jules gets up, opens the door and orders the muppet to get out. A blast of icy air rushes into the ambulance, sending shivers through me.

'Mrs Caron, you're perfectly safe talking to me,' I continue, once Jules has returned to my side. 'And Detective Sergeant Jules Demers is my colleague. We've been working together for many years, you can trust him.'

'Would you rather I stepped outside, Mrs Caron, and left you alone with Maxine?'

She doesn't respond; she seems lost in her thoughts.

Jules casts me a quick glance. 'You were Maxine's teacher, weren't you?'

The silence lingers, she's not budging an inch.

'Mrs Caron,' I say, 'we've found a hand in your living room.'

The survival blanket twitches, the rustling almost startles me, but her eyes are still locked on the same spot as when we came in.

'A hand hidden inside a—' I interrupt myself.

Jules frowns. He's asking me his question silently. Ah, how well my Chickadee knows me.

'—inside one of your side tables.'

I wait a few seconds, mentally pacing up and down, because I have only one desire: to get the hell out of this ambulance and go and see if there's anything to the crazy idea that's just sprung into my mind.

At last I get up and step outside, Jules right behind me, then we're almost running to the front door of the house.

We pull our coveralls on again.

Jules hasn't asked me anything. He's waiting. He's surely the only man who can read me this well.

'Simon!' Now it's my turn to yell his name. 'See if you can open that for me, over there,' I call, pointing to a second side table tucked in behind some plants, identical to the one that revealed the severed hand.

Simon gets to his feet. He looks from one table to the other, then hurries across the living room and crouches down to lift the tray top off the second.

As soon as we've pulled our hoods up, we join him.

The tray top is stuck, so Jules has to hold the table steady while Simon tries to loosen it like the lid on a stubborn jam jar. There's a hollow sound as the top pops open. Céci abandons Philippe Caron's body and comes over to see. I re-enact our earlier scene, reaching my latex-gloved hands around the sides of the glass dome to extract it delicately from the chest.

'Oh, shit,' Céci and Jules curse, practically in unison.

It's a hand with an open palm, this time severed a touch higher up the forearm. The fingers, much longer, are pressing against the glass as if they're feeling for a way out.

'Bloody hell, they really look mummified,' Jules comments.

Céci sets him straight: 'More like dried or tanned.'

'Three times a charm?' he jokes, giving me a what-if kind of look. 'I'm going upstairs,' he adds, making a hasty exit from the living room.

'OK,' I reply, falling into step.

'Do you think there are more?'

'I'll give you a shout if we find any, Simon.'

'I'll start in the entryway,' Céci suggests.

'Perfect.'

I walk across the hallway and am about to go into what looks like the Carons' study when I notice another table to my right, below a window overlooking the garden. I stand right in front of it and feel a terrible temptation to open it.

'I've found another one. Simon, come over here with your camera!'

I can hear his muffled steps as well as a creaking of floorboards over my head from Jules moving around upstairs.

Simon stops in front of the window, takes a few photos and points to the table top. I tip my chin. He bends down, grasps the sides of the table top and pulls it towards him. This one gives more easily.

'One in the kitchen too!' Céci calls from the far end of the hallway. 'What kind of crazy shit is this?'

'We've got another hand,' I announce, seeing the fingers under their dome. 'Simon, can you take care of it? I'm going to have a look in the study.'

'Three times a charm, no kidding,' he mutters, plunging his hands into the table's belly.

In the study, the first thing I see is yet another table.

'Simon!' I yell, not daring to think what these finds could mean, and what – and whom – they'll implicate.

I quickly scan the room and its furnishings: two desks facing one another, bookshelves all the way up to the coved ceiling, a wingback chair, a floor lamp and that side table, a carbon copy of those in the hallway and the living room.

'Nothing upstairs,' Jules reports, finding me again. 'So how many have you found, then?'

'Maxine. There's one in the dining room too,' Céci calls.

'I was going to say five. But that makes six,' I say.

'Six – so far,' he replies.

6
Lucienne
1899

The nannies are seated on two iron chairs between two poplars. The Jardin de Luxembourg has never been so popular; everyone in Paris comes here to stretch their legs.

'Maman, Maman! Look at my cart.'

Jeanne puts her bucket full of gravel down on my dress.

'Jeanne!' her nanny chides. 'You're getting your mother's dress all dirty.'

'Leave her be,' I smile, picking up some of the chips of gravel with my gloved fingers to place them in the hollow of my palm. 'And what is your cart carrying, *ma chérie*?'

'Forage.'

'Forage?'

'Yes, Mademoiselle Saint-Genêt said this morning that there are thousands upon thousands of horses in Paris. I don't want them to be hungry. How many was it, nanny?'

'Eighty thousand.'

'Eighty thousand, Maman, can you believe it? That's rather a lot, I think, eighty thousand.'

'It is, indeed,' I smile. 'And Rose, what are you doing?'

Jeanne rolls her eyes and turns to her sister, who doesn't appear to have heard me. 'She's baking cakes.'

Rose is crouched down, her summer coat sweeping the gravel. She's sprinkling a pile of stones with soil, and getting her chubby hands filthy. Suddenly she stops what she's doing and tugs at the tie of her hat.

'Rose,' her nanny tuts, watching her out of the corner of her eye.

Without taking her eyes off her play baking, my daughter manages to doff her hat.

Her nanny puts down her sewing and shakes off the dust that cakes the hat's pale-pink ribbons, flashing a contrite smile at me.

'For goodness' sake, Rose,' she chides.

My daughter waves her off rudely.

'Rose,' I intervene, my voice rolling into the deepest of tones.

'It hurts here, Maman,' she says, showing me a spot beneath her chin.

'I know, *ma chérie*, but look at me,' I say, tilting my head to show her my veil. 'A worldly lady does not reveal her locks when she leaves the house. Tomorrow, I shall ask Nanny to put yours up with hairpins so it won't smart your skin anymore.'

'Like you, Maman?'

'Yes, like me.'

'*Merci,* Maman.'

Rose pulls a face as her nanny ties a double bow under her chin, but doesn't dare undo it again.

We stay another hour in the gardens, Jeanne's nanny sewing a skirt, and Rose's a set of handkerchiefs. Meanwhile, I listen to my daughters playing and the cheerful conversations of passers-by out to catch a ray of sunshine.

When we get back to Avenue Foch, Jeanne and Rose retire to their quarters, and I to mine. I have a few letters to write and my attire to prepare for tomorrow. I must ask Mary to confirm that my dress suits me, as I can't allow a slip in taste to set those ladies' tongues wagging, or to cause my husband embarrassment.

For, tomorrow, I am to accompany Henri to the Palais Garnier.

We are going with another couple, the de la Courtières. This time I cannot feign a migraine and stay at home with my cousin Mary. I have no choice but to go, turn a cheek to the taunting and make a good impression. But they won't let me in, these Parisiennes, they keep me outside of their impenetrable world, of their codes I don't always understand, and their French, which at times has everything of a foreign language.

I've told Henri I'll be dining in my apartments. I have no desire to spend two evenings in a row with him; tomorrow is already enough.

Once the nannies have turned in for the evening, I go in to kiss Jeanne and Rose goodnight. Mary joins me and we tell them, as we like to do at bedtime, unbeknownst to the household and away from their prying ears, about our Quebec, our Lac-Clarence, her dense forest, her fresh air, her snow that melts in the mouth like a communion wafer and her river of clear waters, a life in colours painted by God and not by men like here, in Paris.

I shut myself in my bedroom later than usual, turning the latch to signal to Henri that I shall not be accommodating him this evening. I fall asleep with a heavy heart and fear in my stomach, thinking about the day that awaits me.

I wake long before morning comes, roused from my bed by dreadful cries. Those of two housekeepers. Two maids. I'm leaving my room just as cousin Mary is about to knock at my door.

A cloud of foul air rushes into my apartments, bringing on a ghastly coughing fit. Mary is breathless too, unable to speak. Thick smoke is seeping under the service door leading to the floor above.

My house is on fire.

I'm stricken by panic. Cousin Mary takes me by the arm and we hurry along the hallway to the central staircase.

'Jeanne ... Rose?' I ask, trembling.

The smoke is burning, stinging so much I can barely keep my eyes open.

'The nannies ... are down below,' a maid replies, coughing.

'And monsieur?'

'I ... don't...' She shakes her head and hurries down the stairs.

I hang on to Mary's arm and we run as quick as can be, holding our breath, our eyes half closed, down to the street.

It takes me a long moment to pull myself together and open my eyes to see our building, the thick black smoke spewing from the upper floors.

Henri, still in his suit, hurries to my side.

'The children?' he questions me, fear darkening his brow.

'...With ... nan ... nies,' I sputter, overcome by another coughing fit.

He shakes his head, eyes wide with dread.

An explosion erupts in the sky, with a rumble like thunder.

In a flash, we're crouching on the ground, unsure where the terrible roar is coming from. From beneath my folded arms, I catch a glimpse of the flames, licking like tentacles from the windows of my bedroom. And the children's.

7
Maxine
2002

You can reproach Marceau for many things, but not her professionalism or her responsiveness. They make the rest tolerable: her savage bark, her total lack of empathy, her aversion to children and family life, and I'm weighing my words here. In mere hours, the municipal hall in Lac-Clarence has been turned into an incident room, and we have everything necessary to unravel this affair, which has proved itself to be more complex than expected; or at least, a dimension has emerged that is radically different from anything I suspected this morning. Seven hands. We've found seven hands at the Caron house. All encased in domes, as if they were precious antiques, and concealed in identical chest tables spread throughout the ground floor.

'Lieutenant Grant?'

'Yes, I'm here.'

Because of the hypothermia, the medics were opposed to us undressing Mrs Caron in the ambulance. Now that her condition has stabilised, forensics are examining her clothes here, at the incident room we've set up. This morning, they were only able to collect samples from the exposed parts of her body. Her hands, her face and her hair.

I picked her up a change of clothes and a pair of shoes before leaving her home. I felt like an intruder, going through her wardrobe, her things arranged with military precision. I had to appreciate the practical side, though. Everything was organised by clothing type, and then placed in order of colour. Unconsciously, I decided on a black ensemble: velvet trousers, a blouse and a wool sweater. Reluctantly, I picked out some panties, a bra and a pair of socks too. Opening the drawer, where everything was folded to perfection, I stifled a sob. It made me think of Mum. The outfit she wore to Charlotte's baptism: beige, but cheerful, frilly and bright. I had washed and ironed the ruffled blouse and long skirt to get rid of the naphthalene smell, then scented the fabric with her perfume. When Dad had leaned in to kiss her, in church, he had smiled. 'She smells like her,' he'd said, stroking her cheek, forgetting for a moment that an envelope was all there was left of Mum. The idea of her, the memories. And he had started to cry at the frigid touch of her hard skin.

On my way to see the forensic technicians and Mrs Caron in an overheated room, I send a message to my daughter, who hasn't replied to my last text.

Mrs Caron's still not reacting to my presence. She's not there. There's an absence in her eyes. She's staring at the wall behind us, perhaps at an imagined window onto the years preceding today's drama. Or who knows, she might be replaying her husband's death in her mind. She always used to speak joyfully of Philippe, the last syllable of his name bringing her a smile, a tenderness that would light up her whole face. As a teenager, I used to think that was so dumb. But not now.

I turn away from her naked body when the forensics woman leads her into the shower. We're in the village hall, and the technician had to clean the dust and debris from the cubicle first. I only allow myself to look at Mrs Caron once she turns her back on me. The blood caking her hair turns the water red. Splashing her shoulders, running down her body. I won't ever stop seeing her as my primary-school teacher. The one who caught me in the shed in the playground one day, comparing attributes with Émile Grangé to see if what Fabrice Daron had told us was true: that boys and girls were meant to 'plug in' to one another! The one too, who treated the class to a birthday chocolate fondue when I turned seven, and who pulled me into a long embrace when Mum died.

'Lieutenant!' The big boss is calling me.

For Marceau, rank trumps everything else. If absolutely necessary, a name is used, albeit only to distinguish one officer from another – but she never uses sex for that purpose. Another of her qualities. I'd better stop now, or I'll end up really singing her praises.

I step out of the bathroom and find Marceau in the main hall. She's chatting to a woman who looks about fifty and is dressed in a remarkably similar navy-blue suit to the one my darling boss is wearing. They share the same natural blonde and the same blue eyes too. But Léonie Marceau's are sparkling with their usual in-transigence, while the other woman's have a gentle crease to them, as do her soft, full lips. Sitting at a desk, Jules is pretending to be poring over the contents of Philippe Caron's computer, but my Chickadee isn't missing a word of their conversation.

'Lieutenant, meet Professor Montminy.'

'Lieutenant Grant,' I elaborate, reaching for a dainty yet rough-feeling hand that shakes mine firmly.

I notice the blue-and-white paint splotching the groove between her fingers.

'Professor Montminy is going to be handling the questioning of Pauline Caron.'

Suddenly the penny drops. This is Ginette Montminy, the forensic psychologist. She trained our very own Emily Roy, the brilliant extra-terrestrial who grew up in Lac-Clarence, just like me, and now works for Scotland Yard.

'I'd prefer to say that I'm going to be accompanying you in this interview, Lieutenant Grant. Is that all right with you?'

'Of course,' I reply, summoning a smile I hope is convincing. As if I could say no.

8
Maxine
2002

'Not now, Sergeant!' Marceau growls at Jules, who's dragging a whiteboard into our improvised meeting room.

Jules straightens up, gives Marceau a glance and wonders what the hell to do with this whiteboard that's now blocking the doorway. He ends up deciding to lean it against the wall out in the corridor, hoping the big boss's barking mood will be merely momentary.

Ginette Montminy has taken a seat at one of the desks and clasped her hands together. She's wearing the sketch of a smile on her face, and it seems to have seeded something remarkably serene in her.

'Lieutenant?' Marceau urges, parking her muscled buttocks on the edge of the table, her skirt rising to reveal thighs that can't have had to work off an ounce of cake or poutine with its sinful chips, cheese curds and gravy, in forever.

I wait for Jules to come in and close the door behind him. He hands prints of the crime-scene photos to Marceau, and she has a look before passing them to the psychologist.

'According to Céci, our medical examiner's preliminary findings, and the forensics team's observations,' I begin, meeting the eyes of Professor Montminy, Marceau and Jules in turn, 'Pauline Caron is responsible for the murder of her husband Philippe. Last night, between ten o'clock and midnight, she stabbed him some thirty times. The cuts on her hands, the blood-spatter patterns on her clothes and face, her fingerprints on the murder weapon – a large carving knife found on the kitchen counter – as well as the prints of her palms on her husband's body and her knees on the floor leave no doubt as to her guilt. Céci should be done with the autopsy soon and have a report for us. That said, the possibility of self-defence can already be ruled out. Pauline Caron has no visible defensive wounds. The superficial nature, size and angle of the cuts on her hands are all consistent with her being the assailant and not the victim.'

I come up for a breath of air. Jules carries on where I leave off.

'Pauline Caron, sixty-five years of age, now retired and formerly both teacher and headmistress of the Lac-Clarence community school. Married for thirty-six years to Philippe Caron, fifty-four years of age, a professor of medieval history at McGill University, a leading expert in the history of Quebec, and an acclaimed author. A very active couple in the Lac-Clarence community. No children. No pets, either. Both have a driver's licence and share one car, a Merc, now at the lab for examination.'

Jules hands off to me again with a glance.

'The SQ were alerted at 8.32 am by a delivery driver who found Pauline Caron sitting outside her home, covered in blood. When the officers arrived, Pauline Caron had them call me. She just gave them my name. Mrs Caron used to be my teacher,' I explain for Montminy's benefit. 'I grew up in Lac-Clarence.'

She gives me a smile. I get the impression she's watching me, observing me, more than she's listening to me.

'Pauline Caron hasn't said a word since the police arrived at her doorstep. She's not responding to questions, not even to mine, but she's allowed herself to be examined by the emergency medics and forensic technicians, putting up no resistance.'

This time, I sigh and it sounds like a chant.

'Were the two of you still in touch?' the psychologist asks me suddenly.

'No, not at all. But my parents would pass things on ... before they died. It's been three and four years now, respectively. Mrs Caron has always been a caring presence. She's a woman who's spent her life looking after others – and her husband. Her actions, this murder ... it's all so completely ... unexplainable. Maybe it's her sense of justice that spurred her to ask for me. She knows what I do for a living...' I cough to expel the frog that's actually more like a cat clawing at my throat. And then I'm left with an infinite sadness.

'You don't seem to be considering the presence of a third party,' Montminy replies.

'That's right. There's nothing at the crime scene, nor anywhere else in the Carons' home, that points to the possibility. And according to forensics and to Céci, all indications are that Mrs Caron was holding the knife that was used to stab her husband. Now, those are just their preliminary findings; we'll have to wait for the official report. And, most of all, hear what Mrs Caron has to say.'

Her eyes glued to the door behind me, Montminy reacts with a series of minute movements of her head.

'We've found seven hands in the home,' I continue, perching Marceau-style on the edge of a desk, but with a pair of tired, shapeless jeans and a posterior that's been plied with Häagen-Dazs for decades. 'Two in the living room, one in the hallway, one in the kitchen, one in the study, another in the dining room and the last one in the laundry room. Each of the hands was mounted on a plinth and placed under a glass dome, then concealed in one of seven identical little chest tables, each with a removable tray top.'

I pause while Jules circulates some photos.

'They've been sent to a forensic anthropologist for analysis, but Céci thinks they're real hands that have been severed and then ... dried, so to speak.'

'And you've no idea of the age of the victims or when they died, I suppose? No way of identifying them?' Marceau asks.

'We've got nothing, right now.'

'What about prints?'

'Only Philippe Caron's, on the glass domes. And there was no dust on the domes themselves, only inside the tables.'

'So,' Marceau goes on, folding her arms across her bosom and leaning back, so her stilettos rise from the greenish floor, 'it seems Pauline Caron might have ... decompensated. Cracked, in other words. To kill her husband with that degree of violence, she must have discovered something about him that shocked her immensely. Something that perturbed or terrified her.'

'Or sent her into a fit of rage,' Montminy adds.

'She's what, five foot four?' Jules interjects. 'For a woman of her age and her build to inflict thirty or more stab wounds, that's one hell of a physical feat. And we found nothing in her home to suggest she's particularly athletic. So yes, it must have been some tremendous anger that she unleashed on her husband. What was the trigger for her murderous frenzy, then?'

'Discovering the hands?' Marceau suggests.

'The thing is,' I say, peeling my posterior off the desk, 'most of the tray tops were easy to lift off the tables. Just by cleaning the house, Pauline Caron could have uncovered what was in those chests.'

'The Carons didn't have a cleaning lady?' the boss wonders.

Jules shakes his head. 'No hired help at all. No gardener either. And it's not like they couldn't afford it.'

'Could the tray tops have come off just by dusting the tables?' Marceau can't have done any cleaning of her own for a while.

'I don't think so, no,' I reply. 'But she would have had to move the tables to vacuum and mop the floors.'

'Maybe he was the one who did all the cleaning?' Marceau goes on.

'I have a hard time believing that,' Jules says. 'Not in their generation.'

'What if Pauline Caron wasn't in the know, and her husband

got a thrill out of thinking those hands were right under his wife's nose?' Marceau insists.

'I don't see how Mrs Caron could not have known,' I intervene, keen to dismiss a suggestion I find so hard to believe. 'There were seven tables in plain sight. Even inadvertently, she must have opened one of them at some point in time.'

'And we don't know when this collection started,' Marceau adds, touching the cap of her pen to her mouth.

'No, but the number of relics alone tells us it's not a recent thing.'

'Good point,' Marceau concedes. She stretches her legs, revealing their shape with a flex of her thigh muscles. 'So we're dealing with a gruesome collector, or a couple of them. Which raises two possibilities. One, that this stuff is murderabilia and he – or they, if they're in this together – are just creepy. Or two, that he or they are killers, of the serial kind, I might add, who've been keeping little mementos of their victims.'

'Or...' I chime in, almost interrupting her, 'Pauline Caron knew about her husband's gruesome collection and let him get on with his little hobby without being into it herself. And then last night, she finds out that he's actually a serial killer and he's the one who's been chopping those hands off. Her whole life comes crashing down, all her certainties, all her beliefs, absolutely everything ... Now that's enough to drive a woman wild with rage by anyone's standards. If you ask me, this theory fits with the facts and the evidence we have at the moment.'

I see heads nodding at me in response.

'But if we venture down the "just collectors" path for a moment,' I continue, pacing around the rectangle of desks, 'the question on my lips is, why hide those hands in various places around the house? I can understand them not wanting to have the things on display right beside their record collection on a shelf in the living room, but why not keep them together in the same room, in a cupboard or a chest?'

I'm interrupted by the sound of my phone ringing. It's Charlotte. I'll call her back after the meeting.

'Sorry,' I apologise, putting it away. 'We also have to look into the significance of the hands. Should we be thinking of them as a retaliation thing? You know, an eye for an eye, a tooth for a tooth. Chopping off the hand of a thief, or a sinner...'

'Don't worry about that for now, Lieutenant,' Marceau cuts in. 'Professor Montminy will take care of the symbolic angle during Pauline Caron's questioning.'

She glides to her feet with a gracefulness I find myself surprised to be admiring. And envying too, perhaps.

'So, let's go through their computers, phones and phone bills, both home and work for the husband, to check for any history of murderabilia sites or other such communities, or even something as simple as emails proving they bought those hands somewhere.'

I note Marceau's use of the plural, 'their'. My theory about Pauline's complicity or culpability is seeping its way into her mind.

'Next, we explore the serial-killer angle. We turn the house upside down looking for crime-scene mementoes, we search the husband's office at the university, we go into their garden with the sniffer dogs. We'll get more drastic with the search if we have to, but only once we've found out more about those hands. And we canvass the neighbours, of course – there don't seem to be many of them – as well as the husband's colleagues at the university and the wife's former colleagues and friends, to get a sense of them as a couple. Come to think of it, has anyone questioned that delivery driver?'

'Not properly, no,' Jules replies, 'but I've got his contact details and I'm planning to call him after the meeting.'

'Perfect. We have a plan. Logistics wise, I've had three rooms set aside for you at the Auberge du Lac. I'd like you to keep boots on the ground here.'

'Sorry, boss,' I reply without an ounce of guilt. 'That's impossible for me with Hugo. He's still too little to leave. I'll have to drive back and forth from Montreal.'

'Can't his sister look after him for a week or two? Charlotte's got a sensible head on her shoulders, hasn't she? And she's practically old enough to be a mother herself.'

If we were still in the Middle Ages, I feel like replying.

'Charlotte's a teenager, boss,' I concede through clenched teeth. 'She's more concerned about her bra size than the child mortality rate in a third-world country. In other words, her skill set doesn't exactly extend to getting up in the middle of the night to put her baby brother back to sleep, or remembering to change his nappy or warm a bottle for him.'

Marceau raises an eyebrow in surprise.

'Sorry, boss, but I can't leave the kids for that long either,' Jules adds, in my defence.

'They're not even your own, Sergeant.'

'They've become my own,' he counters without animosity.

'Professor?'

Ginette Montminy moves with ... I'm almost tempted to say, a certain sensuality. She graces Marceau with a generous, serene smile and hands her the photos Jules passed around.

'I'll gladly take you up on the offer if my interviews drag on, thank you. But not on a Monday, Wednesday, Friday or Sunday evening. That's when I have my four grandchildren with me.'

My bad, I muse, and chuckle to myself. Her pleasant smile was no more than a polite 'screw you'.

9
Lina
1949

This time, I walked a different way after school and I got here much sooner. The bearded ventriloquist greeted me with a nod and Mother gave me a suspicious look. I've come into the same sitting room as yesterday, with a new book.

The click of the door handle startles me.

Try as I might to disappear behind the back of the armchair, my satchel on the floor betrays my presence. I daren't turn around, though, for fear that Sonia or Solange, whatever her name is, might come over and prattle on at me about something or other. I slip what I'm reading under my English exercise book, as a precaution.

I recognise the whoosh of the wheelchair. Anne-Marie parks the old lady in the same place as yesterday and walks away without a word.

I'm hesitant to say hello. I don't feel like striking up a conversation. At the same time, she barely said a word to me yesterday in the three hours we were sitting together. She watched the sun 'die', as she put it, then she picked up her notebook and began to read in silence.

'Hello,' I say to the back of her head.

She raises a forearm from her armrest and merely wiggles her fingers. The sun fans its rays like a star, filtering them through the trees, turning them from blue-grey to orange, only to suddenly change its mind and paint the sky pink, even though it knows the night will erase it all in a matter of minutes.

'If you watch it again tomorrow,' the old lady says all of a sudden, 'you'll see it never expires the same way.'

Foolishly, my gaze falls on my book, and I realise I've neglected my reading.

I don't say anything in reply. There's nothing to say, anyway, and she doesn't seem too bothered about good manners. It's nice. She's frank and direct, with no double talk and no undertones, unlike most people. I don't see the point of double talk. The choice seems simple enough to me: either speak or keep your mouth shut. Hiding a no behind a yes or a yes behind a maybe – honestly, how are you supposed to make sense of that? And why waste time complicating things? It's as tiresome for the person asking the question as it is for the person who has to answer it. And there's another vital point that exasperates me. Why speak, if it's ultimately to say nothing?

And so I plunge into my reading again until darkness falls.

'Well?' the old lady suddenly asks my reflection in the window. 'You must have really done something to end up condemned to whiling away the finest hours of the day in my company.'

I open my mouth, and then I reconsider. Mother has forbidden me from speaking to anyone here about what happened. Mrs Morin did try to suggest that surely, it must have been an accident, but Mother can read me like an open book. I think back to the witches, whispering their insults at me. I wonder if they're plotting their revenge. *Let them try.*

'At your age,' the old lady continues, 'I had a cousin who made me do things ... I didn't like at all.' The mirror image in the pane shakes her head as if to express disgust. 'You know what I did to that pig to stop him coming after me?'

It's my turn to shake my head.

'I set his dog's kennel on fire.'

My mouth gapes in surprise. 'Is that true?'

'Mmmhm. And you know what?'

'I think so. He stopped?'

'That's right.'

I think back to the 'incident'.

'Would you mind reading out loud?' she asks me.

Before, I would never have dared to read Huysmans' *The Damned* to anyone. I'm usually surrounded by sanctimonious so-and-sos who are convinced the Devil's out to get them and might sound the alarm to Mother. But this old lady seems different.

'It's *The Damned*, by Huysmans,' I tell her, all the same.

'Mmmhm.'

'I'm on chapter five already, does that matter?'

'Not at all.'

I open my book, clear my throat, but then stop myself.

'It happened at choir practice. Every time the teacher Mrs Morin made us take a break, Tamara would make fun of me under her breath. She would say these horrible things and Julie would laugh into her elbow. It's always like that with those two witches. They hate me. And the last time, when we were practising for the Christmas parade, I ... I lowered my candle a bit too close to Tamara's long hair ... and it caught fire.'

'A terrible accident,' the old lady says.

I look up and catch the reflection of her smile in the window.

'Yes, it was a terrible accident,' I reply.

10
Maxine
2002

'How would you like to proceed, Professor?'

'Call me Gina,' she replies without looking up from the photos she's examining one after the other, reading glasses perched on the bridge of her slim nose. '"Professor Montminy" sounds stuffy. And "Ginette" – that just reminds me of every time I knew I was about to get a good spanking. And not the kind that leaves you begging for more.'

I respond with an awkward laugh. Has she really just shared a racy remark with me?

'How would you like to proceed, Gina?' I repeat, forcing a smile that must look more like a grimace.

'Do you have photos of their bedroom?' she continues, still not answering my question.

'No, we didn't take any photos upstairs.'

'Did they share the marital bed?'

'They slept together, yes.'

'And they shared a study. By choice, as I understand, and not for lack of space.'

'The size of the house would seem to suggest that, yes.'

'What did Pauline Caron say to the patrol officers, exactly? Just your name?'

'My first and my last name, yes, Maxine Grant. What she always called me as a child. As if the two were inseparable.'

'That was all?'

'That was all, yes.'

She nods, almost imperceptibly.

'Which class did Pauline Caron teach?'

'Just the one. There were very few children in Lac-Clarence back then. She used to split us up into small groups. She was wonderful. It never felt like we were going to school.'

'Did she have her pupils call her "Mrs Caron"?'

I smile as the memories return. 'Yes, and it's hard for me to call her anything else.'

Gina looks up at me. 'How old is Hugo?'

I wasn't expecting any personal questions. 'Eight months,' I end up saying.

'He's not sleeping through the night?'

'Things are ... difficult.'

She smiles. Her eyes are sparkling in a different way, as if Hugo was here burbling in front of her, making her melt with joy.

'And your eldest, Charlotte, how old is she, love?'

The term of endearment does me the world of good, easing the tension in the situation and our rapport in an instant. Children, or maternity, have removed the barriers.

'The ungrateful age.'

Her lips curve into an ephemeral smile.

I adjust my toque, which keeps riding up on my forehead.

I should ask about her own children and grandchildren, but I have only one desire – to go and question Mrs Caron and make some headway in this investigation that's already gnawing away at me.

'You must be burning up in that toque. I've got some dry shampoo in my little booty-call bag. You're welcome to use some if you like,' she ventures, without ado.

I freeze. I don't know if I'm embarrassed or ashamed, or simply grateful. My toque is a stop-gap to conceal the disastrous state of my hair. The boss is definitely one to notice a wrinkle in my blouse or a grease stain on my jeans, while she always looks sharp and well pressed. She's sublime, of course, but it comes at a cost. In my opinion, life's too short to waste time every morning drawing a better version of yourself, only to erase it every night.

I hear myself saying, 'I'd love to, yes. Thanks, Gina.'

She bends down, rummages in her handbag and extracts a flowery little pouch, which she then hands to me. I thank her with a smile, feeling like a teenager caught short for a tampon.

'Shake the bottle and hold the spray about four inches from your hair. Not too close, or it'll turn everything white. Next, massage your scalp for thirty seconds like you're shampooing your hair, then brush. You were asking how I wanted to proceed,' she continues, as if the two conversations were connected. 'I might ask you the same question. That depends on you and ... the sergeant as much as it does on me.'

It suddenly dawns on me that Marceau didn't introduce Jules and Gina, and I've failed to keep her up to speed.

'Jules Demers. Sorry, I should have introduced you.'

'Let's just keep the dialogue open. The worst thing for me is to roll up in a team that feels micromanaged. I'm here to work with you, not for myself or against you. Let's tell it like it is. When things are working and when they aren't. Let's make things simple. Is that all right with you?'

'I'm all for making things simple,' I reply, before excusing myself to take a call from Charlotte.

11
Maxine
2002

Mrs Caron has the same absence in her eyes as when I left her in her shower. She's sitting obediently behind a table, dressed in the black outfit picked out by yours truly, the strands of her usual impeccably smooth bob now flowing wild and free as the long grass.

I sit down opposite her.

Two rooms away, Gina, Marceau and Jules are watching the interview I'm about to begin. There's no two-way mirror here, but a system of cameras to relay my questioning in real time. Gina's asked me to handle the first round. She just wants to observe, for now.

My chair squeaks as I lean against the backrest.

'Mrs Caron?'

She's staring at the door behind me, as if she was expecting someone else. Her hands are resting flat on the table, exposing nails in places still blackened by blood.

'Your husband is dead, Mrs Caron. Philippe is dead. And we would like to know what happened.'

I mark a pause.

'Did he hurt you, Mrs Caron?'

Nothing in her attitude changes. As if she's not hearing my words.

'What was so serious that you took a knife and stabbed him thirty-one times? What did you discover?'

I let out a sigh.

My only desire now is to get out of here. Go home. Make dinner. Get back to our evening ritual. And yet, here I am, in this overheated room, with her, unable to rid my thoughts of her husband, belly and torso in shreds, immersed in a pool of blood that's licking at everything around like an insatiable monster. A picture that's superimposed over a vision of Hugo sleeping peacefully in his crib, arms and legs spread like a starfish, chest rising to the rhythm of his gentle snoring. I don't know why, but my mind wanders back into the past. I can see Charlotte's hair, the long strands I'm braiding over and over, until the plait tickles my thigh – me on the sofa, her sitting between my legs. She's laughing in response to a trick Jerry's played on Tom; my hand's stroking her cheek so she'll stop fidgeting and I can finish her hair. A decade ago. Already.

'Mrs Caron,' I strain myself to go on, 'we've found seven hands in your home. Hands that have been mounted on plinths and protected by glass domes.'

She clenches her fists for a second, then places her palms flat on the table again.

'Were you aware they were there? Or did you discover them last night?'

The tension is mounting. I'm losing patience. I have to keep it together.

'Who do those hands belong to, Mrs Caron?'

I lean forwards and plant my elbows on the table.

'Mrs Caron, talk to me. Tell me what happened in your home, last night,' I insist, tilting my head in an attempt to catch her eye.

I'm watching her every move. I'm waiting for a sentence, a word, the slightest sound. But nothing comes.

'Tell me what happened to you, Mrs Caron.'

I swallow to loosen the knot that's tightening around my throat, to no avail, of course. I have to keep trying. I can't give up at this point.

I sit up, glue my back to the chair.

'Do you remember my husband, Mrs Caron? He was with me at Mum's funeral.'

She's not looking at me. I don't see her move or react in any way. Nothing changes in her behaviour or her posture.

One last crack of the whip, I tell myself.

'I know you remember him, Mrs Caron. He was telling you about the Marco Polo charts he wanted to go and study in South America. That was how he died. Sixteen months ago. On the journey out there. A helicopter accident. He knew nothing about Hugo.'

The taste of my husband's lips comes rushing back to me. His hand reaching out to my belly at night. His absence larger than anything inside me. Our family disunited for always, his departures repeating forever. From one chart to another, one story to another, one death to another, until his own end.

'Mrs Caron?' I insist, one more time.

But she remains shrouded in a silence that gives me the chills and numbs her pain.

It's time to pass the torch. At last.

12
Lucienne
1899

I enter the drawing room in my housecoat, *sans* corset, my hair in a simple French braid. I'm surprised not to see my mother-in-law. We're staying with her while our new home is being prepared.

'Monsieur,' I nod to the chief of police, who's standing there before my husband.

'Madame Docquer,' he replies, with a tilt of the head.

Henri's pupils are dilating with fury. I'm not presentable. I don't care. I couldn't give a monkey's about the gossip. It's not like chins aren't wagging already.

I seat myself in an armchair beside my husband, who's trying to keep a lid on his exasperation.

'What have you found?' I ask the chief of police, holding him accountable to me.

With a glance, he seeks permission from Henri to answer my question.

'I have a right to know how the investigation into the disappearance of my daughters is progressing,' I insist, glaring at the man of the law.

'Lucienne...' my husband intervenes. He would gladly send me away to lie down if he could.

'Henri, if you will allow me,' the chief of police interposes.

Henri acquiesces with a sharp nod of his head, giving the man an impatient wave.

'Madame Docquer, we have not found the bodies of your daughters in the ruins of your residence.'

I practically interrupt the man, my voice reaching all the high notes.

'You see. That's what I told you, Henri. They've been kidnapped!'

'Madame, if I may say, if your daughters had been kidnapped, we would have received a ransom demand.' He marks a pause. 'Yet this is not the case.'

'But it's not even been three days. Surely the ransom demand is coming.'

'Madame, will you think for a moment,' he replies, honeying the insult of his words. 'Why set a fire if the kidnappers wanted your daughters alive to hold to ransom?'

'To cause a distraction so they could make off with two screaming children without attracting attention. Does that not sound like reason enough to you?'

My eyes flit from Henri to the chief of police. Not for a second do either of them seem convinced by my arguments.

'Unless the fire had nothing to do with the kidnapping? I don't know, perhaps it was an accident ... perhaps a fire started in their room? Jeanne and Rose might well have been playing with candles ... when the kidnappers burst in on them, no?'

The chief of police purses his lips and gives my husband a furtive glance.

Reading their closed expressions, I see there's no sense in fighting. I won't be heard by these two men. They're barely listening to me.

'Well then,' I vent as I rise, conceding defeat.

This time, Henri stands. I leave the drawing room without another word to either of them.

Mary's waiting for me in the hall. 'Lucienne, Violette de la Courtière is here to see you.'

'Let her know I'm in no condition to receive her.'

'I've told her, but she's insisting. You know the woman. Better not get on the wrong side of her.'

I sigh, and for a second I consider going to change, then I catch myself. Seeing me in this state might hasten her departure.

I cinch the belt of my housecoat and make my way to the parlour, thinking of the spectacle I'm about to offer, the details of which I know will travel everywhere the skirts of the sublime Violette de la Courtière may glide.

I find my visitor pacing up and down the confined space, parasol still in hand. She hurries over to me and pulls me into an embrace with an intimacy that surprises me. I stiffen at the proximity, the likes of which we have never shared. Her hard corset jabs into the soft folds of my unbridled body – not that this seems to quash her enthusiasm.

'My dear Lucienne,' she gushes, the feathers in her hat tickling my cheek as she steps back.

She inspects me with a maternal eye.

'Good heavens, you're pale. Are you getting proper nourishment, at least? Mary, are you looking after her?'

'Yes, I am looking after her, madame,' my cousin replies, making herself comfortable on the sofa nearest the door.

'Do have a seat,' Violette commands me. 'I fear you might not be steady on your feet.'

We sit side by side on the sofa across from Mary's.

'When will you be able to return home?' she asks.

'The work is going to take a good two years, Henri tells me.'

'Oh, good heavens ... but your husband has another town house on Avenue Foch, does he not?'

I nod. 'Yes, we shall be moving there next week.'

'Very well. What have the police said to you?'

I try to shake loose the knot of anxiety in my throat. 'The chief of police thinks ... that my daughters perished in the flames.'

I lower my eyes to maintain the appropriate decency and dignity. Violette moves closer to me. Our knees are touching. She imprisons my hands in her suede gloves.

'But what does the mother's instinct in you say, my dear Lucienne?'

I lift my gaze to her carefully made-up face. I have to wonder if she's setting a trap I should avoid. I ponder for a moment, unable to think what it might be. And so I tread cautiously.

'I don't think they're dead.'

'I was sure of it!' she immediately cries, with a victor's eyes and smile.

'I beg your pardon?' I blurt in surprise, my reaction speaking before my reason. Clearly, I have trouble keeping my cool and not looking foolish.

'My dear Lucienne, I was absolutely certain you had your doubts about your sweet children being spirited away by the blaze that ravaged your home. And I do agree with you, it makes no sense. They would have found them, like they found the bodies of your servants...'

She catches herself. Hazards a glance at the closed door.

'I was unsure of the Lucienne I was expecting to see,' she admits, giving my hand a brief squeeze, almost whispering now, 'but I can see you've all your wits about you.'

She draws herself tall and continues.

'Now, may I share my thoughts with you, safe in the knowledge that you shall keep all this to yourself? Your husband mustn't hear a word, since I don't care for mine to find out and take umbrage with me.' She doesn't wait for an answer. 'Mary?' she adds, turning to my cousin.

Mary stiffens. 'Of course, madame.'

'Very well.' She smooths the taffeta of her skirt, glances at the closed door once more and then leans closer to me. 'I know a private detective who does a far better job than our police,' she whispers to me. 'I think we should hire him, Lucienne, to find out what's really happened to your daughters. Hire him and await his findings. Once he presents them to us, we shall decide on the course we wish to take.'

I look at her, not comprehending. 'What are you trying to say?'

Her gloved palm pats the back of my hand. 'All in good time, my little Lucienne. All in good time.'

13
Maxine
2002

'Seems like someone had a better night, eh? You don't look so rough as you did yesterday,' Céci calls out as Jules and I walk into the autopsy suite to join her.

'It wasn't too bad,' I reply, trying to convince myself.

'Hallelujah. Before you know it, you'll be able to pee alone again.'

I offer a breath mint to Jules, unwrap mine and toss the white, blue-striped pastille into my mouth. The flavour ices my tongue and my palate, then gets right up my nose, numbing my sense of smell in seconds.

I don't mind the sight of a corpse as much as I do the smell of it. For me, there's nothing human anymore about a body. It's nothing but a carnal envelope, and, surely, what really matters is what's inside the envelope. You have to delve inside the body to find the soul.

'So you're taking up sewing now, are you?' Jules asks Céci, who's busy stitching up Philippe Caron's torso.

'Don't get me started,' Céci sighs, blowing her dark fringe out of her eyes. 'I've been lumbered with a third-year student and twice already today he's puked this close to my feet. Another one who should have gone into dentistry.'

The seamstress puts down her tools and moves over to the stainless-steel sink to remove her gloves and wash her hands.

'It feels like I'm doing household chores today, not performing an autopsy,' she says, raising her voice over the trickling of the water. 'It's hellish. I don't know what he did to his wife, but she really did a number on him. Thirty-one stab wounds, to be precise. Twenty-nine of those were to the abdomen; that's the softest part of the body and the easiest to penetrate. Étienne, no. Get out!' Céci suddenly shrieks and glares over my shoulder.

For a second I wonder if she's talking to a dog. But we turn and see a tall, skinny youth who's frozen solid by the saloon doors that are still swinging behind him.

'Go to the office and type up the findings from the Ballanger autopsy.'

The student leaves without any discussion, eyes glued to his shoes.

'Christ. Like I need him to butt in again and throw up another pool of puke for me to clean. Right, where was I? Ah, yes. Of the thirty-one knife wounds, only two were inflicted to the heart, and right in the middle of it, though the penetration of the blade was only superficial. The depth of the wounds is consistent with the typical strength of a woman of Pauline Caron's age and build. So has she decided to open her mouth, then?'

Jules and I shake our heads in unison.

Céci smiles. 'You make me think of a little old couple, you two. Chickadee and Sweet Maxine.'

'Jules is the love of my life. In every sense but one,' I reply in all seriousness, before crunching the rest of my mint.

'Well, aren't you sweet!' Jules exclaims, exaggerating a charmer's wink.

'You're just saying that because you don't live with him,' Céci goes on. 'The day-to-day's the killer. I spend my days up to my eyes in blood and guts, but nothing turns my stomach more than walking into the bathroom after my husband's been. Nothing like it for killing the mood.'

'Lovely,' Jules muses.

'Wait ... what was I saying?'

'You were telling us about the delights of conjugal life,' he reminds her, handing me another mint.

'Yes, so guess what I've found out by stretching Philippe Caron out on my table? Those thirty-one knife wounds were not the cause of death. I mean, they would have been more than enough to do him in, but that's not the case here.'

'You're kidding?' Jules is flabbergasted.

'What else have you discovered?' I ask, fearing the worst.

'Philippe Caron died as a result of cranial trauma.'

'What?' Jules cries.

'Shit,' I mutter, intelligently. So much for putting this case to bed swiftly. Unless the investigation finds that this head injury was inflicted by Mrs Caron too.

'Have a look at this,' Céci continues, lifting and turning Philippe Caron's head. She points to a wound at the back. 'That's what killed him, in an instant.'

14
Maxine
2002

We're sitting in Jules's car, the heater blasting as we blow on our coffees. My phone rings. I answer it and, same as always when it's the boss calling me, the conversation begins with a bark. I put her on speakerphone.

'Tell me what's happening.'

I can hear her nibbling on one of those seeds of hers that she has to wash down with green tea. Organic. Of course.

'We're just leaving Céci. Caron died as a result of cranial trauma.'

Marceau stops chewing.

'Céci noted two deep wounds to the back of the head, typical of a fall, she says.'

'So did he pass out, then, or have a heart attack?' she asks.

'No, nothing of the sort. He was in perfect health.'

'Anything on the toxicology report?'

'Nothing there, either. It was a heavy fall. Céci thinks he was likely pushed into the chimney lintel and then he landed on a cast-iron sculpture on the hearth. Simon should be getting back to us soon about the samples they collected at the scene.'

Marceau groans at the other end of the line.

'He might well have been pushed by Pauline Caron,' Jules chips in.

'A third party may also have been in the house,' Marceau retorts.

'There's nothing to suggest that,' Jules replies.

'It had been snowing. Any tire tracks or footprints might have been covered over in the night,' I reply.

'For sure, but we've found no clues to suggest that anyone else was there, inside. If Pauline Caron had the force and the anger in her to inflict thirty-one stab wounds on her husband, surely she had the strength to shove him as well.'

'Lieutenant?' Marceau presses me.

'I don't see why she'd lay into her husband's body like that if someone else had already gone to the trouble of killing him. That doesn't hold up. The silence she's sunk into and the psychological shock she's suffering fit with Jules's theory. She killed her husband and can't come to terms with it.'

'All right. Where are you now?'

'Parked outside McGill University. We're going to meet with the chair of the faculty of arts, where Caron taught.'

'I've got the search warrant for his office. I'm sending in a team to collect his computer and files.' With that, Marceau hangs up as abruptly as always.

꩜

Roxanne Bouchard is waiting to greet us at the entrance to the main building. She makes me think of a version of Botticelli's Venus, flourishing in her forties and sculpted in a pair of leather trousers: just as radiant, yet streets-ahead sexy.

'I was afraid you'd lose your way in the maze of the faculty,' she explains, shaking us by the hand, her smile dimpling in delight. 'Come, I'll show you to Philippe's office. Let's take the scenic route,' she suggests, pointing to a long corridor. 'We can speak more freely that way.'

'Had you known Philippe Caron for a long time?'

She averts her gaze from mine and turns it to the floor. 'Sixteen years.'

She clears her throat before she goes on.

'Philippe was a learned man, a man with a passion. But first and foremost he was an excellent educator, which made his courses very popular. He wasn't a teacher, he was a storyteller. This way.' She guides us into a stairwell. 'Philippe never locked his office, only the filing cabinet where he kept the copies of student exams. His students would often drop in to deliver an assignment or return a book he'd loaned them; they would also come by to chat about his class, or about some coursework or reading. I did find it concerning to see students filing into his office, but there was never a single incident to regret. So he must have been doing things right. OK, here we are.'

She unlocks the door, then suddenly removes her hand from the doorknob.

'Sorry. Perhaps you want to, I don't know ... seal the premises?'

'No, if there was that much coming and going, it won't be necessary,' Jules explains. 'Our colleagues will be coming to get his computer and some of his things. Just keep the room locked, like we asked you yesterday.'

'Oh, all right,' she says, turning the knob.

The door opens onto an imposing mahogany desk that has its back turned to a row of three large windows. To the left, a brown leather armchair sits beside a *semainier*: a chest of drawers – seven of them, each with a lock. Shelves stuffed with books line the walls.

'I have a copy of the key. It opens all the drawers,' Roxanne tells me, seeing my gaze linger on the chest.

'Did he have an assistant or a secretary?'

'No, he took care of his own mail and correspondence, with the help of his wife.' Roxanne shuts the door behind us.

'He must've had real charisma,' I continue, going over to one of the walls of books.

'Yes, but let me stop you right there. He didn't use his

charisma or his charm, even less his learnedness, to seduce his students or colleagues. Philippe was entirely devoted to his wife. As she was to him. They were so endearing, the two of them. Whenever they were together, there was space only for them, for their connection, and nothing else. As if they were simply enough for one another.'

A veil of tears covers her eyes.

'A stifling kind of relationship?' I press, somewhat pitilessly.

'No, no, not at all. Not in that sense, no. Sorry, I didn't word that the right way. There was nothing stifling about it. Quite the opposite, theirs was the kind of love that lifts you up, the kind that drives you to become a better version of yourself. You see what I mean?'

No, I don't, but now's not the time to be telling her my life story.

'So ... no dalliances at all, you say, no matter how minor or insignificant, with colleagues, or students? Female or male?'

'None whatsoever.'

'Not even any rumours?' Jules chimes in. He's pulled on a pair of gloves and is tapping away at the computer.

'No. Listen, Philippe was a brilliant and very handsome man. And I'm sure plenty would have liked to end up in bed with him. Me included, when I first landed at McGill. But honestly, if that had been his style, there would've been stories, don't you think?'

She pauses for a moment, trying to collect herself. I'm sure she's going to ask me something about the investigation. I'm waiting, but she can't seem to make up her mind.

'Had he seemed preoccupied or concerned at all lately?' Jules joins in.

'Not recently, no ... but he did about six months ago.'

'What happened?'

'Nothing in particular. I just found him to be a bit ... absent. Like he had his head in the clouds. It went on for a few weeks, just before the summer break. He was spending more time here, in his office, and at his apartment in town.'

Jules and I give each other a look. What apartment is she talking about?

15
Lina
1949

I'm late for choir practice.

Leaving the house this morning, I forgot my outfit for our Christmas concert rehearsal, so I've had to run home and get it now, right before I go to church.

Still sweating, I'm getting changed in the sacristy with the other girls, turning my back to Tamara to avoid her teasing me about my non-existent breasts, my knock knees or something or other. She always finds something that's never bothered me before.

'Do hurry along, girls,' Mrs Morin urges us with a clap of her hands.

I certainly won't be reading *The Damned* by Huysmans to *her*.

We scurry out of the sacristy to take our places in the choir, a semicircle wearing red and white. The boys are dressed in black and white. Luckily, Tamara and Julie are at the other end of my row, far enough away for me to ignore them.

I close my eyes for a moment to cut myself off from them and the nuisance noises a church always amplifies: the squeaking sole of a shoe, a cough, a sniffle, whispers. I block everything out and focus not on the words to 'O, Christmas Tree', which I find beyond stupid, but on the melody. On the vibrations the singing triggers in my mouth, in my throat, in my belly; on the harmony of voices blending one into the other in spite of the distance between us. I focus on all this beauty that's bristling my skin like the cold's chilling caress.

I open my eyes to find myself being called to order by Mrs Morin, who's gesticulating like she's milking a mad cow.

The first thing I see is Tamara's gaping mouth, the look in her eye shifting from surprise to amusement. Then I see her raise her arm and extend it horizontally to point her index finger in my direction. Her laughter is unleashed simultaneously, triggering a domino effect in the choir as they all lay eyes on me.

I lower mine, trying to understand what could be provoking the overwhelming hilarity.

The sight knocks the breath out of me like a punch in the stomach. Streams of red, smearing the white wool of my stockings. On my right leg, it's dribbled all the way down into my shoe. I'm suddenly aware of my sticky, blood-soaked panties.

I feel mortified. Frozen to the spot.

I don't know how to react to the laughing.

The tears are welling up inside me.

I clench my teeth. I can't give them this satisfaction.

'Goodness me! Go and get changed, Lina, what are you waiting for?'

Slowly, I turn my head to Mrs Morin. If I get changed in there, in the sacristy, I'll have to come out and join the choir again. And I'll have to walk outside at the end of the rehearsal. Three times, I'll have to suffer their jeering.

I leave my place and cross the nave, reminding myself with every step to walk calmly, not to give in to the temptation to run, to hold back my tears. Not to release the sobs that are surging inside me, up into my nose. To choke them back. I force myself to ignore the calls to order Mrs Morin is hurling at my back, to forget about the screeching raptors and their laughter I'm leaving behind me. I push the door, which resists for a second, and turn around to shut it quick as can be, eyes down so they don't meet anyone else's.

And then I run, I run in my stockings stained with menstrual blood, because that's what it must be. I run, shivering in the icy air that's burning my ears, my throat and my lungs, crying all the pent-up tears in my chest from these long minutes that have seemed like days.

My legs lead me to the madhouse.

I lower my eyes, once more, as I walk past the bearded ven-triloquist on the door, who barely notices me. For the short distance separating me from the sitting room, I press myself flat against the walls and hope I don't run into anyone, and especially not Mother. Luckily, Solange is the only one who comes by, looking for Léonard, her teddy bear, most likely, and she ignores me completely.

The door is wide open and the old lady is there.

She sees my dishevelled reflection in the window and immediately turns away from her sunset. She lowers a hand to the wheel of her chair and swings it to one side.

All she needs is one look, one second.

'Come,' she commands. 'Push me.'

I hurry over to her wheelchair, place my trembling hands on the handles and turn her to face the door.

'No, no, go that way,' she says, pointing to the other end of the room, her hands righting the direction of the wheels.

There's a hidden door, painted to look just like the walls, that I've never noticed before, with a key in the lock.

I stop in front of it.

I don't have time to step to the side and around the wheelchair before she leans forwards to unlock the door and yank it open a crack.

'Shut it behind us,' she tells me, sitting back, the chair creaking in spite of her small stature.

Inside, she turns to the right and presses a switch.

We're in a room pierced by three tall windows that must be twice the size of the sitting room, with a bed flanked by a bedside table and a wardrobe, and a desk facing the middle window. A bookcase fills one whole wall and the others are covered with paintings in finely sculpted gold frames. There's also a coffee table surrounded by two armchairs and a sofa.

'Open the wardrobe,' she urges me. 'On the bottom shelf you'll find some panties and some white woollen stockings. Take two pairs of panties. Fold the second in two. That'll do as a pad until you get home. You can go behind there to change.'

She points to a folding screen that looks to me like a much bigger version of the things people put in front of a fireplace.

'Just leave your dirty laundry on the floor. The new girl will wash it for you. And you'll get it back clean tomorrow. Your mother won't know a thing. Tell her you lent your overcoat to a classmate who got hers wet. I'll give you something to put on for the way home.'

I wonder for a moment if Mrs Morin will tell Mother about my hasty departure from choir practice. But I know she won't say a word, simply to avoid uttering the word 'menstruation'.

I slip behind the screen, rid myself of my bloody drawers, replace them with Lucienne's, which are a bit too big but will do the job, then I step out again.

'You missed your sunset, and it's all my fault,' I say, seeing the sky is as black as ink.

'Oh, it's not mine. You can still read to me, though. Have you finished the Huysmans?'

I shake my head.

'You'll find it in my library. Everything's in alphabetical order.'

For a second I stand still in surprise. Then my legs carry me to the shelves stocked with books, where I find Huysmans beside Hugo. I reach for *The Damned* and open it on my way to the sofa.

The old lady has wheeled her chair behind the desk; she turns her back on me so she's facing the window, as if the sun were still clinging to a couple of clouds.

'Chapter fifteen,' I announce, sitting down.

'Chapter fifteen,' she repeats, without turning around.

16
Maxine
2002

'You know, I don't believe a word of Bouchard's character reference for Caron,' Jules tells me as he's unlocking the door to the professor's apartment.

Roxanne Bouchard agreed to give us the spare set of keys Philippe Caron had left with his faculty's secretary. So we've decided to go straight there without passing Go, and by that I mean speaking to the big boss.

'After you, *Lieutenant*,' he teases, Marceau-style, holding the door open for me.

The bachelor pad is on the second floor of a luxury apartment building on Crescent Street in Montreal, right in the heart of the Golden Square Mile. I have to hand it to him: the brilliant professor didn't exactly scrimp on his expenses.

The door opens into a narrow hallway elegantly decorated with a tempered-glass and wrought-iron console and a white padded leather stool; three mirrors adorn the wall to the right, and hanging to the left is a reproduction of an Impressionist classic, the name of which escapes me.

I pull on my latex gloves and open the drawer in the hallway console. 'Look,' I say to Jules, handing him the bills I've just found.

'In both of their names? That's bizarre.'

'Not if they own the place together, Jules. Who's to say Pauline Caron didn't share this little *pied-à-terre* and stay here with him after a book launch or a talk, to save the hour or hour and a half drive back to Lac-Clarence at night?'

'Aw, listen to you getting all mushy. Sounds like someone's been reading too much chick lit. No, if you ask me, he put the apartment in both their names for tax reasons, or maybe even just to keep up appearances – even if he was screwing around left, right and centre.'

We follow the hallway to a vast living space with an open-plan kitchen and dining nook that flows into a lounge dominated by a white, leather, U-shaped sectional facing a state-of-the-art flatscreen television.

'Nothing like the bucolic charm of their house, is it?' says Jules.

'It's very impersonal. Makes me think of a luxury hotel suite.'

'More of a shag pad than a love nest.'

'Mmm, good point.'

'Anyway, I can't see any hands being chopped off here, not with a sofa as white as that. Unless he kept replacing it.'

'You're talking like he's guilty already,' I chide, striding across the lounge. 'Wait until we know what's on their computers, Jules. They might turn out to be collectors, that's all.'

'Aye aye, Lieutenant!' he barks over my shoulder, yanking a smile out of me.

I enter the one and only bedroom, which looks just as Scandinavian as the rest of the apartment, with its sleek and obsessively white decor that seems far more dismal than any matte black.

I open the wardrobe and find a combination of manly and feminine things.

'Looks just like Pauline's style, eh?'

I squeal. 'Bloody hell, you scared me there. I didn't hear you come in.'

He carries on regardless. 'In the bathroom, I found exactly the same toiletries and things as she had at their place in Lac-Clarence. The same shampoo, shower gel, day cream, hairspray, eyeliner, body lotion, you name it.'

'So it seems she would come and stay overnight and spend time in this apartment, then.'

'But that doesn't mean her husband didn't have hookups here.'

'Hookups?' I ask.

'That's what I said. He might have had fuck buddies when his wife wasn't around, but there's nothing to say it was women he brought back here. Imagine if that's what Pauline Caron found out?'

'And you think she would have laid into him with that much violence because he was into guys?'

'You'd be surprised how much hate my sexual preferences can stir up. Lac-Clarence is a small community, Max, and that couple were a pillar of it. Imagine that woman's shame. And her anger at a man who never gave her a child.'

I wince. 'I don't know, Jules...'

'Better canvass the neighbours to see if they saw any of his conquests coming or going.'

'Jeez, you're like a dog with a bone, aren't you?'

'Who, me?'

Something startles me again, and this time it's the sound of my phone. I pull it out of the front pocket of my jeans, realising my Levi's feel tighter than ever. Marceau's started braying before I even pick up. Her first word is cut off, and all I catch of it is the dying of her high pitch. She's obviously not calling to share good news.

'Get back to Lac-Clarence right away. They've found something at the Caron place.'

17
Maxine
2002

I'm walking behind Jules, following a trench of footsteps cut by the crime-scene team and their boots. Even though they've packed the path down, we're still sinking up to our ankles in snow. I bet they had fun lugging all their gear through the forest in minus twelve degrees and powder like this.

It turns out the Carons' property extends for dozens of hectares around their home. I thought the woods I could see from the house belonged to the regional county municipality. I'd never have suspected the couple were the proud owners of the surrounding forest.

'Remind me to move to Mexico, will you?' Jules shivers. 'When we talk about freezing our balls off in this country of ours, we're not kidding.'

'Or freezing our tits off. I don't know why I don't keep a pair of boots in my car. I can't tell you what state my feet are in. Frozen to the bone, they are.'

'Yeah, well we're not usually expecting to go trekking in the woods on work time, are we?'

The cabin emerges at last from behind a clump of white spruce and we pick up the pace, like a pair of frozen, starving fair-weather strollers happening upon a welcome refuge.

'It looks like a Hansel and Gretel house, but without all the sweet stuff. Maybe it's the Weight Watchers version,' Jules jokes.

Simon's standing outside, a few metres from the entrance. He's smoking a cigarillo and knocking the ash into a little tin with a lid. He stubs it out when he sees us approaching, and mimics a military salute before leading the way into the snow-covered cabin, which all but blends into the milky background.

The door hinges moan like aching joints. We find ourselves in a single open space, which would be as chilly as outside were it not for the powerful floodlights making my colleagues' work easier. I'm hoping the warmth will help thaw my toes too. Now is really not the time for me to catch my death. That said, I don't think there's ever a good time for your body to give up on you, is there?

I have a quick look around and, other than a big hearth at one end of the cabin, a few hooks here and there on the walls and two milking stools, there's nothing here.

'Kill the lights!' Simon suddenly orders.

'Reminds me of the first and only time I was with a girl,' Jules whispers in my ear. 'I took one look down at her bits and thought to myself, "Do I really have to go *there*?" Anyway, I turned the light off so I could imagine it was something else, if you know what I mean.'

I give him a jab with my hip to shut him up, but I can't help smiling. Darkness envelops us in an instant and I realise both windows in here have been masked on the inside.

'Whoa, look at that,' Jules exclaims as the sudden gloom reveals an abundance of bluish stains, droplets, spatters and pools on the walls and floor of the cabin.

'Bloody hell!' I cry, echoing in spite of myself what Jules said at the Carons' house.

'You can say that again, Lieutenant Grant,' Simon replies. 'The stuff's everywhere. Trust me, there must have been quite the bloodbath here.'

18

Lucienne
1899

Mary wanted to make a detour to see the Pont Alexandre III being built. The newspapers have reported that Lacarrière, the foundry behind the sumptuous chandelier at the Palais Garnier, would be casting the thirty-two candelabras for the bridge and she wanted to see if they had started fitting them. This is far from being the case, though, yet the Exposition Universelle is looming. Every Parisian is griping about the delays to the building works. They'll never be finished in time, and their city will be the laughing stock of the world. *They'll* be the laughing stock of the world. Suddenly, I can picture Jeanne in the carriage with us, the wonder in her eyes, her mouth agape, being such a keen observer, taking such a masculine interest in bridges and other ambitious architectural projects.

I know Mary is thinking of Jeanne too, at this very moment.

I flash her a brief smile, which she returns – acknowledging everything we share. My thoughts turn to the last time I laid eyes on my children, the night they disappeared. I tightened the curlers in their hair before kissing them goodnight.

We arrive at Maxim's, on the Rue Royale, a few minutes early.

Violette is waiting for us inside the café – 'at her usual table', the waiter informs us.

'Ah, here you are, my dear.' She greets me with warmth and exuberance, touching a hand to the sleeve of my black dress. Then she purses her lips and sadness pulls at the seams of her face. 'Mademoiselle Gagnon,' she murmurs to Mary at last, gracing her with a brief nod, to which my cousin responds with the same distance. The purple feathers in Violette's hat are dancing with her every movement. 'I've ordered tea and biscuits for us,' she continues.

'Thank you kindly, Violette,' I reply, setting down my parasol.

'Have you seen how much this place has changed?' she says, with a glance to her surroundings. 'It's bold, but I think it's sublime.' She leans towards us. 'Between you and me,' she whispers, 'I hear they've furnished apartments upstairs for courtesans, the kind who seduce the greats – and I'm not just talking about kings, princes and ministers. I shan't name any names.' She mimes sewing up her mouth with a needle and thread. 'But believe me, there'll be plenty of husbands going home rather later than usual...'

Mary blushes. And I'm no better, myself.

'Have you been out and about?' she suddenly enquires, changing the topic, to my great relief.

'Mary wanted to see how the work on the Pont Alexandre III was coming on.'

'Ah, don't say a word, it's driving me mad how slow things are. I thought they would have built the moving walkway too, or finished the first line of the Métro, but no, nothing. One must wonder if they'll be ready by next April. Paris is going to be one long festival for months. How delightful.'

I nod politely, wondering what imperative has compelled her to invite me here.

'Have you had any news from the detective?' Violette continues.

I allow myself a breath. 'He says he hasn't found anything to suggest that ... that they were abducted. No one noticed anything suspicious in the vicinity of our home, not anyone carrying two sleeping children, or any questionable trunks or packages ... and no ... no screaming either...'

I bite my lip and shake my head. Violette places her satin-gloved hand on mine.

'He thinks that their ... that they ... that they'll be found in the rubble,' I conclude, lowering my eyes.

'All right, all right,' she intervenes, tapping my forearm, as if she's already tiring of my tears and my hesitations. Then she drills her artfully made-up eyes into mine. 'Have you heard of Victor Hugo's little whim? One his wife and son share, I might add.'

I sit up in my chair, squirming inelegantly.

'Of his taste for ... conversations with the beyond?' I venture, hoping not to trip up.

She concurs with a sharp movement of her chin, which reassures me. Her eyes sparkle with excitement.

'Have you read the write-ups of these seances, Lucienne? They're un-be-liev-a-ble.'

I nod. Who hasn't heard of Hugo's passion for spiritual seances? Of the chair he famously saved for passing spirits in his house on Guernsey? During these table-turning episodes, the writer supposedly conversed with Galileo, Balzac, Jesus Christ, Socrates, the dove from Noah's Ark, and even concepts such as Death and Poetry. But most importantly, he was able to engage with Léopoldine, his beloved drowned daughter.

'What do you think, Lucienne?'

Her question takes me aback. Violette does not belong to the class of ladies who ask the views of others.

'I ... struggle to believe it.'

'I'm telling you about it,' she continues as if I had expressed no reservation, 'because the evening before last, I was at a dinner where we were discussing Madame de Thèbes and her next Christmas Almanac.'

'Isn't she the fortune teller on the Avenue de Wagram?'

'That's right. The lady who owes her popularity to Alexandre Dumas – the son, obviously. Well, it turns out she's predicted a great many events and conflicts, which is simply frightful and terrifying when one thinks about it. The mere notion that our future is already written saddens me immensely. As it happens, this Madame de Thèbes is heralding a second Boer War not long from now. As well as a world war at the beginning of the next century. Can you imagine the drama?' She shakes her head with visible concern. 'In short, our hostess was telling me that she had partaken in a Spiritism seance at the astronomer Camille Flammarion's home with an Italian clairvoyant, a certain Eusapia Palladino, who – wait for it – is said to have levitated a table.'

'Levitated a table?' I repeat dumbly, overcome with surprise and curiosity.

'And,' Violette continues as if there's nothing to it, 'it seems that scientists from around the world have come to study this clairvoyant, or medium, as they're known now. As if it weren't enough to lift objects without touching them, it seems she can communicate with the dead and others who have disappeared. She says she can hear them calling for help.'

Nausea sweeps over me. I swallow a mouthful of my tea, which has appeared on the table.

'My God, Lucienne, I've upset you, you're pale...'

I set down my cup and saucer, trying to pull myself together. 'No, I ... I beg your pardon. Please, do go on, Violette.'

She tilts her head, reaches for my hand and grasps it between her palms.

'I'm taking you back to that night ... to the night of the fire. I'm so sorry, my dear Lucienne, so very sorry. I'm not bringing it back in vain, I promise you that. Do forgive my lack of tact, but you're still so young. It grieves me terribly to see you dressed in black at your age. You could go on living, have children again. You're far too young to die of despair. That's why we simply must know what happened to your daughters. And I think that Eusapia Palladino could help you. Help us. To find Jeanne and Rose. Wherever they may be. Up there. Or down here.'

19
Lina
1949

'*The Spirits' Book*, by Allan Kardec,' I announce as I sit on the sofa.

'You won't understand a thing.'

'You'll explain it to me, won't you?'

My little old lady smiles. Her chair is turned to face me.

'So be it,' she replies, adjusting the panels of her damask skirt.

'"Introduction to the Spiritist Doctrine",' I read, leaning comfortably into a soft cushion.

'Do you at least know who Allan Kardec was?'

I shake my head and carry on. 'First of all, I have a question. Do you know what the Louviers possessions are?'

She looks up at me. 'Whatever is making you ask a question like that? Allan Kardec?'

I shake my head. 'Father Tremblay. He's a sort of ... secretary to Father Dion. He heard a lad in the choir talking about possession. By the Devil, I mean.'

'Oh, really? Why would this young man bring up a matter of that sort?'

'He said the Devil touches nothing of what belongs to the divine. That if lightning were to strike, we would be protected, there, inside the church.'

'Mmmhm.'

'Father Tremblay replied that lightning was a divine act, but it could strike everywhere. He said too that some nuns had been possessed by the Devil. And he mentioned the possessions at Louviers. I wanted to know if it was true.'

Again she smiles, but now her eyes are sparkling with ... it's malice, I think that's what I see.

'And why do you think that a man of the Church would lie to you?'

'Have you ever tried walking on water?'

She bursts out laughing. Her liana-like braid slides off her shoulder and down her back.

I wait for her laughter to subside.

'Yes, the possessed nuns of Louviers did exist. It happened in the seventeenth century, in a convent in Normandy, in the northwest of France. There was even a trial that lasted for several years. It seems Father Tremblay is worthy of trust, then,' she smirks.

I'm satisfied with her answer, because I like Father Tremblay. And I'm about to carry on reading, or rather, get started, when she interrupts me – with nothing but a drawing of breath, a suspended thought, a question preparing to hatch.

'You haven't mentioned the choir in a long time, Lina. Since you've just opened the door a crack – by mentioning Father Tremblay – I thought I'd sneak inside.'

She marks a silence to make sure I want to let her in. I turn my gaze towards her. To the braid she's slipping once more between her shoulder and her breast.

'How are things going?'

'Not well,' I whisper, lowering my eyes again.

Since the period episode, Tamara has regained the upper hand. Julie is far more reserved, though, as if she were taking pity on me, but that's no better. Although ... I don't know.

'I want...' I wonder if I can share this with her, the desire that's throbbing in my chest. 'I want to see ... fear in her eyes...'

There, I dared to say it.

I wait.

'Respect or deference, that would be much better, don't you think?' she replies.

'I don't know ... perhaps...'

'Everything stems from your posture.'

'My posture? If I stand up straight, you mean?'

'Not just that. But it's a start. Straighten yourself up.'

I get to my feet.

'No, sit down again.'

I do what I'm told.

'Now, lengthen your back. Imagine there's a string tied to the top of your head and I'm pulling on it.'

I put my spine to work.

'There you go. Perfect. Now open your bust, draw your shoulders back.'

Automatically, I release a deep sigh.

'You see. How do you feel?'

'Powerful.'

She cackles as I sigh with joy once more.

'Interesting,' I continue. 'And beautiful.'

'Perfect.'

She tips and taps the underside of her chin slightly. I mimic her.

'Good. When I mentioned posture, I specifically meant how you react to the insults and provocations. Torturers like Tamara feed on fear and submission. She smiles when she's attacking you, doesn't she?'

I nod my head, yes.

'Do the same thing. Return the smile with a slight tip of your chin, like I've just shown you.'

'Like this?' I ask, trying to reproduce the image that's taking shape in my mind.

'Like that, yes. Mimic her. Smile. Put her in a place of shame. Disarm her. Make your response mirror her question. Have the courage to confront her.'

The prospect of confronting Tamara both excites and frightens me.

'It's like when you're playing chess,' she continues.

'Tamara, she's the ... king?'

'Mmmhm. And you're the queen, but you've forgotten you can move everywhere.'

'So ... if I put her in check ... the chess board is mine?'

'Exactly, Lina. The chess board belongs to you.'

20
Maxine
2002

Jules brings a basket overflowing with doughnuts to my desk.

'Here you go. One vegetarian breakfast, homemade by your very own Chickadee.'

'So long as it's grain based, that's all right with me.'

'Sunflower oil, that's from grains. Flour, well, that's from grains too. Sugar ... does granulated count?'

He manages to get a smile out of me.

We're interrupted by the hurried clicking of Marceau's heels. Gina and her pumps are clacking right behind, but to a different beat. Marceau's are a symphony of quavers, while Gina's are playing crotchets, all swiftness without haste, tempting me to prick an ear.

'I've just briefed Professor Montminy about the Montreal apartment and the cabin found on the Carons' property,' the big boss announces, getting down to business without a word to greet us or set the mood.

'No-Lube Léonie', that's her nickname here at the station. Classy, I know, but what can you expect in a profession saturated with testosterone?

'Sergeant, have you spoken to the delivery driver?' Marceau continues.

Yes, he has. 'All clean on that front, it seems.'

'And someone's canvassing the neighbours on Crescent Street, are they?' she asks, perching on a desk, ignoring the chairs as always.

Biting into a doughnut, I nod. The sugar coats my tongue, caresses my palate. The velvety dough melts in my mouth. A veritable carnal pleasure, this is. A rush of endorphins. For me, there's no softer drug than sugar.

Marceau ignores the basket Jules is holding out to her. I'm sure she's not doing it on purpose. I understand, and respect, her absolute rejection of the stuff. It's a defensive reflex. The doughnut is the embodiment of her two arch-enemies. Fat and sugar, the passionate, copulating couple.

'We're not expecting them to report back until tomorrow morning,' Jules replies for me, unbuttoning his woollen cardigan. 'It all depends on the neighbours they have or haven't managed to speak to.'

'Any cameras in the lobby of the building?'

We shake our heads in unison.

'Are the traces of blood that were found on the chimney lintel and the cast-iron sculpture consistent with the autopsy findings?'

'Yes,' Jules replies. 'Simon's confirmed that.'

'Have you seen the results of the samples that were taken from the Carons' vehicle?'

'Yes, they came in this morning. Nothing.'

'What about the ones from the cabin?'

'Not yet, no. But I'd say we've found the place where the hands were cut off.'

'We *might* have found the place,' I correct him.

'What? You're still not convinced?'

'Not until the test results come in, no.'

'We've got seven severed hands, mounted on plinths under glass domes, hidden in six rooms of the Caron house. We've got a cabin dripping with blood on the property as well, and you're not convinced?'

'Luminol is a presumptive test. Until the results of the samples are in, we can't be sure that it's human blood in there. So no, Jules, I'm not convinced yet.'

Jules shakes his head.

This reminds me of my argument with Charlotte this morning. What used to be discussions two years ago have turned into duels with yelling, crying and doors slamming. It's as if there's a playwright in the room, sprinkling every conversation, every decision, every disagreement with a dash of Racinian drama. I'll be glad when this bloody phase has passed.

Marceau calls us to order. 'Where are we at with the computers?'

'I was just getting to that,' Jules replies. 'We've been tied up with the Montreal apartment and the bloodstained cabin, so Sergeant David's taking care of that. I'd already been through the computer Philippe Caron kept at home with a fine-tooth comb and all I found was word-processing stuff. Word documents, all to do with his research, books, classes or articles he was writing for university publications or magazines. His online history only shows weekly connections to his inbox. Looks like he only checked and replied to his personal emails on weekends. That means no browsing tracks for any basic auction or murderabilia sites. I didn't even find any trace of him accessing porn sites, and that's saying something. He must still be doing the DVD thing. Still, Sergeant David came in behind me and gave things a good seeing-to, if you'll pardon the expression.'

Jules touches a finger to his nose and clears his throat, delighting for a moment in the pleasure of his innuendo. I note Gina's amused smile as she helps herself to another doughnut. And Marceau's total lack of reaction as she waits for what's next, arms folded to a white silk blouse ironed to perfection.

'David didn't find anything either. Same with Philippe Caron's work computer. He only really went online to get into his work inbox, which was merged with his personal email, as it happens. A few hits on the university web portal, but nothing else. Other than that, just Word documents, the same as those on his personal computer. Basically, there's nothing to suggest those hands were purchased online. Pauline Caron didn't surf the web much more. She used her husband's email address and doesn't even have one of her own. On her computer, we found all of Caron's books. Looks like she typed and edited them.'

'The publisher has confirmed that to me,' I comment through a mouthful of my second doughnut as I observe Gina, who's scribbling on her notepad.

'As for their two phone lines,' Jules continues, 'Sergeant David has been a great help to me there as well. Husband and wife shared a landline and just the one mobile, and the contract for those is in Pauline Caron's name. It seems they both used that mobile, because the university would call Philippe on that number.'

Jules refers to his notes with a scratch of his nascent beard. Suddenly, I can sense the coarse bristles of my husband's face on my lips. The delicious tickle that would always draw a sigh of pleasure from me, wherever we were.

I let go of the memory rather than hanging on to it. I know how to do that, now.

'So, on both numbers, not in any particular order, we've got incoming and outgoing calls with libraries, bookshops and other Canadian and French universities where the professor was giving lectures, holding book launches and having meetings. A few restaurants for dinner reservations. And lastly, there's a number they called once or twice a week. Belongs to a couple, Bernadette and Richard Damatian. Pauline and Bernadette volunteer at the school together and they run the choir in Lac-Clarence. *Voilà.* I think I've covered everything. So basically, we've got nothing, not a sausage, to sink our teeth into. It's deflating.'

'Mid-morning, we're meeting with Bernadette Damatian,' I say. 'I suppose the sniffer dogs haven't found anything on the Carons' property?'

Marceau shakes her head.

My phone vibrates in my hand.

'It's Simon,' I say out loud, seeing the name on the screen.

I flip the phone open and put it down on my desk.

'Hi, Simon, I've got you on speakerphone.'

'Ah, right. OK. It's about the validation results of the immuno-chromatographic tests ... er ... I mean the results of the tests on the samples revealed with luminol. They're negative.'

'Wait, which ones are you talking about?'

'The ones from the Montreal apartment—'

'Right, well no surprise there,' Jules cuts in. 'I'd be surprised if they severed those hands there.'

'And the cabin as well.'

'What?' Jules cries, flabbergasted. 'Holy shit.'

'Yes ... well, it is blood, but it's animal blood. Wild game, probably, given the quantity of it.'

'But Caron wasn't a hunter,' Jules tuts. 'We've found nothing in the home to suggest he was, anyway.'

'Maybe ... maybe he told his friends they could use the cabin for hunting? Or maybe some hunters just went in there and made themselves at home?' Simon ventures, as if he's distressed to have disappointed Jules.

'Shit,' Jules repeats.

'Yes. Sorry. Well. No. I mean...'

'Thank you, Simon,' I say, hanging up before Marceau starts barking. She's already rolling her eyes.

Silence follows the clack of my phone flipping shut.

'So ... back to square one, it is,' Jules sums things up.

21
Maxine
2002

'I'd like to begin my interviews with Pauline Caron,' Gina announces at the end of our morning meeting.

'Sure, no problem,' I reply, aware that she's not asking permission, but informing me in an elegant, understanding and quite agreeable way.

'All right if we start right away?'

'Of course. I suppose you'd rather be one on one with her?'

'Yes. Just one question, first.'

I acquiesce with an obliging smile.

'I'd like to know how long she spent outside her front door, before the police arrived.'

'According to the emergency medics, no more than two hours,' I tell her.

Gina turns her face to the right, as if a noise has just attracted her attention, then she nods her head several times.

'She spent the night with her husband,' I say, almost for myself. 'Kneeling by his side. That's what the blood on the floor and on her clothes tell us, in any case. Is that what you were wondering?'

'Yes,' she replies, turning to me. 'Shall we go?'

Gina follows me into the recording-and-viewing room.

Not ten seconds later, Jules pushes the door open behind us. 'She'll be here in a minute,' he tells us.

'Is it possible to film her feet and legs under the table?' Gina asks.

'Yes, you can zoom all the way in,' Jules replies, as the interview room door opens and Mrs Caron appears on the screen.

She's wearing the same clothes as the day before. There's a crinkle in her hair at the back of her head, probably from sleeping on it. The custody officer pulls out a chair for her to sit on, with a screech that makes us wince, even Jules. Mrs Caron obediently takes a seat. The officer removes her handcuffs and leaves the room.

'Look, I can zoom in like this,' Jules demonstrates.

The camera advances on Pauline Caron's legs, which are extended and crossed at the ankles. There's something almost disturbing about the close-up.

'Perfect,' Gina replies.

The psychologist leaves the control room. A few seconds later, we hear a knock at the interview-room door. Mrs Caron doesn't react. Gina enters the room. She's buttoned up her suit jacket and fastened her blouse all the way up to the neck. She closes the door behind her, then pivots on her heels.

'Hello, Mrs Caron.'

She looks down at my former teacher's hands, now free from their cuffs.

'I'm Ginette Montminy. The police have asked me to come in to help you and give you space to speak.'

Mrs Caron's eyes are anchored to the middle of the table. Gina flicks back a blonde lock that's caressing her cheek.

'You're free to fill this space. Or leave it empty, for that matter.'

She lets a silence linger.

I don't know what Gina's filled this quiet of hers with, but it's not heavy. It's anything but. The atmosphere is as light as the wake of a summer thunderstorm. When the sky loses its inhibitions and then has nothing more to say.

'You know, Mrs Caron, I'm a teacher, just like you,' Gina goes on with a smile. 'And even if we're loath to admit it, we all have a favourite student, don't we?'

Pauline stiffens, with just a subtle shift of her bosom. It's almost imperceptible.

Gina extends another silence, then speaks again, slowly and an octave lower.

'There are some people, those who make an impression on me and who matter to me, who, every time I think about them, bring music to my mind. As if there's a melody shadowing their every step. It's not synaesthesia. Just a tic of mine since I was a child.'

Gina smiles once more. A caring, maternal, mothering smile.

'When I think about my favourite student, I feel like singing a song about a bird.'

Without letting her smile slip, she begins to hum a song made popular by René Simard and his pure, angelic voice – one I used to listen to as a child, for months, on repeat.

And as Gina's voice carries the tune with power and precision, I find the lyrics scrolling by in my mind, as if I had sung them just yesterday.

> *These fine mists I know*
> *Winter mornings, pink snow*
> *I'll find it all, today*
> *The white hare, come out to play*
> *Though the bird, the bird's taken flight*
> *And never, ever find him, I might*

Then Gina begins to sing the words in her crisp, clear voice, infusing emotion, perhaps even experience, in every line.

> *...Since I saw the bird fly*
> *I saw the bird leave with my very own eye*
> *I heard the bird cry*
> *So fine, soar so far in the sky*
> *I'd give to you all that's mine*
> *But why won't you tell me a thing*
> *What great secret is yours to sing*

Abruptly, Mrs Caron clamps her legs together and slides her feet beneath her chair. She presses them so tightly, they begin to shake. The rest of her body, her bust, her arms, the face she's exposing to Gina, remains motionless.

> *The secret of a man*
> *It's one I understand*
> *I, you know...*

She utters a sudden snorting sound, then a series of staccato breaths that shake her shoulders. As the sobs shudder through her chest, she lowers her head and seems to shrink.

Gina raises a hand to the camera and gives us a brief nod, telling us not to intervene, singing all the while.

> *I, you know I can say*
> *How sorry the bird went away*
> *If you were to listen to me one day*
> *You'd teach me your every array*
> *Away the bird flies to return*
> *To see him tomorrow you'll yearn*

Mrs Caron lifts her head, shoulders still shuddering, then joins Gina in humming a shaky tune, weak but on track, as if she'd fallen mid-stride and were just getting up, limping, suffering, yet eager to run once more.

Gina keeps on singing, her gaze fixed on Mrs Caron, who's still humming the melody along with her.

> *This is the bird you loved*
> *The jealous bird I judged*
> *If he does return from his flight*
> *I'll tell him you waited all night*

Gina cuts the final note brutally short. It sounds like she's hit the mute button. I can see the words suspended in the silence. Not the lyrics to the song, the ones that are floating between the two of them.

'I'd like to go and rest now.'

I gasp in surprise, and Jules adds a 'holy shit' for punctuation.

'All right, Mrs Caron. I'll walk you back,' Gina stands and replies.

22
Maxine
2002

The three of us are sitting in my car, in silence, on our way to the Damatians' house. Despite Jules's insistence, Gina refused to sit in the front, making a point of not interfering with our routine, being involved without imposing.

She's looking out of the window, offering her noble, elegant self to me in profile. Rounded forehead, straight nose, high, prominent cheekbones, jutting chin – and that practised lock of hers, willowing over her cheek to rest on her shoulder. Since I first laid eyes on her, she's made me think of a Greek statue, with her confident, seamless curves, and the strength and determination she exudes.

'Do you know the Damatians?' she suddenly asks me, meeting my gaze in the rearview mirror.

'Not really, no,' I say, turning my eyes back to the road, embarrassed to have been caught looking at her. 'Their sons are six years younger than me, so we were never at school together. I would run into them in the village, of course. But the last time must have been...' I puff, flipping through the mental pages of time '... a good thirty years ago. I'm not sure I'd even recognise her.'

'What did she do, back then?'

'She and her husband were accountants. But I suppose they're both retired, now.'

Indeed, Bernadette Damatian has lost all resemblance to the slender woman I vaguely knew decades ago. She greets us, asking me if I'm Nicole and Raynald's daughter, by any chance. My affirmative reply is an invitation for her somewhat belated condolences, which beckon the memory of my parents. It's an impromptu but agreeable diversion, once the first, eternally painful second has passed.

She invites us to follow her into the living room, where two armchairs, their backs adorned with crocheted antimacassars, sit facing a narrow two-seater sofa. Jules and I take the sofa. Gina and Bernadette sit down across from us.

'Sorry,' Mrs Damatian says, getting up again. 'I've forgotten to offer you something to drink.'

'It's all right, thank—'

'I'll make you some coffee,' she cuts me off, leaving the room. 'Biscuits?' she asks from the kitchen.

'Don't trouble yourself,' I reply, knowing very well we won't be escaping the biscuits.

'Milk? Sugar?'

Gina grins at me.

'Both!' I cry to make sure my voice carries, before returning Gina's smile.

Jules is much quieter than usual; he seems lost in his thoughts. If Gina weren't here, I would be asking him, tongue in cheek, if his thoughts were clean enough to share. Instead, I nudge a knee into his to bring him back. Startled, he gives me a vague look and blinks like he's just woken up from an unexpected nap.

'Here you go,' Mrs Damatian announces, the clacking of her slippers preceding her voice.

She sets down a tray of steaming cups, teaspoons, milk and brown sugar, complete with a farandole of biscuits laid out on a plate.

'I can't believe what a media circus this whole thing's becoming,' she says, sitting down. 'This morning we walked past the village hall where you and your teams have set yourselves up, and, good heavens, Paparazzi all over the place. A gang of vultures, they are. We've seen the barricades you've put up by the Carons' driveway ... That can't make it easy to do your job, I imagine?'

'They're not helping things, no.'

'Well, I suppose they have to write something for the folk who buy those rags of theirs, don't they? Please, help yourselves.'

A clinking of cutlery fills the silence that Mrs Damatian is preparing to break. I can see her hesitating, shifting in her chair like it's uncomfortable. But the only thing that's uncomfortable is the situation.

'Is it true ... what people are saying?' she ventures, clumsily.

'What are people saying?' I ask, almost meanly.

'That Pauline ... that it was Pauline who killed Philippe.'

I take a sip of my *café au lait* before I reply.

'I don't know, Mrs Damatian. How about you, what do you think?'

She starts shaking her head vigorously. 'It can't be. It's just not possible. No, it can't be Pauline. She...'

Bernadette Damatian can't take her eyes off her knees, or stop seeing her memories of Pauline Caron.

'Fifty years, I've known her. Half a century. She's devoted her life to the school and the children of Lac-Clarence. Our children, my children. We run the choir together, and I help her with volunteer duties at the school. She's a generous, gentle, sweet and patient woman. My mum even used to work with hers. You have to understand, it's not ... it's just not possible.'

I give her a nod of acknowledgement, pursing my lips to show my compassion. To invite her to open up.

'So you must have seen one another quite often?' I ask.

She sniffs, lifts her chin, blinks away her tears. 'Twice a week, on Fridays for choir, and on Wednesdays at the school. We would phone each other regularly too.'

She casts a fleeting glance at Jules, who's scribbling notes in his pocketbook.

'Did you and your husband socialise with them as a couple too?' I continue.

'No, no. That wasn't their style. Philippe spent his time working. Writing, teaching, travelling to promote his books and giving talks, and Pauline would accompany him. They were very tied up. I mean, they would get involved in things in the community – village fêtes, book clubs, parties and all that, so they were far too busy for private dinners with friends.'

'How did they get on?'

'Very well. They were always together and I never saw them disrespect one another. Quite the contrary. Philippe was clearly very considerate of Pauline.'

'He was quite a bit younger than her ... so wasn't Pauline ... anxious, with all those women around him?' I ask.

Almost imperceptibly, Gina furrows her brow.

'Women?' Bernadette repeats. 'No one was circling him. He was a handsome man, for sure, but more of a – how should I say? – a cerebral ... an intellectual. I can't imagine him ... well, you know.' She wrings her hands.

'Pauline's never mentioned any arguments, any disagreements between the two of them?' Jules asks, extracting his nose from his notebook at last.

'They must have had some, like every couple, but Pauline doesn't share intimate things like that with other people. She's not ... forthcoming about her private life. That's not her style.'

'And she doesn't have any other friends, besides yourself?' I ask, helping myself to a sugar-coated biscuit.

Bernadette twists her lips into a dubious pout that crazes her mouth with wrinkles. 'No, not that I know of. People in the choir, perhaps, but she wouldn't see them outside our practices and concerts.'

'No family, no cousins?'

'They didn't have children, or siblings. Their parents had passed away, so no, I don't imagine they did.'

'Have you ever been to their house?'

'No. Like I said, it wasn't their style, and people in the village respected that.' A gentle crease graces her mouth. 'My husband liked to joke around and call them the Duke and Duchess Caron. Not to be nasty, you know, and it's not because they were snooty or anything. It's just that, well, they were a bit like royalty around here, you see.'

'Do you know if they spent much time at their apartment in Montreal?' Jules says.

'It depended on Philippe's commitments. They varied a lot.'

'Did he go there alone?' I ask.

'I'd be surprised if he did. Maybe if he had a talk on a choir night. But Pauline would have gone to join him later.'

'They both had a driver's licence?'

'Yes.'

'Were they into hunting?'

'Hunting?' Bernadette scoffs. 'No, I can't imagine them hunting.'

'And Philippe Caron, did he have any friends?' Jules chimes in again. 'Your husband, for example?'

'No, not that I know of. And no, not my husband. Certainly not,' she insists, turning her gaze skywards with sadness.

'And Pauline never mentioned Philippe going out at all?' I continue, undaunted.

'Going out?' Bernadette echoes. 'No, that man spent his time reading and writing. As my husband puts it, if he ever went to a cabaret, he'd be more likely to bury his nose in the programme than to notice the dress circle's full to bursting.'

I smile politely before finishing my cup of coffee, with the image in my mind of a woman on a theatre balcony, breasts spilling from her cleavage. I can't help but visualise expressions like these. I'm sure I'd give Freud a complex or two.

I put my cup down and stand up. 'Thank you, Mrs Damatian.'

'How awful ... I can't believe she ... it must be someone else. I hope you're looking into that angle, are you?'

I nod, but can't bring myself to look her in the eye.

'Mrs Damatian,' Gina intervenes, 'can I ask you what music Pauline likes to listen to?'

The question doesn't seem like a strange one to Bernadette, whose smile is making her eyes sparkle.

'Oh, she loves Félix Leclerc and Gilles Vigneault. She's a devout fan.'

'And what are you singing in the choir, at the moment?'

'Ah!' she cries. 'The Quebec Symphony Orchestra is celebrating its centenary this year, so we're rehearsing a series of classics. At the moment we're working on Mahler's Symphony No. 8.'

'Do you know if she has any hobbies other than singing?'

'She likes to fill little bottles with sand and turn them into art, you know? Like a picture of a sunset or a bird, using different colours of sand. Can you imagine the patience it must take to do something like that? It would drive me mad.'

In the corner of my eye, Jules grimaces in amusement, and I can imagine the quip on the tip of his tongue: *Well, my dear Bernadette, it seems it ended up driving her mad, too.*

'Hey, big tits,' Tamara hisses.

Obviously, my chest is as flat as a bread board. All I have are 'rose buds' – that's what Mother calls them. Not that they're in any hurry to bloom.

Tamara cranes her head to grab my attention before she finds a seat in the pew.

I stiffen.

Here we go. *En garde* for the next assault.

This time, she's the one who's late. We've spent two hours decorating the church for the year-end celebrations and Tamara disappeared just before they sat us down to go over the order of events for the Christmas concert.

Here I was, hoping she wouldn't show her face again. I found myself breathing a different way when she wasn't here. Too bad that doesn't happen very often.

'Look,' she whispers, staring at my breasts. 'They're growing.'

Stupidly, I look down at my non-existent chest, and she laughs out loud.

I notice that Julie barely smiles and turn my attention back to Father Dion and Father Tremblay, who are taking turns to explain the finer details of the event to us as Mrs Morin nods her agreement.

I extend my spine and lengthen my back as if someone were

pulling on a string tied to the crown of my head. My shoulders draw back and release my bosom. As if by magic, I instantly feel less small, less squashed. I feel that I matter, that my voice matters.

I respond to Tamara with a smile. A smile I hope is broad, generous and genuine.

She frowns imperceptibly. My reaction has taken her by surprise.

I sustain the smile, and find it's getting easier to hold.

'At least I know where to put my socks ... on my feet,' I whisper back to her, stretching my mouth and tensing my cheeks with a tilt of my chin that boosts my confidence even more.

The girls sitting between us bite their lips to stop themselves from laughing.

Obviously I'm not the only one to have noticed that Tamara's breasts seem to change size and shape regularly. But since she's the king on the chess board, no one dares to upset her, and so no one has ever brought this up.

Julie simply lowers her eyes.

Tamara glares at me. 'What are you on about? Don't talk rubbish,' she murmurs, tugging at her woollen cardigan.

She sits back in the pew, combing her fingers through her blonde curls, which are much shorter since I burned the ends off. Then she turns her gaze to Father Tremblay, who's speaking.

I smile, and don't have to force it this time.

Twenty or so minutes later, after I've nearly fallen asleep several times, we get up at last and retrieve our overcoats from the pews at the back.

Mine is not where I left it.

I turn and look around; someone might have moved it.

'Looking for this?' Tamara pipes up, pointing to a pile of stained fabric at the far end of the very last pew.

It takes me a second to make out my coat beneath the rags. Then I recognise the cream buttons I replaced at the neck.

Tamara has fastened red-stained panties and stockings to the sleeves and pockets of my overcoat. She picks it up by the collar and swings it to and fro, rags twirling gaily. She's elated.

So that's why she was late. Ugh, she's such a freak.

My whole body tenses, not with shame, but with a blind fury that makes me want to scream. To roar. To pound my fists into the nasty wretch. To make her bleed.

I bump and bruise my way to her along the wooden pew.

'Give it to me,' I order, reaching out my hand.

'Or else what?' she taunts me, with a tip of her chin.

'Or else, it's more than just your hair I'll burn next time. It'll be all of you, from top to toe.'

She drops the coat, and I can't see an ounce of fear in her eyes. Only defiance.

I pick up my overcoat and sit down in the pew. Then I set about undoing the safety pins she's used to fasten these rags stained red with ink or blood; God only knows how she's done it.

It's not working, I tell myself as I focus on the task at hand.

I can't force respect and deference on the king.

24
Maxine
2002

Jules has just dropped us off at the Carons' house in Lac-Clarence.

Before he drove away, I asked him what had been weighing on his mind, back at the Damatians' place. 'Just an argument with Marius,' he assured me with a weary smile. Then off he went to our incident room at the village hall to phone Sergeant David for an update on the canvassing of the Carons' neighbours in Montreal. It was a call he'd rather make from a landline because the mobile reception here, in the sticks, leaves a lot to be desired.

Gina takes off her coat at the foot of the stairs, hangs it over the banister and pulls out a compact camera and digital voice recorder. From her scarf she liberates her blonde mane streaked with strands more silvery than grey, then she strides across the hallway and enters the living room.

The forensic teams have vacated the premises. The house reposes in an oppressive silence. I almost want to stomp my feet to bring a bit of life into the place. It reeks of death. The trails of blood along the hallway carpet don't help. Neither does the dried blood that darkens the living room. The pool has been mopped up, but the stain looks even bigger without Philippe Caron's dead body wallowing in it.

Gina glosses over the gruesomeness and goes straight to the bookshelves on either side of the TV. She tilts her head to see the words on the spines and reads some of the titles out loud into her voice recorder. She does the same with the records and CDs. She examines the paintings and lithographs on the walls, commits them to memory. A naked young woman, her back turned, in an attic; an old woman sitting at a table in a hovel; then, hanging between the windows, a more than imposing reproduction depicting some sort of celebration, men and women dancing naked among others who've drunk and eaten their fill.

'Can I take that little bottle of sand with me?' Gina asks, pointing to a minuscule vial sitting beside a candle on one of the shelves to the right.

'Yes, of course. We'll do the necessary paperwork back at the incident room. I'll get it,' I say, pulling a transparent bag from my pocket and hugging the wall to go and retrieve it.

'Is it hard to be back among the dead?' she asks me, seeing right through my efforts to slalom between the bloodstains.

'Very.'

'It's the baby effect.'

'Even well into my forties?'

'That makes it worse still,' she smiles.

She takes a photo of the two centaurs or demons that are perched on the mantelpiece, one at each end.

'Where I see an X on the floor, does that mean there was a table there with a hand in it?' she asks.

I nod.

'And they were all on the ground floor, were they?'

'Yes. Come on, I'll show you.'

Gina follows me out of the lounge and into the laundry room – through the only doorway on the left side of the hallway, just inside the front door.

'There was one there,' I say, pointing to the X marked with adhesive tape beside the tumble dryer.

Gina frowns. And closes her eyes for a second.

'All right,' she says, as if answering her own silent question.

'The third one was in the kitchen, over there.'

We cross the hallway, both mindful to step over Mrs Caron's bloody footprints. I point to an X on the floor below the window.

'And there was nothing on these tables? I mean, there were no trinkets, candlesticks, plants, lamps or … anything that might have just been left there, like a book, a pair of glasses, a remote control?'

'Nothing at all. On any of them.'

We make our way to the next room, the dining room, and I show her where the table was, tucked to the right of a sideboard. Gina spins and leans to one side, as if she's mentally calculating the dimensions of the room.

We move on to the Carons' study.

To the right, on the way in, the psychologist pauses in front of a glass case, the top two shelves of which are filled with literary awards – there are fourteen of them, by my count. On the third shelf a large sketchbook sits on a lectern of sorts, open to a page with a drawing of a bell in a circle of Latin words, together with an inkwell and a quill. And on the fourth and final shelf, also on a lectern, is an old edition of *Macbeth*.

'That sketchbook belonged to Sir Arthur Conan Doyle,' I clarify with a tap of my index finger on the glass. 'It's chock full of notes and drawings for his Sherlock Holmes mysteries. We've had it authenticated.'

Gina takes some photos, then moves on to the couple's twin desks.

'This is quite something, isn't it?' I say.

'Yes. A great deal of love. Or obsession.'

'Or both.'

She replies with a smile before photographing a duct-taped X on the floor. She also takes a few snaps of two paintings hanging one above the other between the windows overlooking the garden, the only space not filled with books.

'The table was jammed up that close to the desks?'

'Yes, it was pushed right up against them.'

Gina stretches the minutes as she browses the books lining the walls, but this time she's not recording any voice notes. Then she returns to Mrs Caron's desk and opens a folder containing a thick sheaf of loose pages.

'Philippe Caron's manuscript in progress,' I explain.

She lingers over the first page, leafs to the next.

'Can I take this?' she asks, closing the folder.

I nod a yes.

On the way out, I point out the location of the seventh and final table, at the end of the hallway. Her acknowledgement comes with a few minute movements of her head. 'I'd like to see their bedroom.'

'Go ahead, I'll follow you,' I say.

'What else is up here?' she asks as we're climbing the stairs.

'A guest room, a bathroom, as well as quite a large box room with cupboards full of linen and old clothes. The bed's not made up in the guest room. I doubt they had a lot of visitors.'

'No attic room under the eaves?'

'No, there's nothing up there.'

Gina has a quick look around the guest room and the box room, takes her time in the bathroom opening drawers and making voice notes, then enters the master bedroom. She opens the wardrobes, examines the clothes and underwear, photographs the painting that hangs in pride of place over the bed – a copy of a famous Rembrandt, I think. Then she takes snaps of the bedside tables. On Pauline's, there's a half-empty bottle of lubricant, a bottle of sweet almond oil and a tube of hand cream. Philippe Caron's has a stack of three books topped with a pair of reading glasses.

'Why film Pauline's legs earlier, during her interview?' I finally muster the courage to ask, as Gina's having one last look around the bedroom.

'Because that's the part of the body we always forget to control, the one that betrays us. We'll think to feign consent or pleasure, but our lower limbs will slip our mind. Now, for example, you're

here with me and you're listening to me, but look at your feet,
Maxine. They're pointing towards the way out.'

25
Lucienne
1899

My heart's not beating, rather it's been frolicking and pounding since I left the house with Mary. I can hear it hammering at my temples louder than the carriage hooves on the cobbles.

When we arrive at Violette's, my throat is dry, my mouth pasty.

Violette told me this would be an intimate seance, and we would try only to make contact with Rose and Jeanne. Still, I'm expecting to find a good twenty people at the gathering. All of Paris knows about our tragedy now, and I find it hard to believe that Violette could resist the temptation to make a spectacle of my drama. The story is still front-page news in the gazettes and Henri has had to ask for the chief of police's help to shoo away the reporters and onlookers from outside our front door. But in the drawing room where we are introduced, there are only three others, chatting with our hostess: a slight woman with a solid, unfortunate face, a younger brunette of a mischievous beauty and an enormous man with an impressive moustache, holding a notebook in one hand.

'Ah, my dear Lucienne,' says Violette, coming to greet us and drawing me into a warm embrace.

She gives me a smile spiked with sadness and gratifies Mary with a nod.

Perhaps I should stop doubting her. Violette has done more for me these last few weeks than my own husband.

We advance into the group, and I find myself being inspected like a curiosity. I almost want to hold Mary's hand.

'Let me introduce you to our companions in this evening's adventure. This is Lucienne Docquer, and here is her cousin, Mary Gagnon. Madame Palladino – Eusapia,' she announces, gesturing to the elder of the two women, 'the formidable medium who will be conducting our seance.'

So this is the famous Eusapia Palladino. I imagined she'd be more ... spectacular, less ... common. Younger, too.

She extends a hand, which I'm about to shake when she accosts me with a strong Italian accent.

'May I take this off for you?' she decides, pinching the end of my glove.

I consent, wondering if she's going to read my palm like Madame de Thèbes. But she tugs off my glove and simply squeezes my hand while she reads my face.

'Moina Mathers.' The second woman introduces herself to me, extending long slender fingers.

Her name rings a bell, but I can't quite place it.

'And this is the great Arthur Conan Doyle, a man with a passion not only for his very own Sherlock Holmes, at least as far as the public believes, but also for Eusapia.'

'*Enchanté*, madame,' he says to me in a barely blemished French, his smile disappearing behind his thick moustache whiskers.

'Holmes seems to be more of a bother to you than anything else,' Moina Mathers jokes. 'Just to think you were forced to bring him back to life! What is an artist if he no longer decides the life or death of his characters?'

'An actor, madame,' the author replies with a smile.

Violette roars with a hearty laugh that seems almost out of place in the weighty atmosphere hanging over her drawing room. Or perhaps it's the knot I can feel in my stomach that's casting a shadow over things.

'Madame Docquer, would you allow me to take a few notes

regarding the seance?' Conan Doyle asks me. 'I shall not mention your name; rather, it is Eusapia's gift that is of interest to me.'

'Yes, of course, please do so.'

'Thank you, madame. I do appreciate it,' he replies with a grateful smile.

A moment of hesitation interrupts the flow of the conversation.

I wonder why Eusapia Palladino hasn't asked me anything about the fire or about my daughters. I know Violette's spoken to her about that night, and I'm certain in great detail, but she's only crossed paths with Jeanne and Rose on a handful of occasions, and very briefly at that; I don't see what she could have told the clairvoyant about them.

At Violette's request, I've brought with me an object belonging to them, small enough to hold in the palm of my hand: the ribbons I would tie in their hair on Sundays. Eusapia has not mentioned these.

I daren't bring an end to the silence with my questions. Violette is our hostess; we shall follow her lead.

'Would you like something to drink before we begin?' she asks, as if she has been reading my mind.

We decline with a shake of the head, eager for the evening to commence.

'My dear Eusapia, do you need anything at all?'

Eusapia shakes her head slowly.

We follow Violette to a round table at the far end of the room, in a darker corner. Eusapia invites us, Violette and me, to sit by her side. Mary takes a seat to my left and Moina Mathers, beside Violette. Arthur Conan Doyle remains standing, behind Eusapia.

'We're going to form a chain,' she says in her song of an accent, opening her arms. 'Place your hands like this.' She shows us, offering hers to us. 'Turn your right palm to the ceiling, and your left to the table.'

We do as we are instructed somewhat awkwardly, hesitating a few seconds as if suddenly confusing our right and our left.

'That's it, very good. Now, without changing that position, take your neighbour's hand in yours.'

I place my left palm against Mary's and offer the right to Eusapia.

'Good,' she says, with a glance around. 'Now, close your eyes for a moment, while you take a long breath in and an equally long breath out. If you would like to open them after that, you may do so.'

I close my eyes.

She inhales deeply through her nose; I imitate her. For a fraction of a second, her hand stiffens in mine. Then she expels the air slowly the same way. I exhale too, dropping my shoulders.

'I am Eusapia,' she announces in the same voice, without artifice. 'I am Eusapia and I am seeking Jeanne Docquer; and I am seeking Rose Docquer.'

My heart is swept away. We've barely begun and already it's at a gallop.

'I am Eusapia, good evening. Good evening to all. I am seeking Jeanne Docquer and Rose Docquer.'

Her words drift apart from one another, lingering

Mary's hand clenches in mine. A shiver runs down my spine.

'Jeanne?' Eusapia asks all of a sudden.

Abruptly, I open my eyes. I'm trembling.

I look around in a panic.

Obviously, there's no one else here but us.

Eusapia squeezes my hand and I realise I've let go completely. I tighten my grip and close my eyes again.

'Rose?' she continues. 'Jeanne, Rose, your maman is here.'

My chest is rising to the rhythm of my hurried breath. My corset has never felt so restrictive.

'Don't be afraid. Your maman won't be angry with you, Jeanne. Nor with you, Rose. She's not here for that. Your maman is here because she's worried.'

In spite of the room's warmth, a chill sweeps through me. In spite of myself, I snort to get rid of these shakes.

'Your maman wants to know if you're all right. She just wants to know if you're all right.'

Eusapia lifts our hands off the table then knocks three times on the wood.

'If you're in danger. If you're afraid, Jeanne, Rose ... if you're afraid, your maman wants to know that, too.'

Suddenly, my hand is propelled upwards. I open my eyes.

The table. The table. It's knocking at my hand.

What the...?

'Jeanne. Rose. Good evening,' Eusapia continues, in the same calm tone.

I begin a breath that becomes more like a sob.

Mary opens her eyes, gives me a brief glance. I close mine again in response.

'Rose? Shhhhh ... your maman is here. Right beside me.'

Eusapia lifts my hand and knocks on the table again, but this time the three strikes are closer together.

'Jeanne, Rose, come to me. There ... it's all right, everything is all right ... shhhhh...'

My stomach and my back are girdled with cramps. I squeeze Mary's hand to fight the pain.

'Jeanne. Rose. Tell me, and tell your maman what happened ... we're listening...'

Now the table knocks against both of my hands, sending a ripple of fear around the circle.

We all open our eyes. Violette. Moira. Mary and me.

But not Eusapia.

The table falls to the floor with an almighty thud.

Without releasing our hands, Eusapia tilts her head to one side. Then she straightens it with one swift movement and opens her mouth wide, hollowing her cheeks, rounding her back, tucking her chin to her chest, like a cat about to throw up a hairball. For a few seconds she remains in this position, then her torso relaxes; she draws herself tall and opens her eyes once more.

She's staring straight ahead, between Mary and Moina.

'Jeanne and Rose are trapped,' she says. 'They are imprisoned. There's no way out. They can't breathe, and there's no way out.'

26
Maxine
2002

'Good afternoon, Lieutenant Grant ... or rather, good evening.' The forensic anthropologist greets me with a firm handshake. 'Patrice Lemay.' He ignores the ravenous eye Jules is giving him.

'Hello,' I reply, glancing at Gina, who's still as cool as a cucumber.

Patrice could have been on the cover of a fashion magazine or strutted the catwalk for any of the great designers. But he chose to spend his life in a lab playing knucklebones. His work stimulates him intellectually, and his expertise delivers answers for detectives and for victims' families. Still, he'd be earning a far better living if he put his best face forward.

'Well, this is a first,' he begins, moving over to the table where he's arranged all seven hands, detached from their plinths.

They're on their backs, some so clenched and spidery they might be mistaken for arachnids with missing limbs. Others look more ... relaxed, I'd say, for lack of a more appropriate adjective. But all of them seem like they might flex an index or middle finger at any moment.

'I know, any creepier and you'll drop dead,' the anthropologist adds with an apologetic smile.

He turns to retrieve a pair of gloves.

'Right, then. These hands – and they're all right hands, as it happens – have not been mummified, but preserved using a rather special process. I'll get to that in a second. But first of all, I want to keep your expectations realistic. I can't just conjure up a life history of their owners for you, they're far too heavily altered for that.'

He shrugs, his own hands outspread.

'My work consists of restoring what has been "altered", but in this case, it's very difficult.'

'Difficult or impossible?' Jules asks, with no attempt to hide his impatience.

'Let me explain: I've found particles of verdigris.' He snaps the latex on his index finger. 'Saltpetre, too,' he continues at an instructional pace with a tug on his middle finger now. 'As well as traces of salt, and peppers,' he concludes, adjusting the glove on his ring and little fingers.

The look in our eyes must be priceless.

'I'm not kidding, and yes, you heard me right. Salt. And peppers, not pepper. As in, these are the result of a salting or pickling process. It's quite peculiar. None of the phalanxes and no chunks of flesh are missing, if you're thinking about acts of cannibalism. Perhaps the rest of the body, but not the hands or the forearms. On that front, everything seems intact, for lack of a better word.'

He reaches for a hand – one that looks flatter than the rest.

'Another thing: I've found traces of wax on the finger ends,' he declares, pointing to the tips.

Silence sets in.

'The same wax on all the fingers?' I venture.

'The same type, yes. On all the digits of all the hands. Just plain, ordinary candle wax. But I can't tell you anything more.'

'So you can't speak to the age or sex of the victims at all?' I try.

The anthropologist shakes his head.

'Or give us any idea when the hands were severed?'

Patrice purses his lips in visible frustration. 'No, I'm sorry.'

'Not even if they were severed ante or post mortem?' I insist.

'If they were severed post mortem, it was before any advance in the decomposition process, so no more than a few hours after death.' Patrice exhales with a deep sigh. 'The only thing I can provide you with is their DNA.'

'You can extract their DNA?' Jules blurts.

The forensic anthropologist gawps at us. 'Of course I can. What made you think I couldn't?'

'You painted such a pessimistic picture, I thought the hands had been "altered" to such an extent there was nothing to be gained from them,' I say, quoting his own expression.

'I know I can only be of minimal assistance, but still...' he adds, and I wonder what I've done to rub him up the wrong way.

'I suppose you're not heading back to Lac-Clarence?' Gina asks us as we're getting in the car. 'Do you feel like having a bite to eat? I don't know if you have someone to look after the kids.'

'I have to get back home to watch the girls,' Jules replies. 'Marius has capoeira practice. Why don't you come over to our place? Maxine, Charlotte's taking over from the nanny tonight, isn't she?'

After a second's hesitation, I nod, realising I don't really have a choice.

'Perhaps you'd rather go home and see Hugo, though?' Gina suggests.

Is it that obvious?

'It'll do me good to have some adult time,' I'm reluctant to conclude.

27
Lina
1949

'It's not working,' I say before I've even taken off my coat on my way into her room.

'What's happened?'

She wheels her chair towards me, moistens her thumb and wipes something off my cheek.

'You had a red mark on your face. I thought you'd scratched yourself. What's been going on?'

'I don't understand. There are a dozen girls my age in the choir. So, why me? Why does Tamara always pick on me?'

'Because you're an easy target,' she explains, unbuttoning my coat. 'Your mother's raising you on her own, so you don't have a father who can stand up to hers and tell him how cruel his daughter's being. You like your own company, and you're into different things than others your age.'

She drapes my coat over the arm of the sofa.

I sit down and grab a flowered cushion to wedge between my thighs. I plant my elbows in it, and massage my cheeks with my fingertips.

'She played another trick on me ... She's never going to stop. Not to mention, Mother's never going to come and stand up for me.' I sigh heavily. 'What can I do? Trust in God, like those two idiot fathers of the Church? Believe that Tamara will be punished in the end? She'll get her comeuppance when I punch her in the face. There's no God, and no more cheeks to turn.'

I raise my arms in surrender.

'I'm sorry, but I can't believe in a god who thinks I have no soul,' I add.

Her gaze lingers on mine. She's never spoken to me like a child, and now she's looking at me like an adult.

'I mean, I don't want to pray to him, you understand? Praying to him would be like disavowing myself.'

She's still observing me, listening to me religiously, dare I say.

'If I had to pray to someone, I'd rather pray to the Devil.'

'The Devil? Why's that?' she asks.

'Because he doesn't disown women. *Au contraire* – he chooses them and calls them to him. After all, witches celebrate him on the great sabbath, don't they?'

She nods her agreement.

'He also accepts that we have reprehensible desires – like mine to take revenge on Tamara – and he allows us to indulge in them without judging or punishing. Perhaps he just has a sense of good and evil that aligns more with mine.'

'Meaning?'

I'm thinking, wondering if God only exists because Satan exists, and vice versa.

'I don't know...' I reply, conceding defeat. 'How about you? Who or what do you believe in?'

'Whichever one will listen to me.'

'And how do you go about being heard?'

'You have to ask, but always in abidance with the set rules.'

'Set by whom?'

'By the Church, if you pray to God; and by the witches, if you pray to the Devil.'

'I know God's rules. "Turn the other cheek" and "help thy neighbour". Blah, blah, blah. I don't believe a word of it. Why would that god, in his own house, allow someone to treat me like Tamara does? There's no sense to it.'

I stop myself and down the water she's just served me in a single gulp.

'Do you know the witches' rules?' I ask her, wiping my mouth on my sleeve.

'Go fetch *Witchcraft, Magic and Alchemy* by Émile Grillot de Givry.'

I get up and go over to the bookshelf.

'It's right beside Huysmans,' I remark, on finding the title in question.

'Yes, a curious coincidence. As it happens, it was while reading *The Damned*, in 1891, that Grillot de Givry, another Frenchman, began to develop an interest in the invisible forces at work in our world – the very forces that conspired for you and me to meet. When I say "invisible forces," I'm talking about magic, about alchemy and about divination – together more commonly known as the occult. This work by Grillot de Givry is going to be your bedtime reading, Lina. It will be the only book on your nightstand until you've finished it. And we shall speak again when you return.'

'Maxi!'

The eldest daughter of Jules's partner barrels into the living room in her pyjamas and leaps into my arms. Her lavender-scented hair is still damp; it's sticking to my cheek, reminding me of Charlotte and her sopping-wet poolside hugs at my parents' place in the summertime. The crumbs of her biscuit tumbling onto my thighs, her delicate lips, the pearls of water on her eyelashes. My body once more becoming a nest for hers.

'Are you stockpiling hugs or something?' Jules jokes as he joins us in the living room with a second pair of pyjamas in hand.

'If only you knew.'

'Hugo's not here?' the big girl asks me, sweeping away a curl that's strayed into her mouth.

'No, sweetie.'

Her expression slides from elation to sadness. 'Ah.'

'Where's our other little dancer?' I ask her.

'She's a dinosaur now,' Jules informs me.

'No, Dada, a stegosaurus.'

'Yes, sorry, a stegosaurus.'

'You'll get your daughter back,' Gina says to me, taking a sip of her beer. 'Everything passes, even the ungrateful age. The getting up in the middle of the night, the nappies. Everything comes in cycles. "This too, shall pass"', she declares, miming the air quotes.

'Sounds a lot like family therapy to me, very Jacques Salomé,' Jules grins, brushing his eldest's hair.

'Not to disappoint you, but it's Hollywood rom-com through and through. That's what the hotel bellhop says to Julia Roberts in *My Best Friend's Wedding* when she's wallowing in a pile of poo, so to speak. So here's looking at you, Paul Giamatti.'

'The lady said poo,' pipes the youngest, tottering in with her bare bum cheeks for all to see. 'We don't say poo at the table.'

'You're quite right, missy,' Gina grants her. 'We have the same rules as your dada too. "Poo" has no place at the table. But right now, we're not eating.'

'Is that true, Dada? Is that the rule? If I'm not eating, I can say the word at the table?'

'Thanks, Gina,' Jules winces. 'Come here, you, let's get you into your PJs.'

'Does that mean yes?'

'Yes, it means yes.'

'Will Daddy say the same thing?'

'We'll sort it so he says the same thing, yes.'

Dada Jules's reply is met with a broad smile and eyes gleaming with joy and mischief.

'Poo. Poo. Poo ... poo ... poopoopoo!'

'Come here, you and your poo-poo mouth. Let's brush those teeth of yours and get you into bed. You too, muffin. Off we go, it's sleepy time.'

I get two hugs, and I close my eyes for both.

Jules disappears with his two rays of sunshine and Gina and I savour the silence as we sip our Molsons.

'So you don't live with your daughter's father anymore?' I ask, not taking my eyes off the foam that's surging up the neck of my bottle, like it's trying to escape.

'We've never lived together.'

'Oh, I'm sorry...'

'No, no, don't worry, Maxine, you're not treading precariously at all. He was a friend. We had one night of passion and I got pregnant. We decided to keep Léa and raise her together. We got on splendidly, and we still do, but we weren't compatible on a ... functional level, if I can put it that way. We weren't in love. That logic was perfectly fine by us, but you can imagine the scandal in my family and in his. Mine were mainly concerned I'd drop out of my studies or end up being a single mum. Léa's father is twelve years older than me. I knew he'd do his part, and do it properly. I was sure of it. And he's been a great father. Present, and available. We brought Léa up together and now he lives on the other side of the country.'

'But you stuck around. He didn't.'

She tilts her bottle to one side, making her beer dance. 'That's true,' she admits. 'Perhaps us women, we're the ones who stay close to the nest.'

'Because we *are* the nest.'

'You have to tell us, Gina, how the heck you can be a grandmother four times over,' says Jules, strolling into the living room. 'Because seriously, you're how old? Fifty...'

'Two.'

'Fifty-two years old,' Jules repeats, grabbing himself a beer and joining us. 'And your daughter?'

'Thirty. Léa's done the opposite to her mother: she's filled her life with children. While going through med school, too.'

'With your help,' I comment.

'With the father's help, most of all. I just help with keeping house.'

'And you love that.'

'Oh God, yes. Stuff they're not allowed: not my domain; homework: not my domain; time-outs: again, not my domain. With me, there's none of that. It's all about having fun, discovering things and enjoying pure, unbridled pleasure, or as close as.'

'You have them quite a lot, from what I've been able to gather.'

'I did lay it on a bit thick with Marceau, but I do plan my time around my daughter's and my son-in-law's. I see my little munchkins at least twice during the week, and on weekends I always have them over at some point or another. I moved closer to their place to make it easier.'

'Have you never thought about moving in with your daughter?' I ask.

'Are you kidding, Maxine?' Jules scoffs. 'How are they supposed to have any intimacy as a couple?'

'More like, how would *I* have any intimacy?' Gina protests.

Jules nearly spits out his beer and has to stifle a laugh.

'Just because I'm past the halfway mark in life, it doesn't mean I can't enjoy all the pleasures. I've got eyes too, you know, and I'm able to see certain anthropologists with a gift for snapping knicker elastic!'

'Ah, thank you Gina!' Jules exclaims. 'Maxine always gives me a guilt trip about the divine Patrice Oh-do-it-to-me-please.'

Gina roars with laughter, and it's contagious. Jules gets a serious case of the giggles too – as one belly-shaking wave subsides, another one rolls in, so it's a while before they both catch their breath.

'Why don't you give yourself permission?' Gina suddenly asks me, as Jules gets up to fetch another round of beers.

'To do what? To enjoy all the pleasures you're talking about?' I ask, aware I'm on the defensive.

'If you say so,' she replies with a wink, her friendliness an invitation for me to get down from my high horse.

'Oh, the traps you psychologists set,' I grin.

I hesitate for a second. Then I decide to come out with it. Or the beers will do it for me.

'Have you seen me? I'm spilling out everywhere.'

'Oh, no you don't, Maxine,' Jules intervenes.

'When I sit down, I feel like my bum squishes out in a puddle.'

Gina puts her beer down. 'Jules, you won't be offended, will you?' she says.

'Me? Never,' he replies.

Gina stands up and slips her skirt down from her waist to her hips, revealing her stomach. 'Look. Have a look at this. Does this look like a flat stomach?'

'No,' I admit, lowering my eyes.

'Wait, I'm not done yet. Are you sure the kids are asleep?'

Jules nods, his curiosity piqued.

I'm squirming uncomfortably in my seat.

Gina wiggles her skirt over her hips and lets it fall to her ankles, revealing a pair of hold-up stockings. Beige panties. She unbuttons her blouse, slips it down her arms to uncover a matching bra. She's curvaceous. Silky. And sensual. She's sublime.

'Well, I can assure you, this flesh, these mounds and valleys of my fifty-something body in the prime of life, none of it's preventing any man, or any woman, from desiring me. From loving me. Or from finding pleasure in doing so. This carnal envelope, how much does it count for in the grand scheme of desire and love, eh? Think about it, Maxine. If I were to ask you, right here, right now, to tell me about whatever love affair or roll in the hay you've had, I guarantee you'll never say, not even once, "oh, his abs!" or "ooh, la, la, that six-pack!" or even, "mmmm, those big biceps, those perfect pecs!". Not once.' She buttons up her blouse. 'Never, Maxine. You'll tell me how he would stroke a thumb over your lips before he kissed you, how he used to lick his lips when he was cooking, how he'd twirl a hand while he was reading. How incredible the slightest touch of his fingers would make you feel. The way he'd hold a cigarette in the corner of his mouth, even though you hate cigarette smoke. How the sound of his voice would make you want to close your eyes because it was simply music to your ears. Desire is far more complex and cerebral than a flat stomach. When it manifests, it's physical, but what sparks it is purely chemical, and that means cerebral.'

'Well, when you said you were having women over, I never

dreamed I'd come home to this,' Marius quips on his way into the kitchen.

We all realise what a scene he's walked in on, and Jules and Gina laugh out loud. Before he goes through to the bedroom to get changed, Marius draws me into a hug, then shakes Gina's hand as she waddles towards him, pulling up her skirt with no hint of a blush.

'Now, Sergeant Jules Demers, you should explain to this man of yours how we came to be doing psychology over the kitchen counter,' Gina murmurs.

'Not to be confused with "doing the psychologist over the kitchen counter",' Jules guffaws.

29
Maxine
2002

'Need me to bottle-feed you some coffee?' Gina smiles from her seat in our improvised conference room.

I feel nauseous.

'Can't the nanny stay over one night a week so you can breathe a little?' she suggests, placing her notebook on the table. 'Or what if your daughter does the ten o'clock feed so you can get a bit more sleep?'

'It's all right ... it'll pass,' I reply, suppressing the unpleasant memories of my recent nights. 'I am going to get a coffee though. Would you like one?'

'Just take a load off your feet. I'll bring you one.'

I don't protest, and take the opportunity to close my eyes for a moment before the day gets going. It's already weighing heavier on me than the last few have.

'Here you go,' says Gina.

I'm startled by the sound of her voice. She's put a steaming plastic cup in front of me. I must have dozed off. The clicking of Marceau's heels sounds the rest of my alarm. I swig a mouthful of coffee and take off my parka.

'The top brass have agreed to us holding Pauline Caron here at the incident room for another few days,' the big boss announces as she enters the room. 'That'll make our job easier for any re-enactments and interviews, that sort of thing. Sergeant?'

'I'm coming!' Jules calls from the corridor.

'How are you going about IDing the hands, Lieutenant?' she asks me, perching her cheeks on the table.

'We're focusing on missing persons in the area, casting the net wide in terms of dates,' I reply, swirling my coffee. 'From 1964 – that's two years before the Carons were married – to the present day. Even though I'm leaning more towards the victims being female – because all the women we've interviewed go on about how handsome Philippe Caron was and what a magnetic presence he had – I'd prefer not to rule out men for now. Nor young adults, either,' I add, feeling my morning nausea strike again. 'We're comparing the DNA from the hands to all available samples. It's going to be a long and tedious process, but I don't want to take any shortcuts. There are still too many unanswered questions for us to isolate a victim type.'

'Where are we with the neighbourhood canvassing in Montreal?'

'All done,' Jules confirms, putting his notepad down before he takes a seat. 'The apartments in that building are almost all leased through agencies. The occupants come and go, and no one knows their neighbours. Sergeant David did an admirable job, though. He asked the owners for a list of their tenants and anyone passing through, then he contacted them one by one, but nothing's come of it. I don't think that angle's going to take us any further.'

Jules pauses for a moment and stares straight ahead.

'Not to take a shortcut or anything,' he continues, giving me an insistent look and a half-smile, 'but if we focus on the serial-killer angle, which seems the most logical to me given that we've found no transactions whatsoever to support the murderabilia theory, we should consider that Philippe Caron severed those hands in collusion with his wife. There's nothing to prove it, I know, Max, but there's nothing to rule it out either. And lastly, the reason for keeping such a collection is hardly relevant at the moment. So whether it's an "eye for an eye" thing or something to do with cannibalism or gruesome trophy hunting, I don't think we should dwell on that for now.'

'I think Jules is right about that last point,' I reply, pushing aside my empty cup. 'We have to think outside the box and instead of getting caught up in the why, we have to determine the how and therefore the where. If we discover where the bodies were cut up, we'll know how the victims were killed, as well as why ... and by whom.'

I lay my palms flat on the table.

'Right,' I continue, staring at my fingers. 'If we disregard for a moment what we know about the Carons – in other words their respectability and their close, loving relationship – and consider just the raw facts, stripped bare of all warm, fuzzy feelings, what does that leave us with?'

'A crime of passion?'

'No. What we have is a remote residence surrounded by woods. A worldly couple protective of their privacy. No cleaning lady, despite them being very busy and clearly having the means. No secretary or assistant either for Philippe Caron, the university professor and successful author. It's his wife, even, who types and edits his work. No pets, which is rare indeed for a couple without children living in the middle of the countryside. So the Carons wanted to be isolated, away from prying eyes.'

I'm letting my thoughts unfold without taking my eyes off my hands.

'We've gone over the house with a fine-tooth comb. No traces of blood other than Philippe Caron's, no basement, nothing in the attic space, no secret rooms, nothing. There's nothing suspicious about their apartment in Montreal either. So where were those hands severed, and where are the bodies? Everything about the Carons' behaviour indicates they've protected their home and their woods like a sanctuary. So that's where I'd be tempted to search. I mean, they had a car, but we've found no traces of anything in there, and besides, moving a body anywhere off their immense property would be extremely risky. I know the sniffer dogs haven't detected anything yet, but I'm sure that's where the answer lies, in the woods around the house. There must be somewhere in proximity to their home, in the surrounding forest, where he or they killed and cut up the victims behind closed doors.'

'And where's their record player?' Gina cuts in.

I look at her, uncomprehending.

'Pauline's a huge music fan. They've got a mind-blowing vinyl collection, but I haven't seen a turntable anywhere at their place. They must have one somewhere.'

30
Lina
1949

I arrive in Lucienne's room with a head full of questions and ideas. Crazy ideas. I don't know where to start.

I set the Grillot de Givry book down on the sofa and sit beside it, hands on my knees.

'Take off your coat, will you?' she suggests, closing the notebook on her thighs.

She looks at me with a smile on her lips, toying with the end of her braid. I glance over my shoulder and get up to close the door. Someone may well come and open it again, but hopefully I'll have a moment to ask her a few questions in peace.

I sit down again. Sigh a brief, but loud, sigh.

'Did you go to the sabbath? Did you encounter the Devil? Does he really have horns, and the chest of a man and the hooves of a goat, like Baphomet?'

She bursts out laughing. 'I imagine you're going to ask me if I fly a sail from my broom as well?'

'Yes,' I reply, in all seriousness. 'Witches really existed, didn't they?'

'Oh, they exist.'

'Even the Church used to acknowledge their existence, right?'

'Yes. And burn them, for that matter.'

'And the Church wouldn't have gone to the trouble of hunting and burning them if it didn't think they were dangerous. It celebrated them too.'

'No, the Church didn't celebrate them, Lina. It sought to eradicate them – because it feared them.'

'Still, it's incredible they were represented on the doors of churches, don't you think?'

'Are you thinking about the cathedral in Lyon, in France, that Grillot de Givry mentions in his book?'

I respond with a swift nod of my head. 'A naked witch straddling a goat and holding a cat by its paws. Quite ... vulgar, don't you think? Why the obsession with nudity?'

'Because the energies we're made of, the one's that travel through us, can only move freely and effectively when we're naked.'

My cheeks feel warm. I think I'm blushing.

'See your reaction, there? Your cheeks turning pink, that's a response acquired under the influence of the Church, which has made sex a sin. You're still young, Lina, to be broaching such subjects.'

'No, I'm not. And I know how ... sex works. How babies are made. All of that.' I lower my eyes. It's distasteful to talk about 'that'.

'You're embarrassed,' Lucienne goes on, as if I'd spoken my feeling out loud. 'But you have no reason to be. We owe our birth to an act the Church condemns as soon as desire and pleasure enter the equation. There were scientists, like the German, Mesmer, who conducted experiments that could have changed medicine and even our entire existence, if we hadn't muzzled them – simply because they went against Catholic religious doctrine. Whatever name you give them, the fluids, the energies that inhabit our body are extremely powerful. If we knew how to use them, we could heal ourselves.'

She marks a pause and picks a chocolate from the bowl on the coffee table.

'You don't just see witches sculpted on the walls and doors of churches, you see demons too. Like the representation of the

Baphomet atop the main portal of the Church of Saint-Merri in Paris.'

I shake my head. I can't believe it. 'A demon at the entrance to a church? So they're really turning the other cheek! But why? Why invite the Devil into the house of God?'

'No one's inviting him in. He stays outside, at the door.'

'Still, he's the one who's watching over those who enter and leave, isn't he?'

'Who's observing them, rather.'

'Do you think it's to guard against satanic possessions?'

'No, I don't think so. You know, baptism is an exorcism. The child, born possessed, must be cleansed and delivered, hence the holy water.'

I wonder what Father Dion would make of that.

'Same as death, for that matter. The last rites cleanse us of our sins.'

'Do you believe it's possible to communicate with the dead?' I ask.

Lucienne cocks her head, sweeping her braid across her book. 'Are you thinking about your father?'

I bite my lip. One day, Mother slapped me when I told her the stories I'd heard walking home from school.

'I'd like to know what he really did during the war,' I say.

Lucienne leaves me time, as always, to make a choice. Whatever it is, she never gets angry.

'I've heard people say that Dad was responsible for torturing prisoners. And he took pleasure in killing.'

'And you want to ask him if that's true?'

I nod my head.

'If that were the case, would you be disappointed? Sad? Shocked?'

I look at her, not grasping where she's going with this.

'Do you think it would be nice to hurt someone who hurts you?' she asks me.

I'm thinking about Tamara. And so is Lucienne, it seems.

'Yes, but to go from that to killing...'

'Even though we were spared the fighting here, you've heard the war stories. You know that life and death weigh less heavily than in peace time. Your father certainly obtained information that saved hundreds, if not thousands, of lives by killing just one person.'

'All right, but enjoying it is another thing entirely, isn't it?'

'Perhaps he didn't enjoy the act, only the result,' she replies.

I like that theory. Suddenly I see Dad in a different light. His memory no longer seems to have the power to ravage everything in its path. Perhaps he was in fact a hero, and Mother is telling the truth.

It's my turn to lean forwards and reach for a chocolate. I pick the round one with a dusting of cocoa powder. It sticks to my teeth and the roof of my mouth, so I take time to swallow it before asking my next question.

'What about you, have you ever communicated with the dead?'

Lucienne dusts her woollen dress with the back of her hand. 'Yes.'

My mouth gapes as images of whirling sheets fly around my mind. 'Did ... did you see ghosts?'

'No.'

'But ... how, then?'

'Through a medium. The equivalent of the witches Grillot de Givry writes about. A medium is a connection between the world of the living and the world of the dead. A medium is a person the dead can speak to, a person through whom they can send us words and messages.'

'But ... how do mediums and witches summon the dead?'

'They possess an energy, a fluid, that opens a kind of channel between the two worlds. Like the Witch of Endor, remember? Grillot mentions her in the book.'

'Yes, the witch of witches.'

Lucienne smiles. 'If you like, yes.'

'So, who did you summon from the dead?'

With the back of her hand, she caresses the cover of her notebook, then she turns away and her gaze flees out the window.

'My daughters.'

Gina enters the interview room, skirts the table and places the vial of sand in front of Mrs Caron, touching a gentle hand to her shoulder. Their eyes meet. Gina smiles and sits down, but without maintaining eye contact, as if to leave the teacher wanting. Unless this is a way of showing respect, I don't know. Pauline follows her with her gaze, before looking down at the vial. She caresses the curves of the glass, touches the tiny cork. She doesn't dwell on the colours, nor on the art inside, a black bird flying over sunset-orange dunes.

Without releasing the serene smile from her lips, Gina suddenly shakes her head. Mrs Caron lifts her face towards her.

I step closer to the screen, forcing Jules to do the same, since I'm blocking his view. I want to be sure I don't miss something.

'You've done a lot for your husband, Pauline. A hell of a lot.'

Mrs Caron shifts her focus to the vial, picks it up in her right hand and curls her fingers around it.

'I think Philippe's talent was as much yours as his. I think you shaped him. Guided him. But he had something you don't. Charisma – that uncommon aura. You noticed it, felt it, the first time you met him. And so you modelled, sculpted and polished Philippe; you forged his character.'

Gina sighs.

'Being a couple, loving one another, is all about being a team, supporting one another, one feeding into and one feeding off the other. And it goes both ways. But sometimes the equation isn't balanced, because the things you exchange aren't quantifiable. What's the presence of the one we love worth? Their support, their faith in us, the things they do to encourage us to give the best of ourselves? The right partner can change the course of a life. They can make our existence sparkling, thrilling – or miserable.'

She pauses, looks up to the ceiling, then lets her gaze glide down to Mrs Caron, as if she's following an insect's flight.

'There's always that age-old debate: do people change? Do we squander our time striving to polish, shape, transform, morph someone else? Ah?!' she exclaims, opening her hands like she's asking the question to an audience. 'Both affirmations are true: people don't change; their desires do. Their aspirations. Their priorities.'

Gina leans back in her chair and crosses her legs. 'I've read the manuscript you were in the process of editing.'

Pauline rounds her back, shifting in her seat and clenching her thighs together.

'What happened, Pauline?' Gina asks, moving to the edge of her chair.

Pauline's squishing the flesh of her fingertip with the cork. Little, insistent, impatient exertions of pressure.

'What could possibly have driven you to kill the man you devoted your life to? What did that man do to you?'

Gina rests her forearms on the table. She's waiting. The silence stretches into the stillness that forebodes a rumble of thunder or the breaking of bad news.

'Those edits to your husband's manuscript, Pauline, they were for you to address, not him.'

Mrs Caron seizes the vial of sand and folds her arms across her chest.

'It was you who wrote your husband's books, wasn't it, Pauline?'

32
Lucienne
1899

Violette has asked me to meet her at the Tuileries. And to come alone.

Mary did not disapprove of, or condemn, my choice to go without her: she knows that Madame de la Courtière is our greatest ally in Paris. She's taken us under her wing. It can't hurt to do as she bids.

'My dear Lucienne,' Violette says, drawing me into a tender embrace in the shelter of her parasol.

She slips her arm beneath mine and leads me to an empty promenade. For the first time, it seems she's struggling to find her words.

'So ... have you heard any news from the private detective?'

My heart feels like it's going to pound out of my chest. I take a deep breath, trying to calm my anxiety.

'He told me yesterday he was going to stop investigating.'

'That's what I feared.' She clamps a hand on my forearm. 'What do you think has happened to your children?'

I lower my eyes. Our boots are kicking up sand from the path, sending clouds of dust to sully the hems of our dresses.

'Precisely what Eusapia Palladino said: they're trapped. Imprisoned. They can't breathe, and there's no way out.'

Violette nods several times in silence.

'So you believe in Eusapia's powers, then?'

'Who could doubt them after the seance the other night? The table moved. I felt it move beneath my fingers. And she was able to contact Jeanne and Rose.'

'Shh,' she commands, curbing my enthusiasm.

'Sorry. To be honest, I ... had my doubts before I met her...'

'As did many of us, my dear. Myself included, some years ago.'

Violette pauses as we cross paths with a couple she greets cordially. She waits for them to move along before she continues.

'But once one has witnessed this communication with the beyond, or spiritual communication, as perhaps was the case with your daughters, one can no longer doubt what is there.'

My mouth feels dry. I decide to ask the burning question that's on the tip of my tongue. 'How ... how did you come to agree to that?'

She smiles. 'The road was long. Let's say that when I met Moina Mathers, to whom you were introduced at my house, it changed my life entirely. She's the sister of Henri Bergson, did you know?'

So that's why her name rang a bell. Moina Mathers Bergson. The sister of the great philosopher. Of course.

I nod silently.

'I met her when I was losing my babies. Oh, what a horrible time that was, Lucienne ... I would pray ... I would spend my time praying to God to grant me a child. Then my dear Moina opened my eyes to another truth, a kind of ... inner peace, by introducing me to new ways of thinking, by broadening my spiritual horizons. Through her, I met...' She releases a deep sigh, one to erase names. 'I met men and women who showed me who to ask, and how. When at last I directed my prayers to he who knows how to listen, the only one, I fell pregnant. Five times in a row, Lucienne. My five precious children you know today.'

She gives me a radiant smile. 'There are two sides to every realm, Lucienne. It all depends on the position from which you choose to view the world. Think for a moment: who do we pray to? A god who thinks that we women are inferior to men; for this god, we are the product of a piece of man, the rib of Adam. Yet who are the bearers of life? We are. We are not nothing; we are everything. We are the goddesses of this world down here, Lucienne. And still, the Church that serves the god we pray to has wondered, and some continue to wonder, if we, we women, are human, if we possess a soul.'

She stops, turns to me and clasps my hands in hers. 'What I'm trying to tell you, Lucienne, is that you're like me. Like I was at that time in my life. You're in search of another truth, and you're ready to open up to something else. And I am here, ready to guide you.'

We've marked out the Carons' property and divided it into three zones.

Gina insisted on coming along with Jules and me. We're combing the north to northeast area where we located the hunter's cabin that's given us so much false hope. Two teams of local patrol officers are searching the remainder of the estate.

'Do you really think she wrote her husband's books?' Jules asks Gina, tugging his hat over his ears. 'Or were you just looking to get a reaction?'

Gina waited twelve minutes for a response from Pauline Caron. Every one of those minutes seemed to last an eternity, and I'm hardly exaggerating. Jules and I were glued to the screen. The tension was as palpable in our viewing room as it must have been between the two women. Then Mrs Caron got up, using her chair for support, the vial of sand squeaking against the metal of the backrest with a kind of whimper. Suddenly realising she was still holding the glass, she placed it gently on the table before asking to leave the room.

'There was something toxic going on between them,' Gina explains, exhaling clouds of steam. 'In their marriage and in their dynamic. I don't know what, exactly, but this thing is enmeshed in the very foundations of their relationship. I still don't have anything concrete to share with you, though, sorry.'

'You mean something more toxic than setting up seven hands, like beacons, on the ground floor of their house? I mean ... something besides that? Something about the way they functioned together in their relationship?'

'Yes, it's one – or maybe more – of the elements that defined them as a couple, but I can't quite put my finger on it. Sorry, with all these hands, maybe that wasn't the best choice of expression.' She smiles with a sniffle, then wipes her nose with the back of her sleeve.

'Careful, it's slippery,' I warn them, scaling a mound of snow.

'What do you have in mind?' Jules asks me, catching Gina just in time.

'Are you all right?' I ask, pausing for a second.

Gina nods and tucks behind her ear a blonde lock that's been beating time in front of her face with an elegance I envy.

'I was wondering what we're looking for here,' Jules tries again. 'What are you expecting? Another hunting cabin? A cave?'

'I don't know exactly, but I can't see them having a go at the bodies out in the open. Even though the woods belong to them, there would always be the risk of someone coming across them. So there must be some place under cover. What type of place, I have no idea.'

'So you think the Carons were in this together? Lieutenant Grant's finally made up her mind?' he grins.

'Well, I do have a hard time believing Philippe Caron went behind his wife's back. She knew what was going on. She can't not have, with the kind of conjoined relationship they had. Their desks sitting face to face, sharing the one mobile phone, her replying to his messages and even writing his books for him...'

'Maybe that's the thing,' Jules insists. 'What if it was the only way for him to exist outside their codependent relationship?'

'By cutting off hands?'

'Symbolically, amputating hands makes perfect sense in their case,' Jules goes on. 'The hand is the embodiment of action, of doing, of independence. Philippe Caron must have felt powerless, incapable of acting how he wanted, chained to an authoritarian wife who steered, perhaps even sanctioned, his deeds. That makes sense, doesn't it, Gina?'

'It does make sense,' she replies, not looking up from her boots as they carry her through the debris of frozen roots and branches.

'But why kill him, then, and with that rage, the overkill so typical of a crime of passion?'

'No idea,' I reply, before gulping a breath of air that burns my throat.

'Whatever it was, it must have been huge ... something completely traumatising, for her to react that way, right?'

'If we're dealing with a sociopath, or rather a couple of sociopaths,' Gina intervenes, 'then their emotional bearings, their sets of values, if we can even say that, are different from ours. If something happened and she perceived it as a violation of their trust, some kind of unpardonable act, that's all it would have taken for her to react with such heightened violence.'

'Ha!' I suddenly exclaim, planting my feet in the snow with a distinct lack of grace.

Jules and Gina stop in their tracks. My sergeant whistles, clear as a bell.

'Respect,' he says. 'Now that's impressive, Grant.'

Hearing only my heart running riot in my chest, I pull out my phone and check for a signal.

'We've found something,' I announce to Marceau.

'Give me your coordinates,' she yaps on the other end of the line.

34
Lina
1949

It's the perfect afternoon for my expedition with Lucienne. The sky is clear, the air fresh, the sun mild, as if nature were expecting us, and just the idea of it makes me smile.

Well, I say 'expedition', but we're just going for a stroll in the Clarence Manor grounds. Lucienne wants to show me something. It'll be a chance for us to talk, too, without anyone spying on us. In her room we're always interrupted at one point or another by a nurse or a housekeeper. Even Mother likes to stop in for a few seconds before going on her way. It reassures her to see me with my nose in a novel or a school book in my hands. Mother has not been called in to see Mrs Morin or Father Dion again, and she sees me smiling now, she said to me the other day on the way home. Lucienne had just told me Mother had thanked her for giving me time and attention. My little old lady replied that she was delighted to be enjoying my company.

'Why did you say you were grateful for spending time with me?' I ask, pushing her wheelchair along a path lined with trees stripped of their leaves.

'You know, before this was a rest home, it was a—'

'Yes, I know they called it the madhouse.'

'I came here during that time.'

'But you're not mad. Just sad.'

She reaches out to me with a gloved hand. I nestle mine in hers.

She squeezes it, then rests her elbow on the armrest. 'Sadness made me flirt with madness. I cut myself off from everything and everyone.'

'What happened?'

'I'd stopped eating. I'd barely speak to anyone anymore.'

'Mother says that losing a child is the worst thing in the world, the worst of all suffering. You lost two of them. Solange, too, she lost her son. He drowned, Mother told me.'

'Léonard, yes.'

'Like her teddy bear?'

'Mmmhm.' Lucienne turns away and draws a bracing breath of air in through her nose.

'When did you get better?'

My questions hangs between us for a moment, and the silence is filled by the crunching of the chair's wheels on the gravel.

'I don't really recall.'

'Why didn't you go home again?'

'Because Clarence Manor became my home.'

'But what about your family. Didn't you miss them?'

'Go to the left here,' she tells me when we come to a fork in the path. 'I wasn't close to my parents, nor to my husband.'

'Didn't they come and see you?'

'My husband never did. My family would come on my birthday.'

'And at Christmas?'

'Not at Christmas, no. Stop here. We'll walk the rest of the way.'

I park the chair, make sure the brakes are engaged and help Lucienne to get up. Leaning on my arm, she slowly unfolds herself, takes a good ten seconds to find her footing, then steps forth to lead the way.

'It's behind this mound,' she says, not taking her eyes off her feet. 'We'll skirt around to the right, it's flatter.'

Her left hand is clutching my wrist; her right, my forearm. I'm focusing on the ground right in front of my feet too.

I don't look up until Lucienne stops.

We're standing in front of a small, rectangular brick building. The stone roof makes it look a bit like a turret on a fort. There's a column standing at each corner, adorned with a garland of pine cones. The wooden door is painted red, and the paint is peeling here and there. It really is a curious building.

'Is it a tomb?'

Lucienne smiles, then slips a hand into the pocket of her coat and pulls out a key, which she hands to me.

'This is for the top lock. The bottom one doesn't work. And no, it's not a tomb. Quite the opposite. This is a place of life and rebirth, Lina. You'll see.'

35
Maxine
2002

The English call it a 'folly'. A garden extravagance. A building surrounded by green space, which serves solely to make casual strollers scratch their heads and ponder whether they've come across a theatre, a storage shed or a cenotaph. In our case, I wonder if this isn't all three at once.

Jules, Gina and I came across this folly combing the north to northeast corner of the Carons' property. The top of one of the columns was sticking out of a scruffy thicket at the summit of a hillock. From a distance, it looked like someone had carved a pine cone out of stone and hung it from a tree like a Christmas decoration. We scaled the slope in a matter of strides and found ourselves looking at a building around four by three metres in size. A roofline like battlements, red bricks tarnished by cold and blackened with moss; a heavy wooden door that must have been painted red at some point, weathered by snow, with two rusty keyholes.

'So, is this place going to painfully destroy our hopes too, do you think?' Jules asked me. He always gets testy when he's feeling anxious. I don't think I'm barking up the wrong tree. Not this time. But I can't be sure until we have a look inside. And the problem is, we haven't been able to do that. For the simple reason that this folly is not actually on the Carons' estate, but on the neighbouring property. And that belongs to the Lelangers, an influential dynasty that's ruled the roost in Lac-Clarence for the past two centuries. In other words, we could have picked an easier bone to dig up. And so we've trudged back in frustration to the incident room with our proverbial tail between our legs to wait not-so patiently for Marceau to secure a warrant. It's going to be a good forty-eight hours, since the top brass are falling over themselves to make sure a legal avalanche doesn't come barrelling down on them.

Now Jules and I are in the viewing room and Marceau has just come in to join us. The big boss has found a perch beside me, hands stuffed in the pockets of her navy-blue pleated slacks, the big lapels of her blazer spilling over her trim forearm muscles.

'Here's how we might go about speeding things up,' she sighs.

No barking, no yapping of orders, just a conditional statement. I wonder where she's going with this, though it's clear she has a shortcut up her sleeve – which is a first.

'You could go and see Yvonne Lelanger, Lieutenant. In Montreal. Ask her if she would agree to sign an authorisation for us to look inside that outbuilding pursuant to our enquiries into the murder of Philippe Caron. Quite simply because we want to leave nothing to chance and it's important to turn over every stone that warrants attention. With the weekend coming, it'll be much faster to get her permission in writing than to wait for a warrant. We'll still get one, of course. But her cooperation will make our job easier and allow us to move on to the next phase of the investigation, and of course, we'll be sure to publicly praise her valuable assistance and readiness to help.'

'Would you like me to ... frame things that way?'

'Not if you have a problem with that, Lieutenant.'

'No problem at all. That said, you might run into one once we open up that folly.'

Her gaze seems to float for a moment. 'I know, Lieutenant.'

'I'll do a debrief with Professor Montminy after her interview with Mrs Caron, then I'll hit the road.'

'Good,' she says, turning to the video monitor.

Gina's just taken a seat in the interview room, across from Pauline. This time, the psychologist isn't smiling. She's tapping on the table between them.

She reminds me of a pianist.

'Pauline, I'd like to go over the sequence of events with you.' Gina's staring down at her virtuoso's fingers. 'All we have, in the living room where Philippe died is evidence that incriminates you, Pauline. Every stain, every drop of blood, every print points to the same conclusion: you assaulted and killed your husband.'

Mrs Caron turns to face the wall to her left, as if there was a window there.

'The detectives have deduced that you pushed him.'

Mrs Caron's eyes flicker to the door of the room, giving the impression that someone has just knocked and is waiting for permission to come in.

Maybe she's expecting to see me.

Gina looks up now and locks her in her sights, invasive, insistent.

'Did your husband push you? Shove you, or shake you? Before you killed him, Pauline? What really happened?'

Pauline's eyes wander out beyond her imaginary window.

She knows that if they meet Gina's, she'll be drawn in, she'll be cornered, and she'll break. That's the impression her flighty posture gives me, at least. Or perhaps that's what I would do, if Gina were hounding me that way.

'You must have had to leave your husband lying on the floor, Pauline. Then walk out of the living room. Go across the hallway. Enter the kitchen. Open the drawer. Choose a knife. Pick it up. Close the drawer again.'

Gina allows herself to take a breath.

'Then you must have gone back into the living room. To kneel down beside your husband and stab him. Thirty-one times.'

Mrs Caron blinks. Her eyelids open and close slowly, like a lizard lazy from the sun.

'It's time to talk, Pauline. Time for you to make yourself heard, to give your version of the facts, before it's too late and there are no more deals to be made.'

Pauline must be imagining her forest through that window.

'Pauline? We've found your little extravagance in the gardens.'

Pauline frowns. It looks like she doesn't know what Gina is talking about.

Could I be wrong?

'We've found your folly, Pauline. Tucked away on the Lelangers' property.'

Pauline closes her mouth. It's been open a fraction until now. She presses her thighs together.

'I wish I'd seen his eyes,' she suddenly whispers. 'When I stabbed him. To see his surprise. His pain. His grief. Not from leaving me. From having to go. I wish he'd seen me too, seen me take back everything I gave him. Everything I gave him that he didn't deserve.'

36
Maxine
2002

'Shasha!'

I hiss it in a whisper, beginning to question this curious habit from when Hugo was born.

I don't get an answer.

'That was the doorbell, Shasha,' I insist, whisper-hissing my heart out.

'Stop calling me that,' my daughter chides, sidling down the hallway, past the bathroom door. Even in here, I can't get two minutes to myself.

'It must be Gina, Sh ... Charlotte. Tell her I'll just be a minute. I'm—'

'Yeah, all right, I get it.'

But I don't hear her voice, or the hinges of our front door.

'Charlotte?'

'Yeah, Mum, just a sec!'

'Keep your voice down,' comes my automatic reply.

There's a knock at the front door now.

'Bloody hell,' I mutter, abandoning my throne.

'What do I do?' my daughter asks me. It sounds like she's glued her lips to the bathroom door.

'Well, go open up.'

'But what about Hugo?'

'Keep your voice down. I'm coming.'

When I meet them in the entryway, Gina's shaking her head in despair.

'Sorry, I hope I didn't wake Hugo, did I?' she whispers. 'Your daughter assures me I didn't...'

'I ... I'll go see,' says Charlotte, disappearing down the hallway.

'I rang the bell, then I cursed myself for doing it. So I thought I'd better knock the second time.'

'Oh, don't worry about it,' I smile, pulling on my parka.

Charlotte comes back to my side and stands rooted to the spot, tugging at the sleeves of her pyjamas.

'Is he out for the count?' I ask.

She nods, forcing a smile.

'If anything happens, you call me, all right?' I say, sweeping a lock of hair from her forehead.

'What do you think might happen?'

I decide not to answer. I'd rather avoid a scene in front of Gina.

'He might wake up?' Charlotte carries on.

'I'll wait for you outside,' Gina says.

Charlotte lowers her eyes. 'Go on, Mum. Sorry. It's only one night. It's all right. Everything's going to be all right.'

I cup her cheeks in my hands, reel her gaze in with mine. 'I know, sweetie. I trust you.'

'Where are you sleeping?'

'Marceau's booked some rooms there for the team.'

My daughter nods her approval. I give her a kiss on the nose, the way I would when my hugs were still precious and needed. Then I grab my overnight bag and shut the door behind me.

'Can I leave my car here?' Gina asks me, with a tip of her chin towards the Lexus parked out front as we carefully navigate the icy steps on the front porch.

'Sure, no problem.'

'I'll come back to Montreal with you tomorrow. There's no sense in us taking two cars.'

'No...' I reply, still struggling to tear my thoughts away from Charlotte.

'She's at that in-between age,' Gina comments, as if I've spoken out loud. 'That too shall pass.'

We arrive at Yvonne Lelanger's house twenty minutes later.

At the entrance to the property, we announce ourselves to a camera that looks like an eyeball. We're buzzed in through an imposing electric gate encased in a stone archway with a keystone bearing a coat of arms, then we make our way up a never-ending driveway, which snakes through snowy grounds, and park on the forecourt of the house.

To my great surprise, it's the heiress herself who answers the door to her Westmount mansion. Since the death of her parents, some ten years earlier, this fierce businesswoman has presided over the family empire with a firm hand and formidable flair.

Yvonne Lelanger is dressed in a pink-and-white suit with black stripes. Dior, Chanel – whatever it is, it's very French, and very chic. She's eating a banana, just swallowing a bite.

'Good evening, Mrs Lelanger. Lieutenant Grant, and this is my colleague, Professor Montminy.'

I'm about to add a 'thank you for agreeing to see us', but I catch myself in time. It's crazy how money lures people – or maybe just me – into misplaced reverence. I don't see why I should be thanking her, a woman who must have someone to iron her socks and peel her banana for her, any more than a single mother who works sixteen hours a day and has only just put her kids to bed when I come knocking at the door to piss her off with my damned neighbourhood enquiries.

'Yes, good evening. Sorry, I've just got in the door,' she apologises, mincing her words and munching her banana.

An awkward silence sets in.

It dawns on me that she's not planning to invite us in. So I hand her a pen and the form to grant us entry to the folly.

'I've spoken with your superior officer,' she tells me, taking what I've given her. 'You're from Lac-Clarence, it seems?'

'Yes.'

She leans on the parapet to sign the document.

'How delightful,' she replies, as if to highlight the only thing we'll ever have in common.

She produces a mechanical smile for me as she hands back the document. And my pen.

'Thank you,' I reply, as generously as possible.

'But of course. In no way would we wish to hinder a criminal investigation.'

With that, Lady Lelanger turns on her heels and returns to the warmth of her very own castle.

'Is it just me, or...'

'No,' Gina replies as she gets back into my car. 'To her, we're a couple of beggars, my dear Maxine.'

I sit behind the wheel and pull my phone out of the pocket of my anorak to text Marceau and let her know we have the signed authorisation. Then I quickly check for any other messages before placing the device in the centre console.

'Is everything all right at home?' Gina asks.

'No news is good news,' I sigh, feeling a lump of sadness rising in my throat.

'Trust her. She's not a child anymore, she's a woman.'

'She's going to great pains to remind me of that,' I reply, starting the engine.

'And that worries you.'

'And then some.'

We're on our way back down the driveway. The gate opens as we approach, as if it knew the abuse I would hurl at it if it didn't.

Out of the blue, Gina begins to hum a song that gives me goosebumps. I even wonder if I'd started to hum it without realising. My husband used to sing this melody time after time to Charlotte when she was little, at bedtime, until she closed her eyes.

'*You are my sunshine,*' Gina ventures, in a voice that warms me as much as it chills my heart.

Since there are some things we can never fully grieve.

I swiftly wipe away a tear before moving my hand to the gearstick and clasping my fingers around it.

'*My only sunshine...*'

Still singing, Gina wraps my hand in the warmth of her caring palm.

'*You make me happy when skies are grey. You'll never know, dear, how much I love you. Please don't take my sunshine away.*'

37
Lina
1949

I take the key Lucienne hands me.

'I've got some oil, in case the lock needs a little lubricating.'

'Has it been a long time since anyone came here?'

'Ten years. Just before the war.'

I try to insert the key, but I encounter resistance.

Lucienne pulls a small bottle out of her pocket, takes the key from me, drips a few drops on its teeth, rubs them in with the pad of her index finger and hands it back to me.

I try the key in the lock again, turn it, force it a little, and at last there's a click. I pull the door and swing it open against the wall. The hinges yowl like a tortured cat.

A pungent, musty odour seizes the chance to escape.

The room is dark and murky. There's nothing in there but a side table, pushed into one corner, with a few candles lying on their sides and a box of matches warped with damp, all covered in dust and cobwebs.

'It's some kind of shelter,' I say.

I turn around and offer my arm for Lucienne to lean on. We step inside together, leaving the door open to let the light in.

'What is this place, Lucienne? Did you used to come here?'

She sweeps every nook and cranny with her gaze, from floor to ceiling, as if she's looking for something. And she's smiling. A smile drawn by memories, by joy as well as regrets.

'Did you come here with your secret lover?' I tease.

She laughs. The echoing of her laughter brings a little life into this place, which I find quite depressing, with its twisted webs and dead insects hanging here, there and everywhere.

'Yes, with my secret love, I suppose.'

'Ah-ha,' I reply with a wink.

'You'll have to keep candles burning in here for a while.'

'What else was here, before?'

'Before?'

'Before you came with your sweetheart.'

'We had a few blankets and an oil lamp.' She advances a few steps, touches her hand to the wall. 'It's not that damp. Just needs some airing out. I'll give you some incense. You should burn some regularly to get rid of this musty smell that's getting in the way of us seeing anything more than these grey walls.'

'It is a bit dreary,' I admit, not daring to say any more.

'Soon, you'll see, it will be very different.'

Her eyes are roaming greedily around the room, as if she's embracing her long-lost lover.

'I'm going to give you the key, Lina. It's the only one; don't lose it.' She leans closer to me. 'This will be your lair.'

Shivers run through my body.

'So, here I'll be in peace to try and ... find some answers ... to communicate with Dad...'

'You'll be able to ask your questions and make your demands, yes. And I'm sure you will be heard, Lina.'

We've followed the path trodden by the crime-scene investigators from the Carons' home to get here. The folly is veiled by a garish blue tent, attached to its facade, and is illuminated by powerful floodlights. A stream of white coveralls is flowing in and out of the canvas flaps in the silent ritual typical of every crime scene. I'm not sure whether it's the respect, reserve, discretion and decency only death, brutality or inhumanity can impose, or whether the men surrounding me are silent simply because they're incapable of doing two things at once.

'They're just getting set up and haven't opened the door yet,' Jules tells me, releasing a cloud of white into the night. 'There you go.' He points behind him to a box containing protective clothing.

I give him a nod and grab what I need. I don the necessaries, heart pounding in my throat and at my temples, legs shaking with cold and trepidation. What if I'm wrong? What if this folly isn't where the Carons perpetrated their crimes? What if it only dashes our hopes, like last time?

Simon's voice surges from inside the tent. 'We're ready!'

I pull up my hood and lead the way to the door of the folly, followed by Gina and Jules.

'Lieutenant Grant, Professor Montminy,' Simon greets us.

We respond with strained smiles, Gina's perhaps more generous than mine.

Two crime-scene technicians in white hoods are standing in the way, in front of the door. The swishing of their coveralls suddenly gives way to the roaring of a power saw, which cuts through the wood like a knife through lard. The technicians fold back on its solid iron hinges the left-side panel of the door so that it's resting against the outside wall like a shutter. The way is now clear for us.

I go in first. A strange smell, sweet and spicy all at once, fills my nose in an instant. I notice a switch to my right and press it, illuminating a bulb on the ceiling. Not a moment later, my ghostly shadow is projected onto the walls and floor of the folly by a floodlight some bright spark has set up right behind me.

'Turn that off, will you!' I bark, a bit more sternly than I had intended.

My shadow vanishes and allows the interior of the folly to emerge. The space can't be any bigger than a dozen square metres. The walls are lined with the same dirty concrete as the floor. To my left, a metre or so off the ground, a bucket is hanging by its handle from a brass garden tap plumbed in to the wall. In the middle of the room is a wooden table about two metres long by sixty or seventy centimetres wide. Against the far wall sits a small refrigerator beside a rustic chest of three drawers. On the chest lies a little black case.

'All that's missing is a buddha. Otherwise I'd swear I was at my acupuncturist's,' Jules quips behind me. 'Drawers?'

I nod and make my way over to the chest while Jules goes for the fridge, the hinges of which squeal like a train pulling into a station.

'Max...' he calls, no sooner have I laid a hand on the case. 'Have a look at this.' His tone is urgent, alarming.

Jules is kneeling in front of the open fridge door. I shuffle over and kneel beside him.

It's not a fridge. It's a freezer, with various compartments inside. Jules is holding the first one open, his eyes glued to the contents:

test tubes sealed with corks and topped with frost, buried in roughly cut sponges, I suppose so they won't break when they're opened.

I reach in and pluck out one of the vials. It's labelled 'SEQ68'.

'What the...?' Jules blurts, catching his curse as if he's in a sacred place.

I stare at the burgundy liquid, transfixed, wondering if Pauline and Philippe Caron have racked up as many dead bodies as they have tubes of frozen blood.

39
Lucienne
1899

I can hear my mother-in-law as soon as the front door shuts behind us. She's not shouting, but her voice booms every word as if she's performing on stage. I also detect Henri's silence. She's the only person who can mute him without saying a word. A stance, a sigh, a sign of disapproval or discontent suffices. Henri lowers his eyes, listens religiously and silently for the duration of his mother's visit. Mary jests that he fears her more than the guillotine. That's not far from the truth. It was my mother-in-law who arranged our marriage. Not Monsieur Docquer senior, no, but Madame Docquer. Or 'Maman', as she insisted I call her from day one.

I know she's waiting for me, her eyes locked on the drawing room and Henri's on the rug.

Mary, walking down the hallway by my side, gives me a fearful glance. All I feel is apathy.

'Good evening, Maman,' I say, entering the room.

My mother-in-law is seated in one of the armchairs flanking the side table. Her outdated, puffy dress makes her look fatter than she really is. I lean down to embrace her. The mixture of perfume and sweat emanating from her clothes turns my stomach.

'You're home late, Lucienne. What were you doing at Madame de la Courtière's until such an hour?'

'I wasn't at Violette's. She was hosting a reception at Mollard's.'

'Maman' raises a suspicious eyebrow.

I can imagine my mother-in-law's shock if she were to learn of our spiritism seance the other evening with an Italian woman versed in the practice of levitation. It would give her a stroke, I'm sure.

I suppress an urge to laugh by coughing into my fist.

'Henri approves of and encourages my friendship with Violette,' I continue, finding my voice again. 'She has been an unwavering source of support to me since ... since the accident.'

I'm not allowed to call the 'accident' an abduction or a disappearance. To 'Maman', Jeanne and Rose are dead.

'Besides, Henri would have been with us this evening, had he not been held back by some pressing business.'

'Gentlemen always have ... business to deal with, Lucienne. Perhaps they may not in Lac-Clarence, but here in Paris, this is the case. Do remember that.'

I turn to Henri, whose gaze is floating between the side table and the armchair in which he's sitting.

'Madame de la Courtière has friendships I disapprove of,' my mother-in-law continues.

I don't intend to defy her and spark a flaming rant condemning everything that doesn't relate, directly or indirectly, to the Church. So I keep my mouth shut.

Suddenly, she casts her bovine gaze on my cousin. I stiffen.

'Mary, leave us be,' she commands. 'And shut the door on your way out.'

Mary knows there's nothing I can say.

My mother-in-law waits until she's disappeared before she goes on.

'Henri tells me you've not been receiving him since the accident.'

Anger stuns me for a second, then shoots through me like an arrow. It gives me a shameful, repulsive feeling to think of my mother-in-law inviting herself into my bed.

'It's time for you to get back to business, Lucienne,' she adds, as if she needs to spell it out to me.

In my mind images begin to attach themselves to her obscene rhetoric. I clench my teeth so tight, a drop of blood erupts in my mouth.

'Will that be all?' I ask curtly.

My mother-in-law nods and looks like she's about to get up. Henri comes running to her aid.

I make no attempt to stir or step in her direction.

'Well, good night, then,' I conclude and turn on my heels, jaw still clenched tight, fury in my belly.

I stamp my booted feet up the stairs like a child in a temper. Every strike of the heel gives me a rush of pleasure as I imagine it driving a hole into that old nanny-goat's forehead.

I shut myself in my room and find a note Mary has slipped under the door. She, too, has retired to her apartments for the night.

I make my way over to my dressing table.

Since the disappearance of Jeanne and Rose, I've asked my chambermaid to put my correspondence in one of the drawers, since when 'Maman' comes to visit, she takes it upon herself to open it, and I fear she may happen upon a letter from Violette. We have passed the information, or rather, the visions from Eusapia, to the private detective. To my great surprise, he is viewing the matter with much interest. It seems spiritism has more followers than I thought. Especially here, in Paris.

I open the middle drawer and leaf through the letters until I find a missive from my friend. Then I sit down and break the seal. The paper inside contains nothing but a date and a time. Three days from now. I'm quivering with impatience.

A series of brief knocks at my door come as an unwelcome interruption. I barely have time to tuck away the letter from Violette and close the drawer of my dressing table before the door opens. My husband is standing on the threshold, hesitant to enter.

I see my chambermaid scurrying over to help me undress and prepare for the night. Henri shoos her away.

I don't say a word. What is there to say? The outcome will be the same, anyway. I know he'll spend the night in my bed, and he'll wake me more than once, each time more aggressively, more resentfully than the last, as if I'm forcing him to toil away between my thighs. Then, first thing in the morning, he'll go off again to tend to his urgent business, as will I to mine. To Violette and this invitation I'm dying to know more about.

40
Maxine
2002

'Look at the writing on here,' Jules says, opening the second drawer of the freezer.

It contains three sponges: two holding half a dozen test tubes, and a third with only one.

Carefully, I remove one of the vials, read 'WS67' on the label and place it back in its sleeve.

'They all say the same thing,' Jules confirms.

He closes this compartment and opens the one below. This time, there are three sponges again, the first two dotted with six vials, and the last with five.

'Look,' he says again, extracting one of the test tubes. This time, I read 'SEQ70'. 'Same here, they're all labelled "SEQ70".'

Jules shuts the freezer door and we stand up again.

The space is so cramped that the forensic technicians working behind us are going to ingenious lengths not to tread on each other's toes. Gina's observing us from the doorway.

We move to our right so we're standing in front of the chest of drawers.

The black case on top looks to be made of leather, or imitation leather. I open both clasps simultaneously, wondering if I'll find a selection of scalpels inside. Or teeth. Or ... That's when I notice the grilles in the sides of the case and understand what this is.

'It's a portable turntable,' Jules announces, before I've had a chance to share my own conclusions.

'Yes, I just realised that when I saw the speakers,' I say, lifting the lid.

I step aside so that Gina can see the record player.

'There must be vinyl in there,' she says, almost to herself, pointing to the drawers of the chest.

'And what else?' Jules places his hands on the handles of the top drawer, inviting her to guess.

Gina smiles and accepts the challenge. 'Bath towels. Tissues. Rubbish bags. Disinfecting or cleaning products. Candles. A lighter.'

'Why not matches?'

'Not practical. It's too damp in here. Take a look around. It's basic, to say the least. Everything in its place.'

'And a place for everything,' I complete with a smile, remembering my father and his workshop.

'An incense burner too,' Gina adds.

'So that's what I could smell when we came in,' I exclaim. 'It reeked like a church.'

'Curious comparison,' Jules comments as he opens the top drawer. 'Although, with that collection of hands and those vials of blood, anyone would think we're holding Holy Communion in here. Right then,' he continues, riffling through the contents with his gloved fingers. 'Here, we have ... a metal box with a ceramic incense burner ... pillar candles and a lighter – good job, professor – one, two ... four records. Mozart's *Adagio KV 356* and *Rondo KV 617 for glass harmonica*; then, Holt Sombach and Donizetti, for the same instrument – which for your information, ladies, was to be played with wet fingers – and finally, Mozart's formidable opera, *Così fan tutte*. Interesting, this obsession with the glass harmonica...'

'Why?' Gina asks.

'Because Mozart was a great friend of Doctor Mesmer's, if that name rings a bell?'

Gina nods. 'The creator of "mesmerism", or animal magnetism,' she replies.

'Means nothing to me,' I hasten to say, before the conversation turns too obscure.

'Well,' Jules explains, 'Mesmer was quite a controversial doctor in the eighteenth century – German or Austrian, I don't recall which. He would use magnets to treat his patients – or to not treat them, depending on whether you asked his followers or his critics. According to his theory, a universal fluid flows through us all, and to put it simply, any imbalance makes us ill. Mesmer would use music in his therapy, and he had a predilection for the glass harmonica. It was during a visit to his home that Mozart first discovered the instrument to which he would devote his final piece of chamber music. The composer also included a reference to mesmerism in his opera, *Così fan tutte*. So to me, it seems obvious that whoever listened to this music was aware of that connection.'

'I notice you didn't say *she*,' I point out.

'That's right, Lieutenant Grant. I'm not going to get ahead of myself and state that it was Pauline Caron until we find the imprint of her buttocks on this table. That's it. Nothing else in this drawer.' Now Jules closes the drawer and moves down to the next one. 'Towels, rags, paper towels, a ... household cleaner, two sponges like the ones in the freezer ... and a pair of scissors. And now in this one,' he continues, opening the third and final drawer. 'We have ... an axe, a knife and four leather belts, arranged in pairs. Lovely...'

'In pairs?' Gina asks.

'To be used as straps,' I explain, pointing to the narrow examination table. 'To keep the victims immobile and—'

I'm jolted out of that thought by the sound of my phone. It takes me a good ten seconds to extract it from beneath my coveralls.

'You have to leave the premises, Lieutenant.' It's Marceau's voice, parched and weary.

'What?!' I shriek.

'Pack everything up. Right away.'

'Why?'

'Yvonne Lelanger's lawyer just called me. The authorisation she signed for us is null and void.'

41
Maxine
2002

'Relaxing weekend, I see, Sweet Maxine?' Jules quips, coming to sit beside me.

I realise it's been forever since I last looked at myself in the mirror.

'I can't hide anything from you, can I?'

'Believe me, you're not hiding anything from anyone. The nights still aren't getting any better?'

I shake my head.

'Want some more coffee?'

I hesitate, eyeing my empty cup. 'I'm going,' I announce with a yawn. 'Can I get one for you too?'

'Don't get up.' He gives me a pat on the hand and stands.

'Am I really that pitiful?' I force myself to smile.

'You don't want to know.' He gives me a kiss on the top of my head and leaves the meeting room.

On Friday night, Yvonne Lelanger and her husband invoked quite the array of noble reasons to justify pulling the plug on our search of the folly. They know very well it's only a matter of days before we get a warrant, but they're trying to buy time so they can sweet-talk their financial partners. Finding oneself with a crime scene in one's garden, connected to a murder that's made the headlines, no less, is as devastating for one's reputation as it is for one's wallet. And so we have to wait until the warrant comes through.

The loss of my parents weighed far heavier than usual on me this weekend. I found myself longing for a Sunday with them. Hugo in their garden, tasting snow and giggling with glee, his cheeks and nose rosy from the cold. Charlotte tipping her head back and laughing with abandon, her long brown curls dancing to the joy of the moment. Sometimes, I wonder if I'll ever see my Shasha smile again. She's not been herself at all. Not since her father died.

I miss my parents too. So much. We used to spend our weekends with them. My husband would come back from one trip, only to go off on another. 'Your breeze of a bloke' my father used to call him. I never wanted to leave my job to follow him around. I could have. We didn't need my salary. But I've never been much of an adventurous soul. And even less of a follower. There was no way I could live out of a suitcase and settle for being the tag-along wife. My husband and I always loved each other from a distance. Maybe that's why the intensity never waned, because in the waiting there was more room for love than for routine. The everyday was exceptional. Everything felt like a gift: lying in bed, listening to him brush his teeth on the rare occasion he'd be joining me; the slippers he'd shuffle with every step and kick off in the most unlikely of places, the slippers that still sit at the foot of my bed. And my desire for him, for us, that never left me.

'Shit, shit, shit,' Jules is hissing as he returns with two cups of coffee and Gina on his heels.

The psychologist places her notepad in front of her.

'What is it?' I ask, taking the coffee he hands me.

'We haven't been able to analyse the blood samples from the freezer in the folly,' Marceau announces on her way in.

'Why?'

'Yvonne Lelanger's lawyer has objected to it.'

'Her lawyer has objected to it...' My echo fades into silence.

'Do you have any good news to share?' I snap, aware of the lack of respect in my tone.

'Not officially, no.'

I look up to Marceau. I don't know what's driving her in this case, but this is the second time I've seen her taking a shortcut.

'OK,' I reply, waiting for the rest.

'I asked Simon to proceed, unofficially, with examining the prints.'

That means Simon spent his weekend in the lab. On his own, to top it off.

'The inside of the folly is plastered with Pauline and Philippe Caron's prints,' Marceau elaborates.

'Yes!' Jules punches a fist in the air.

'And only theirs?' I ask, mustering a bit of energy.

'Yes. On the axe, the belts, all over the place. Any leads on what's on the labels of those vials of blood?'

'We're mulling it over,' I reply. 'But I don't think it's anything to do with the names of the victims.'

'Too simplistic?' Marceau wonders.

'It's more that the identities of the victims weren't important to them, I think.'

'So what would...?' Marceau leaves her words trailing and reaches for her phone, which won't stop vibrating in her blazer pocket. She raises it to her ear.

We remain silent, like a trio of well brought-up siblings, listening to her murmurings of assent.

'We have our search warrant,' she announces, snapping her phone shut.

I breathe a sigh of relief.

'I'll call forensics and give them the go-ahead to test the freezer samples,' Marceau continues. 'And I'll send the crime-scene team back to the folly to finish gathering evidence. I'll get a search under way for those seven bodies too. Should we start by fanning out in a twenty-metre radius?'

'Twenty metres at a time makes sense to me,' I reply, visualising the terrain. 'If they committed their crimes in the folly, they can't have moved the bodies very far.'

'Do you think they'd have run the risk of burying them or getting rid of them on the Lelanger property?' Jules asks.

'Well, they certainly ran the risk of using that garden extravagance of theirs. The Lelanger estate is huge. Forty hectares. The Carons must have known that their wealthy neighbours would never venture so far from the manor house and so close to their place.'

'I wonder where the key is, though. And how they got their hands on it.'

'Maybe they fitted that lock themselves?'

'I don't know, it looks pretty vintage to me.'

Another immense wave of fatigue barrels into me. I release a long, slow puff of breath, and massage my brow.

'As far as the hands are concerned,' Marceau chimes in, 'they're still cross-referencing genetic profiles with missing persons, but there's nothing conclusive to report yet. Professor?' she asks, turning to Gina now.

Gina's staring at Marceau, twirling her pen in her fingers like a majorette with her baton.

'Bernadette Damatian mentioned her mother when we met with her,' she replies, after a pause. 'She used to work with Pauline's mother, I gather?'

'That's right,' I confirm, surprised that Gina would recall this detail.

'Do you know where?'

I shake my head.

'Do you know if she's still alive?'

'I think so. Otherwise I'd have seen an obituary. Everyone knows everything in Lac-Clarence,' I add, to soften my somewhat abrupt reply. 'Would you like to meet with her?'

She gives me a silent nod.

'To ... find out more about Pauline Caron?'

'To try, at least. And I'd like you to come with me, Maxine, if you don't mind. I think she'll be more willing to open up if you're there. You're from here, if you see what I mean?'

'Yes, of course. Do you want to interview Mrs Caron first?'

Gina bites her lower lip.

'You'd prefer to wait,' I answer for her, wondering what she really has in mind.

Gina's gaze flicks to her notes. 'Her prints confirm her presence in the folly. But the portable turntable and those records suggest that she was much more than a consenting victim.'

42
Lucienne
1899

Violette's carriage is waiting at our front door.

She opens the carriage door and motions for us to hurry up, adjusts her summer coat and shuffles over so we can seat ourselves.

'I'm sorry, but I'll have to cover your eyes,' she tells us, producing two black, satin blindfolds.

Mary and I exchange a glance, then I turn my back to Violette. My body feels charged with an almost carnal thrill.

Violette ties the blindfold without a word. I've never known her to be so quiet. I was expecting to see her exalted, barely able to contain herself; and here she is, the picture of hieratic calm. She who always exudes enthusiasm and takes eagerness to another level is now demonstrating a restraint that seems very out of character. The joy curling on her lips is intense, yet intimate, almost internalised.

My mask now in place, I sit back in my seat and lose myself in the swishing of our skirts and the impatient whinnying of our horses.

During the journey, I listen to Paris as if I'm discovering the city's voice. There is far more to hear while travelling these avenues than the mere hammering of horses' hooves on cobblestones and the sputtering of the odd automobile. Paris is buzzing with the racket of street vendors, with the cries of children, with hearty, joyous laughter. As carriages draw to a halt, parasols click open, steps clack down, heels clatter along hurriedly, heavily or wearily.

After a while, Paris falls silent and I sense we're reaching the countryside. I've been so absorbed by this game, I have no inkling how long it's been since Violette tied the blindfold over my eyes. I listen to the crunching of the gravel and the grass as we pass by. Even the smells are different in the country. The landscape is pure.

Suddenly, the carriage stops. A long creaking sound tells me a gate is opening. Then our carriage is on its way once more. Now the wheels seem to be rolling on sand. It must be a driveway, in a park or a private estate.

I can feel a hand caressing the back of my head. My skin bristles with goosebumps.

'We're here,' Violette tells us. 'I just wanted to make sure your blindfold was still tight, to make sure it doesn't slip when you step out.'

My throat is throbbing, my mouth dry with anticipation.

'Please sit tight, Mary, someone will come for you. Lucienne, you come with me. Gather your dress the way you normally do when you step out of a carriage.'

I bend down, sliding a hand the length of my leg to grasp a fold of fabric, then lift my skirt and petticoat.

'Now lean forwards,' Violette instructs me, exerting a gentle pressure on the top of my hat.

I feel for, and find, the step with the toe of my boot, then alight from the carriage with the aid of my friend.

The heat is the same as in Paris, but the air is less stifling, despite the lack of breeze.

I've only taken a few strides when Violette stops me. 'There are four steps for you to climb. They're quite high.'

I lift my foot.

'A little lower,' she guides me.

Behind me, I can hear the sound of Mary's footsteps and her guide repeating the instructions Violette gave me.

We enter a building I presume to be a manor house, given its remoteness and its acoustics, since our heels are clicking on tiles.

My heart is pounding like mad. I have no idea what awaits us. It hasn't occurred to me for a second that I could be endangering Henri's reputation – as well as that of my family. Since I received Violette's note, I have harboured only one desire, to discover the secret of this soiree, this encounter or ceremony. Nothing else has mattered.

We stop. A squealing sound, a lingering moan keeps us from moving for a moment. It must be a door, a tall and heavy one, so dramatic is the opening. As it closes behind us, a rustling breaks the silence. I sense a gentle touch, a flowing of breath, a floral scent.

Another caress at the back of my head, and the blindfold falls.

43
Lina
1950

I've had to wait more than a month for this moment.

I've been coming to this shelter in the gardens every day. First I cleaned the place from top to bottom to clear all the dust, cobwebs and traces of mould from the walls and ceiling, then I aired it out and burned the incense Lucienne gave me. She's also given me some blankets and an oil lamp that will give out more light than just the candles.

I've had to wait more than a month, because I can't make my demands just any time I like. Lucienne has been adamant about this: the spirits may only be summoned on very specific dates. And the first date of the year is the second day of February: Candlemas.

Mother is no longer controlling my comings and goings. She knows I'm spending my spare time with Lucienne. If, by chance, she happens to pay a visit to Lucienne's room to check on me while I'm out in the garden, Lucienne has agreed to tell her I've gone to fetch some laundry for her, or a book, or a bite to eat from the kitchen.

No matter what, I have a few hours ahead of me.

I fold my panties and place them on the top of my pile of clothes.

I'm shaking. More with anticipation than from the cold.

This is the first time that I've been naked and have taken the time to look at this body, my body, the one Tamara has tormented with so much mockery. The first time I've allowed myself to do so. The shape of my breasts is more pronounced. I look more like a woman than a child, now.

I reach into my satchel for two pouches I've sewn from scraps of fabric. From the first, I extract a square cut from one of Dad's old shirts and keep this in my right hand. From the second, I remove two of Tamara's hairs I've sewn to a scrap of stocking stained with red ink, one of those she pinned to my coat, and this I hold in my left hand.

Lucienne has told me I must abide by certain rules, like the sorcerer's calendar and the magic circle where I am to stand, and I must meticulously recite the incantations and prepare the ingredients of the potion, failing which, Satan will not listen to me. However, I may choose how my ritual unfolds or 'compose my own music', as she says.

I stand at the centre of the circle, facing Och, the Sun, whose symbol I have drawn at the very top. The flickering flames of the candles are projecting pools of yellow that waver from floor to ceiling with every draught. My skin is bathed from top to toe in a golden light that shimmers over my stiff, cold nipples.

I raise my arms to the ceiling in a V shape, marking Venus to my right and Mars to my left. To Venus, who is only Love, I raise my father; to Mars, who is but war and conflict, I brandish Tamara.

I can't feel the cold anymore, just a mixture of excitement and apprehension.

I close my eyes and chant with conviction:

Bagabi laca bachabé
Lamac cahi achababé
Karrelyos
Lamac lamec Bachalyas
Cabahagy sabalyos
Baryolos
Lagoz atha cabyolas

Samahac et famyolas
Harrahya

I'm waving the scraps of fabric like flags, tipping my head back as if someone or something on the ceiling's drawing my attention.

Bagabi laca bachabé
Lamac cahi achababé
Come, hear me!

Karrelyos
Lamac lamec
Bachalyas
Come, listen to me!

Cabahagy sabalyos
Baryolos
Come, answer me!

Lagoz atha cabyolas
Samahac et famyolas
Come, help me!

Harrahya
Make Tamara leave! Banish her! Punish her!
Hurt her like she's hurt me!

Harrahya
Harrahya
Harrahya

My feet are drumming a beat on the floor. My knees are rising to my waist, my head is swaying side to side. A curious wave of warmth is spreading upwards from my lower belly to my heart.

It's him.
He hears me.
He's listening to me.
I can feel it.
I clench Tamara's scrap of fabric in my fist and I dance, dance, dance, until my legs give way beneath me.

44
Maxine
2002

'Sorry, it's my day for having Mum to visit today,' Bernadette Damatian explains, inviting us in.

'Thank you for meeting with us,' I smile.

'We're the ones who should be apologising for encroaching on your family time,' Gina adds.

'It's no bother at all, quite the opposite. Mum's thrilled to have a visitor, and especially a pure, dyed-in-the-wool Clarençoise. Mum,' our hostess announces, as we go through to the living room, 'this is Lieutenant Grant and Professor Montminy. Ladies, this is my mother, Anne-Marie.'

'Hello there,' I say, shaking the hand of the elderly woman in a wheelchair.

She has a firm grip. Gina steps forwards in turn to greet her. We take a seat on the narrow sofa.

'Ah!' Anne-Marie cries, slapping her brown wool trousers, a winning smile creasing her harmonious face. 'A woman lieutenant with the Sûreté and a professor in...?'

'Clinical psychology.' Gina fills in the blank with a grin.

'How lovely,' she gushes, her grey eyes gleaming with interest.

'What can I offer you?' Bernadette asks us.

'Coffee, Bernie, coffee. Women of their calibre drink coffee. Or am I mistaken?'

'Not at all,' Gina grants her. 'Coffee is the drink of warriors. Tea is the beverage of the wise.'

'But who likes wise women, eh?' Anne-Marie replies, giving us a wink.

Bernadette winces with embarrassment and slips away to the kitchen.

'So, Pauline Caron...' the elderly woman leads, with an air of mystery. 'Lisette is no longer of this world, thank God. This whole affair would have been the death of her. It'd be the death of any mother, for that matter. I gather from the news that Pauline didn't do things by halves.' She shakes her head. 'I like to think I'm a good judge of character, but Pauline ... little Pauline ... it's beyond me. He must have been taking a hand to her, that big husband of hers, it's just not possible otherwise. When a woman loses her rag, there's always a man to blame. And it's always something to do with the nest. A man fleeing it, or not wanting to bring a child into it.'

'Here you go,' Bernadette chirps, placing a tray full of cups on the coffee table.

'The last time we saw your daughter, she told us you used to work with Lisette, Pauline's mother?' Gina ventures, with a discreet thank-you to Bernadette.

'Yes, we worked together in a rest home. Lisette was remarkably courageous. I had a lot of admiration for her. She raised Pauline on her own. Her husband died during the war, in the camps. He was a resistance fighter. A Frenchman.'

With a smile, Anne-Marie accepts the cup her daughter hands her, and it seems that her first sip carries her off somewhere.

'What kind of a child was Pauline?' says Gina, coaxing her back.

'Never one to bite her tongue, not with her mother at least. Always had her nose in a book, too. I think they used to give her grief about that at school, you know.'

'Pauline was bullied?' Bernadette interjects in surprise. 'Are you sure, Mum? As I remember, she was always quite a popular girl.'

'No, Bernie, that was later on. You're a bit younger than her...'

'Still, Mum, she was the one who gave that reading at the service for Julie Gauthier, do you remember that?'

'Of course I remember. Everyone around here remembers that. What a terrible thing that was to happen. Poor child. Her parents never got over it,' she says, shaking her head.

'Who was Julie Gauthier?' I ask, putting my cup down.

'A young girl in the village,' Bernadette explains. 'She was run over by a car. It was in the early fifties.'

'As I was saying,' Anne-Marie continues, 'that was *after* Lisette had to take a harder line with Pauline and keep a closer eye on her after school.'

'What happened?' Gina asks.

'Pauline used to skip school. Not to antagonise her mother, but to get away from some bullies, I think. She always used to come home with torn clothes, exercise books that weren't hers, and who knows what else. So after school, Pauline would come over to our work. That was when she started to change. To change into the person you remember, Bernie. That more ... popular girl.'

Anne-Marie pauses to adjust a pin in her white bun.

'What was it that ... sparked this change, in your opinion?' Gina asks.

'Lisette had no time to pay attention to her daughter. Being a single mother is hard enough these days, but imagine what it was like after the war.'

Anne-Marie releases a sigh.

'I don't know if this is what helped Pauline ... but she became acquainted with a resident almost as old as I am today, and the woman acted like a grandmother to her. She would lend her the ear Lisette couldn't, for lack of time and energy. That poor old woman had lost her zest for life after the death of her two daughters in a fire. Pauline started reading to her, and slowly but surely, we began to hear them chatting and laughing. The girl became a ray of sunshine around there. That "rest home" we worked in, Lisette and me, was more of a prison than anything else, if you ask me. They used to lock up women who'd become a burden to their wealthy families, or to the justice system. In fact, when it first opened in the middle of the nineteenth century, it was a psychiatric hospital. Things changed after the war. Lisette and I had trained as nurses, so they hired us in the blink of an eye. The job paid incredibly well. And for Lisette, that money was very welcome. Clarence Manor closed ... at the end of the sixties, or in the early seventies, didn't it, Bernie?'

'I have no idea, Mum.'

'Yes, you do. It was when that old heiress passed away that her family took back possession of the manor house, here in Lac-Clarence. They converted the rest home into their country house.'

My fingers clench around my coffee cup.

I open my mouth to ask the question, but Bernadette beats me to it.

'Which heiress and which manor house are you talking about, Mum?'

'Good God, Bernie,' Anne-Marie tuts. 'You make me wonder who's the old mad hatter here. I'm talking about the Lelangers' manor house, a couple of kilometres away from the Carons' place. The heiress was Lucienne Lelanger – the elderly woman who befriended Pauline.'

45
Lina
1950

I'm walking through the forest, following the path from school I've not taken for months to go and see Lucienne. I've made myself go that way to inflict the punishment I deserve. To remember not to make certain mistakes again.

I'm walking barefoot. It's not cold, but the twigs and stone chips are digging into the soles of my feet. I embrace the pain of every step. It reminds me of my stupidity, my gullibility, my ignorance and my naivety.

I shouldn't have got caught up in the game
In her game, in their game
I shouldn't have gone with them
On the outing Father Tremblay led
I shouldn't have mixed with the others
Thought I was one of them
I shouldn't have let my guard down
I shouldn't have done as they did
Tasted the river water with open hands
Then wanted a taste with the tips of my toes
I shouldn't have taken my shoes off
My socks
Rolled up my trousers
Cried with joy because they were splashing me too
Not ignoring me

Lost myself in the laughter of others
Joined mine with theirs
Felt our joys weaving together
I shouldn't have let myself go
Thought I had a right to be reckless
Thought she'd forget that I'm the one who makes her victorious
I shielded my face from the splashing
Got up to run with the girls, away from the boys
Then Father Tremblay called us back
I retraced my steps to the riverbank
Hunted for my shoes while the others were lacing theirs up
Saw Tamara's jubilant smile
And understood I'd never find them

I've arrived at Clarence Manor.

I don't care if I run into Mother or anyone else. My feet are a mess. They're sticking to the tiles with every step I take. Leaving a trail of brown and red behind me.

I push open Lucienne's door. Her gaze falls on my muddy, bloody toes.

Her face turns to stone.

'Go fetch two towels and two pads from the cupboard,' she instructs. 'Get my basin too.'

I do as she says.

I clench my teeth as I cross the living room to fetch what she's asked for. The pain is becoming intolerable. I clench my teeth so I won't cry.

I bring everything over to the coffee table.

'Lie down,' she commands, gesturing to the sofa beside her throne of a chair.

I obey.

She lays the first towel in her lap, gently lifts my legs by the calves and rests them on her knees. She pours the water from her teapot into the basin and soaks the other towel in there.

The tears are coming in torrents. I'm coughing to keep them at bay. Biting my lips.

'It didn't work,' I murmur.

Lucienne stares at me as she tends to my wounds.

'She wasn't supposed to keep torturing me...' My voice is up and down, all over the place.

There's a breath caught somewhere between my belly and my throat, and I cough it up.

'I ... I asked Dad to stop Tamara. I asked him to help me stop her. To make her stop bullying me. To just make her stop!'

I'm huffing more than crying. I clench my teeth, sniffle my sobs. *Stop crying*, I beg myself. *Good God, Lina, just stop crying.* I sigh, take a deep breath and squash my anger deep down in my chest. I only have myself to blame.

'Maybe I didn't do things properly.'

I cry out in pain. The cut beside my right toe is a deep one. Lucienne continues to clean out the crevasse, oblivious to my cries. I wait for her to move on to the next wound before I elaborate.

'Still, I followed the recommendations of John Dee – you know, Queen Elizabeth I's astrologer – down to the letter. Girardius too. As well as the words reported by Rutebeuf. I went with the method you advised. I don't understand.'

She dries my right foot and wraps it in the cloth pad.

'Perhaps time is what it takes, Lina. Time for the spirits to hear you, to deem you worthy of their listening, to answer your calls.'

Maybe that's true. Or maybe Tamara is a demon and none of those I'm summoning can do a thing against her.

Lucienne is tending to my other foot now. She sends the new girl, who isn't a girl anymore, to find me a pair of clodhoppers. I have to tie the laces around my ankles to keep them on. My feet will hurt for a few days, and to stop the cuts bleeding and help them scab, I'm not to walk on them, she advises.

When I leave Clarence Manor, I feel more indifferent than angry or hateful. I limp home, every step a reminder of my choices. My poor choices.

The whole time I keep going over the ritual in my mind, again and again, wondering what I forgot, what I should have said and done differently.

When at last I get to our street, I'm so lost in my thoughts it takes me a moment to recognise the silhouette emerging from the darkness in front of my home. It's Julie. She draws herself tall when she sees me coming. I notice my shoes, sitting side by side on the top step of the porch, my socks still stuffed inside them.

'I'm sorry, Lina,' she says, her gaze shifting from my shoes to the ground at her feet. 'I don't know why she…' She shakes her head and bites her lip. 'I'm so sorry…'

She looks up at me for a second and gives me a furtive smile, then she walks away.

46
Maxine
2002

'I'd like us to talk about Lucienne Lelanger, Pauline,' Gina says, closing the interview-room door behind her.

Pauline smiles. The shape on her lips suddenly gives flesh and blood to this dehumanised form that bears nothing of the woman I knew. Mrs Caron has become a complete stranger to me. Except in this one brief moment when, like a dried flower stuck between two pages jogging the memory of a whole summer, her smile revives a fragment of my childhood.

'Lucienne was your saviour, wasn't she?'

Pauline cocks her head to one side. She seems to be pondering Gina's question.

'She gave me life.'

'The life you lived. Did Lucienne Lelanger bequeath you part of her fortune?'

'Only a plot of land when she died. I had my house built on it. What I was referring to was the ethereal aspect of our relationship.' Now I recognise the teacherly tone of Pauline Caron, her phrasing, her measured voice. 'She taught me how to weave my own existence, one thread at a time.'

'Lucienne was like a mother to you.'

'No mother could have brought me what she did. Our relationship was free from the constraints of education and duty. It was an apprenticeship. It was freeing and stimulating.'

'What did she teach you?' Gina's picking up the tempo, as if she's trying to make Pauline Caron open up spontaneously.

'Not to come across as common ... or vulgar, but Lucienne taught me to honour my desires.'

'To accept them?'

'To honour them.'

'I suppose you're not alluding to carnal desire?'

'Carnal desire is but a means to an end.'

'Yet you know nothing of childbearing, Pauline. You've not been a mother.'

Pauline seals her lips for a second. Then: 'I've carried children and created far more than any mother.'

'Are you talking about your career as a schoolteacher?'

'I'm talking about the light I bring shining from the void.'

'Where are the bodies of those you severed hands from, Pauline? Where are your victims?'

'They're not victims. If they were, we wouldn't have cut off their hands.'

'You and Philippe?'

Pauline turns and looks at Gina. 'Do you have that little thing of a— ... of sand on you?'

'Why sever those hands? What good are they to you?'

Pauline turns her head to the far wall. 'They're no good for anything, now.'

'We've found your prints, and Philippe's, in the folly.'

'Do you know why, or rather, for whom, that outbuilding was built? Lucienne's great-grandfather had it put up for his son, who wanted a tower where he could play soldier and stand guard. But one time, when he was out hunting, the great-grandfather mistook his son for a deer. So the story goes. And he shot him dead. Yet he should have known his son was playing in the vicinity. You would have smelled a rat, as a psychologist. As far as you're concerned, there are no accidents. Only manifestations of the sub-conscious. Freudian slips ... or successes, in the end.'

'Who does the blood in the vials you kept in the freezer belong to?'

Pauline tips her chin, as if she's trying to keep her head above the quicksand, snatch a final breath of air before she goes under. Resigning herself.

'What purpose did they serve?'

'To change the way of things.'

'And did you change the way of things, Pauline? Did it really work?'

'Yes, very well. Until the end.'

'What end?'

'Until Philippe died. The end.'

'Until you killed your husband, Pauline. Until you stabbed him thirty-one times.'

'Yes, until I stabbed him. Thirty-one times. But we've already talked about that, it's...' She catches herself, swallows her words and gives a sigh. 'It's like in *Macbeth*. Everything begins with an encounter, a prophetic encounter with a witch. If Macbeth's path had never crossed that of the three witches, he would never have killed King Duncan. Lady Macbeth or no Lady Macbeth.'

There's a knock at the door. It opens a crack.

Gina turns her head and marks a two-second pause. Then she gets up and leaves the room without a word to Pauline, whose gaze falls first on Gina's back, then on the door closing behind her.

A moment later, Marceau and Gina enter the viewing room.

'We've just found three bodies near the folly,' the boss glumly announces.

'Ah, at last,' Jules exclaims. 'Now we can start identifying those hands.'

'Not so fast. These three bodies are intact.'

Another caress at the back of my head, and the blindfold falls. I blink my eyes open and see Mary by my side, who, like me, is casting a curious gaze around her. We're standing at the entrance to a torchlit room. There are white drapes covering what seem to be three windows. Two women I've never seen, bare-headed and dressed in dark linen robes, are cloaking in black a table set at the centre of a circle painted on the floor. A coarse, white stroke of a brush, marked by symbols whose meaning I cannot decipher.

One of the women pushes a round cart to the outside of the circle. On it, the other woman sets down some sort of chalice covered with a lace handkerchief, as well as a crudely poured candle, which sits atop a candlestick in the shape of a clenched fist. The first woman reaches for a perfume burner and places it on the table. I recognise the floral scent I smelled on arrival.

Violette leads us along the wall and we stand where we can see the whole length of the main table. The door is to our left.

My heart feels like it's beating everywhere except in my chest. I have absolutely no idea what to expect. I cast a furtive glance at Violette, whose face is the picture of inner peace and abundant joy.

Both attendants suddenly begin to sing. Their voices bathe the room in a softness which, I don't know why, reminds me of waves rolling on the shore.

A woman dressed in a burgundy toga now enters the room, followed by a younger, naked woman, whose blonde hair is cascading down her back and over her breasts. Her locks bear the characteristic wave of a bun that's just been undone. She's looking straight ahead as she walks with no hint of shame, indifferent to our presence.

She lies down on the table, arms by her sides, feet facing the door, hair flowing free. In spite of the warmth in the room, her nipples are standing proud and her body is covered in goosebumps, as is mine. The torchlight has turned her milky skin to gold and sends shadows dancing all around, licking at our feet and the table legs, as if we were dipping them in the blackest of waters.

The woman in the toga stands facing us, in the circle, by the naked girl's belly. She raises her arms to the ceiling in a V shape. Then she closes her eyes and begins to chant.

Bagabi laca bachabé
Lamac cahi achababé
Karrelyos
Lamac lamec Bachalyas
Cabahagy sabalyos
Baryolos
Lagoz atha cabyolas
Samahac et famyolas
Harrahya

Her voice blankets the song of the two women. I can't understand a word of her incantation, and yet I sense she is speaking to me.

Arms still raised to the ceiling, she inhales, exhales and then chants even louder.

Her two assistants approach the girl on the table. The first lays a red ribbon over the girl's heart, the other drapes a pink, ruffled cloth over her private parts, then they both return to their places.

The toga-clad officiant circles the table, picks up the chalice and removes the handkerchief. Then she stands by the naked girl's head and holds the chalice over her.

> *Bagabi laca bachabé*
> *Lamac cahi achababé*
> *Come, hear me!*

She tips the chalice and a reddish liquid rains on the young woman's forehead, splashing off the bridge of her nose as she closes her eyes, flowing down her cheeks and into her ears.

It's blood, I'm sure it is.

The priestess advances to the girl's shoulders.

> *Karrelyos*
> *Lamac lamec Bachalyas*
> *Come, listen to me!*

She pours blood over the girl's left breast.

> *Cabahagy sabalyos*
> *Baryolos*
> *Come, answer me!*

She moves down the table and drizzles the girl's belly, filling her navel as she goes.

> *Lagoz atha cabyolas*
> *Samahac et famyolas*
> *Come, help me!*

Then she empties the rest of the chalice over the girl's privates.

Harrahya
Make Madame de Langlois go away! Banish her! Punish her!
Punish her for robbing Béatrice of her husband!
Make Madame de Langlois go away! Banish her! Punish her!
Harrahya
Harrahya
Harrahya

The priestess is drumming her feet on the floor, chanting in time to her beat. Her knees are rising to her waist, her head swaying side to side.

It's you!
You hear me
You're listening!
I can feel you!

She stops, gasping for breath, and covers the girl's face with one hand. Then, with her right index and middle finger, she traces a bloody line down from the crown of the girl's head, across her neck, down her chest, between her breasts, over her belly, her crotch, down her left leg to the foot.

The priestess is praying with passion, tracing the same line again and again, the blood now forming a near-black film.

Harrahya
Harrahya
Harrahya

I'm surprised to find myself repeating these words with her, carried away in this life-breathing movement, like I'm witnessing a birth or a rebirth.

Suddenly, I sense a wave of warmth spreading upwards from my lower belly to my breast. The pleasure I feel is immense and unbelievably intense, a carnal coming that's weaving an improbable web from my heart and my mind to my crotch.

And, as if she can read my thoughts, Violette slips her hand into mine and together we sing, crying in ecstasy.

Harrahya
Harrahya
Harrahya

48
Lina
1950

I put my satchel beside me on the sofa and cast a swift glance to the bedroom door. Lucienne nods her head. She'll warn me if someone's coming. The coast is clear.

I open the leather flap, remove the glass jar and hold it in my lap. 'Do you think I'll have enough?'

Lucienne smiles. 'More than enough, yes.'

I'm eyeing the viscous liquid. It's much thicker than I imagined.

I've set traps for hares before, seen Mother butcher more than a few, but I've never slit one's throat. I don't know if the way I collected the animal's blood was the best method. Admittedly, I hadn't given it a thought until I had the hare's body in my hands.

Today, it's the twentieth of March. Tomorrow morning at four thirty-five will be the ideal time for another ritual, since it will be the arrival of spring.

I place the jar back in my satchel.

'Mother is on call tonight. I told her I hate being home alone. She's given me permission to stay a bit longer with you.' I smile proudly. 'She'll be home in the morning between six and half past. I want to time it as close as possible to four thirty-five, you see. I thought I'd go out to the garden around half past three to get everything ready. By four thirty-five I'll be summoning the spirits to rid me of Tamara. Or rather, of the hold she has on me. I'll be done by five or half past, so that gives me at least half an hour of wiggle room, just in case.'

'You could go out to the garden straight from here and start the ritual earlier.'

'That won't stack the odds in my favour, though, will it?'

'The night is more auspicious than the early morning. Not to mention, if you're going home at five in the morning, you might run into people in the village. It's risky, Lina. Midnight is perfect.'

Lucienne is right. The woods around the shelter will shield me from sight, whereas crossing the village would leave me perilously exposed. I don't know how I'd explain why I'm out in the street in the early morning.

Though my thoughts don't stray far from what awaits me a few hours from now, we spend the evening chatting about Paris during the Belle Époque. Lucienne tells me all about the Palais Garnier, the Tuileries, her long and uncomfortable corseted dresses, her fancy hairstyles studded with diamonds.

When her clock strikes eleven, my heart quickens. I put on my coat and pick up my satchel with a shiver of pleasure.

'Lina.' Lucienne stops me as I've about to leave.

I turn around. She's at the window.

'One moment. There's someone outside. Wait a minute before you go.'

I join her at the window, and the surprise I see is almost enough to mute the music in my heart.

It's Mother. Mother and Tamara. Mother and Tamara hurrying away into the night.

Lucienne looks at me.

'It's Tamara...' I reply to her silent question, feeling a lump in my throat at the sight of that monster of a girl by my mother's side.

Lucienne frowns.

They're going around the back of the building, towards the gymnasium. Mother has her arm around Tamara's shoulders like a shawl, holding my tormentor's blonde curls captive in its embrace.

Feeling unsteady on my feet, I cross the room and leave without a word.

As I make my way down the back stairs, I tell myself I'm going to confront them. Challenge them. My rage at my mother's betrayal builds with every step that takes me closer to them. To me, it looks like that protective arm is nurturing the demon who's poisoning me.

When I step out into the courtyard, they're nowhere to be seen. There's no light, no door standing ajar or just closing. They can't be far away, though. I head for the gymnasium. What can the two of them be doing in the middle of the night? Where are they going? What's brought them together?

The gymnasium door is closed. The lights are off. I skirt the perimeter anyway. Pricking my ears, listening at every window. Nothing. Frustration bleeds into anger. Good God, where are they?

I retrace my steps.

It really looked like they were heading for the gymnasium. I can't see what they'd be doing in there, but I was sure they were going that way. In that direction.

Perhaps Mother's gone back to work and Tamara's taken off through the woods?

Perhaps.

I wonder about the summer pavilion, down the garden path. It's closed for renovations. Why would they go in there? Among the scaffolding and paint pots?

I have no idea. But I have to go and see.

I run to the pavilion, clutching my satchel to my chest, now not so much with anger as with an unpleasant feeling, like I'm treading on a floor that's shaking and splintering beneath my feet.

As I approach, I can see there's a faint light shining from one of the inner rooms. I skirt the building and crouch down as soon as I find the source. The light is illuminating the back of my mother's head.

Suddenly, a muffled cry rings out.

My heart lurches into my mouth, bleeds into my ears, pounds at my temples. The nearest way into the building is a set of French doors. They're open. I sneak inside without closing them behind me.

I'm guided by Tamara's cries and pleas. I'm not concerned about the sound of my footsteps because her screams are now covering them. I'm comforted by her shrieking, because whatever is happening, I know that monster is suffering, and my mother is on my side, because she's making her suffer.

They're right behind the next door. I push it open. There's no point hiding. I'm not thinking anymore, to be honest. I just want to see her face. Her eyes, her forehead, her mouth, twisted in pain.

She's lying on a table, her legs butterflied open and splayed apart.

Mother is leaning down between her thighs.

'Bite down on the blanket,' Mother tells her.

Tamara's breathing is rushed and ragged. Her arm shoots out bizarrely to one side, as if she's reaching for someone's hand. She manages to grab hold of the edge of the blanket she's lying on, stuffs it into her mouth like she's going to devour it, then starts screaming again, yanking her head off the table, her face dripping with sweat, nostrils gaping with her muffled cries.

That's when she sees me.

Her face creases through the tears, like she's somehow surmounting the pain. She wheezes. 'Don't say ... don't say a...'

Mother turns and sees me too.

Tamara's privates are covered in blood. So are the towels beneath her buttocks. As well as Mother's hands.

'Lina, get out!' she snaps, before turning back to Tamara.

I don't want to leave.

'The towels,' Mother suddenly says.

I'm staring at Tamara. There's nothing jubilant about the look on her face now.

'Lina!'

Mother's voice rattles off the bare walls. I realise she's talking to me.

'Bring me the towels. Behind you. Now!'

I spin on my heels. There's a pile of towels on a metal cabinet. I grab them with both hands and pass them to my mother.

She immediately pulls away the blood-soaked rags and tosses them behind her, near the door, then replaces them with the fresh ones I've brought her.

'Now go,' she says in a firm but surprisingly calm and clear voice, punctuated by Tamara's tears and her dog-like panting. 'Don't worry. I'm taking care of your friend. Everything's going to be all right. She's going to be all right. Aren't you, Tamara? It'll be all right.'

Tamara moans in response.

I back away, unable to take my eyes off my subdued rival. I nearly trip over the bloody towels on the floor, and freeze.

My thoughts turn to the jar of hare's blood in my satchel.

Tamara's blood would be so much better.

I gather up the whole pile and carry the bloody rags away with me. I stop by the door to roll them up and stuff them into my satchel.

My breathing is as short and loud as Tamara's. But I'm not in pain. Quite the opposite, in fact.

I run off into the woods. Towards the shelter.

I have Tamara's blood.

49

Lucienne
1899

We're sitting in the carriage in silence.

Violette tied the blindfolds over our eyes again before we left the room, and took them off once we were past the gate. Now, like Mary and me, she's gazing out the window, lost in her thoughts. There's something curious about the calm she's exuding, as if her mind has had its fill.

She hasn't asked me what I thought of the ceremony, nor how it made me feel, since she saw and sensed we were overcome by the same exaltation and the same, dare I say, faith. What will the next step be? What is there to learn? How will the learning process unfold? With whom? Violette? How long will it take? There are so many questions I'm dying to ask her, though I know it's not the right time.

'Was it Satan they summoned?' Mary asks, cutting short my train of thought.

Violette turns to her as if only just noticing she's here.

'Yes,' she replies with no further explanation, turning right back to gaze at her reflection and the dark night beyond the glass.

It suddenly occurs to me how much trust Violette has placed in me. In us. Not once has she urged us to keep our lips sealed about this ritual, this ceremony, this black mass, whatever it's called. This too, she will tell me. I must simply be patient.

I think about that young woman who wanted to drive a rival out of her life. And who summoned the Devil to do so.

'She wanted to take back possession of her husband,' I say, as if to myself, musing that in her place I would have asked for precisely the opposite.

'Her husband, as well as her life as a respected, respectable lady.'

I can still see her lying there, on that table, her blonde hair cascading over the edge, down to the floor, lending her an air of the Renaissance Venus. I wonder if her wish will be granted, and if so, how long she'll have to wait for it to happen.

The memory of the priestess bloodying the woman's milky skin carries me away for a moment.

There's a question burning on the tip of my tongue. I doubt Violette will answer it, but I decide to ask her all the same, and refrain from encumbering myself with circumlocutions.

'I was wondering if the blood used in the ritual is of a particular ... provenance?'

Mary turns to stone.

Violette keeps staring into the darkness as if she hasn't heard me.

'This ... religion is not one of relinquishing or repenting,' she whispers, her gaze still immersed in the night, 'but of acknowledging one's desires and recognising that they are legitimate and natural. Desires one may heed without judgement. Satan arms us so we may defend ourselves. What is required comes at a price, Lucienne, like everything. A price greater than a simple prayer. And the only offering he accepts is blood. Pure blood. The purest of all.'

I think about the famous painting by Goya in my grandfather's collection, of the woman handing a plump baby to Satan.

'The blood of a child,' I murmur.

We arrive home as the clock strikes two in the morning. As I step out of the carriage, I see the lights are on in the drawing room. I wonder what Henri could be doing. He's not the type to stay up late. No sooner does he return from one of his evenings of 'business' than he turns in for the night. He knows I'm with Violette – she said she was inviting me to a party with her actress friends. Henri approves of our friendship. What husband would not approve of my socialising in such a circle? Violette holds the purse strings of a considerable fortune, far greater than that of her husband. Monsieur de la Courtière thus affords his wife unprecedented freedoms, for she is his banker.

I step across the threshold and, leaving Mary in the doorway, I go through to the drawing room without removing my hat. There I find Henri and the chief of police, both in evening dress.

Without looking up at me, my husband waves a letter in my face.

'What is it?' I ask, in an anxious voice.

'A ransom demand,' replies the chief.

50
Maxine
2002

'I was hoping you'd found the bodies,' Patrice Lemay says to us, with a nod of his chin to the seven hands laid out on a steel table.

The forensic anthropologist moves to the next table, where a skeleton of a body awaits. The three of us follow like eager students.

'No. We're expanding our collection, though,' Jules replies. 'We were fed up with doing the Addams Family thing.'

'The Addams Family thing?' I ask, shaking my head.

'Oh, come on, you must know about the hand that has a mind of its own? Their servant. "Thing", they call it.'

For a second, a hand in black and white springs to mind.

'It was more *Harry Potter* I was thinking about,' Patrice replies, without taking his eyes off the bones. 'But that's a generational thing, I suppose.'

Jules looks at me, aghast. 'We must not have seen the same *Harry Potter*,' he snaps.

Patrice doesn't seem to pick up on Jules's shift in mood.

'I'm talking about the latest film, the one about the Chamber of Secrets, that just came out in November. When Potter is in Knockturn Alley, at Borgin and Burkes, he ends up fighting with a hand on a plinth that looks just like yours. What if you're dealing with a couple of wizarding apprentices?'

'They don't seem like novices to me.'

'So you're still searching for the owners of the hands?'

'The bodies can't be far away,' Jules says, almost to himself. 'We found these three right by the cabin.'

Now, bizarrely, something Pauline said comes to mind. Or rather, a hesitation in her words.

'Patrice, I know this isn't necessarily your area of expertise,' I blurt, 'but would it be possible to determine, by examining the ashes of a ... by examining ashes, if they contain fragments of human bones?'

'It won't be easy, if they're powdered.'

Jules winces.

'That said, if there are some fragments of bone or teeth, it's more likely.'

'What are you thinking about?' Gina asks me.

'The little bottles of coloured sand that Pauline Caron would make as a hobby, according to Bernadette Damatian. The pleasure I could see it gave her when you handed her one. And the fact she asked you if you still had it. Did you hear the hesitation, the pause in her sentence when she brought it up? She was going to say something other than "sand". She started to say "a—", and then she caught herself. I did wonder, "a *what*?". But what if it wasn't "a *something*", but instead a word beginning with the letter "a", like ... "ashes"?'

Gina slowly nods, as if the horror of my suggestion is chilling her blood.

'We haven't found the slightest trace of those seven bodies,' I continue. 'The sniffer dogs haven't picked up a scent on the Carons' property or around the folly. So maybe, and I stress the maybe, the Carons burned those bodies?'

'Burned? But where?' Jules cuts in.

'I don't know ... nearby?'

'The only places with a chimney in the vicinity are their house and that hunter's cabin. It's not like they'd be doing that in the open air.'

'If the bodies were dismembered in the folly, they might have been transported, I don't know, in plastic bags? Big garden waste bags. Then tossed on the hearth and burned.'

'But surely that would have left some debris. What would they have done with it?'

'Spread it out in the countryside somewhere, in the forest. And Pauline Caron would have kept a handful in those bottles of hers. A souvenir. As serial killers do.'

'But she already had the hands, right?'

'Would you mind if we got back to the matter at hand, for lack of a better way to put it?' the anthropologist cuts in. 'As I told you earlier,' he carries on, 'I haven't had time to unwrap the two other bodies but I will as soon I'm finished with her. It'll be a much easier job than dealing with the hands, because we have the teeth. And let's just say that teeth go, ahem, hand in hand with prints and identification. Yay!'

'So it's a woman?' I ask, deadpan.

'At the end of puberty, a young woman's pelvis is around twenty-five percent broader than a male's of the same age,' Patrice explains, tracing the outline of the body part in front of him. 'Because of the hormonal changes to prepare her body for the necessities of childbirth, if I'm not mistaken. Oestrogen, I believe. Then when menopause occurs, the pelvis contracts, so that by the time she's around seventy years old, a woman's pelvis is around eight percent narrower than that of a female of childbearing age. What I can already tell you here – call it a preliminary observation – is that your victim is female and was between fourteen and eighteen years old when she died, because she had not finished growing. So, this is the body of a child.'

51
Lucienne
1899

'Maman' refused to have Mary come along.

'It's a family affair,' she proclaimed.

I retorted that Mary is part of my family.

'Not ours,' she chided.

And so there are three of us in the carriage travelling to the tip of Île de la Cité, behind Notre-Dame, mother and son sitting side by side like a grieving couple, showing a united front.

Nothing has happened since the ransom demand. No more letters. No news of my daughters. No instructions. Nothing. And so, the chief of police has asked us to go to the morgue to try and find my children.

I'm not worried. I know Jeanne and Rose aren't waiting for me at this dubious thrill bazaar to which Parisians flock like pilgrims – up to a million visitors a year, says Henri, for his mother's benefit. My charming new friends brought me here, not long after I first arrived in the capital. They found it terribly amusing to show this side of Paris to a young Québécoise, fresh off the boat and a long way from her own land. I had no idea the place was a morgue back then. We were approaching the sublime and majestic Notre-Dame, and I felt like I was in a waking dream, in the company of these Parisiennes who were treating me as their equal. Faithless and fascinated, I had even left Mary behind to go with them to the 'house of glass', as they called it with an air of importance and mystery. Naive as I was, I had pictured a grand place like the Hall of Mirrors at Versailles, concealing the kind of cabaret ladies like us weren't supposed to frequent. Until the very last moment, I had foolishly thought this was an adventure for aristocrats dying of boredom. Until we arrived at a place that was far from palatial, and where I found myself staring at dead bodies in glass display cases. These cruel women had been expecting me to faint, or vomit, which would have been quite spectacular, and undignified for a lady of my standing. But, having spent my childhood skinning, gutting and butchering the game my grandfather brought home, a handful of banged-up bodies had not the slightest effect on me. Not that this prevented me from becoming the target of their ceaseless mockery.

And now I'm back here again.

'Maman' steps down from the carriage holding a handkerchief to her nose, convinced she's about to visit a slaughterhouse. As if the stench of death were floating all the way out here. How ignorant. They've been storing the bodies in refrigerators for at least fifteen years. What the devil is this old hag imagining? That the corpses on display in these windows are putrefying before people's eyes?

I've not been back to the morgue since that fateful evening, when it dawned on me that for all of Paris and its high society, I would always be the Québécoise who married Henri Docquer. But oh, how wrong I was. Now I am Madame de la Courtière's *protégée*.

We're shuffling along in the crowd of sightseers, Henri tending an arm to his mother, whose corpulence and puffiness are challenging her gait. She turns to me, her face creased with exertion and dripping with acrid sweat.

'You could at least put on a suitable expression, daughter of mine.'

'I'm not worried. I know Jeanne and Rose aren't here, Maman.'

'You know nothing, Lucienne. You only have hope. And your

hope is standing in the way of this whole family beginning to live again.'

This whole family. My mother-in-law and her annoying tendency to overinflate.

A young woman greets us and takes us to the 'family room'. She ushers us through the main hall where they brought me the last time. The gawpers are gathering at the railing, whistling in fright at the sight of the naked bodies on display in the harsh light, their modesty at least protected by leather aprons.

There are three tables in the room we enter. And on them, lined up tightly side by side, lie five little girls who look like they're sleeping. One of them must have drowned. She's not yet been undressed and her wet clothes are clinging to her skin. Besides the mud on her, which smells nowhere near as bad as my mother-in-law, nothing about this sight is unbearable or repulsive.

'See, I told you so,' I say, my tone brimming with arrogance. 'Jeanne and Rose aren't here.'

She doesn't rise to it and just waddles to the door, using Henri's arm as a cane.

The return journey rolls by in a soothing silence, as if for the first time since the beginning of our marriage, my voice has been heard. I have just shown them that mine carries as much weight as theirs and is worth listening to.

When the carriage draws up at our door, the chief of police is waiting on the porch. I wonder who could have informed him already that we failed to identify Jeanne or Rose at the morgue.

Henri helps his mother to alight and is about to greet the chief when he is interrupted by a salvo of screams. The door opens to reveal Mary being restrained by two police officers. She's flailing like a wild animal, kicking out at the two men who are twisting her arms to dodge her blows.

I'm clinging to my seat. My knees are knocking in horror.

My Mary. No, they can't take my Mary away from me. Not her. Let them take it all away from me, but not her.

Her whole body relaxes when she sees me. Her face creases with uncontrollable tears. She gives up fighting, and the police officers seize the chance to tighten their grip.

'They're taking me away, my Lucienne. They're taking me away.'

An intolerable pain tears through my chest and splits me in two.

52
Maxine
2002

This morning, when I took Hugo out for a walk, the cold all but paralysed me. Now a hellish wind has picked up too, and I wonder how Yvonne Lelanger can be standing outside, waiting for us on the porch of her manor house.

She's got a chunky scarf wrapped around her neck and is hugging her arms to her chest as if that could combat the gusts of glacial air whipping at her cheeks. This time, she invites us into her home.

'The manor house was built at the beginning of the nineteenth century,' she explains, walking us through a hall lined with mirrors and jarring reflections, across a floor that looks like a chess board. 'It was converted half a century later into a psychiatric hospital, then it became a rest home after the war. 'My parents renovated it completely when Clarence Manor closed in the early seventies, thinking it would be nice for the family to come back and holiday here. When my husband and I took possession of the place four years ago, we just redecorated the interior. This way,' she guides us.

We follow her through to a cosy lounge, heated by an imposing fireplace. There are two sofas framing a rectangular, wrought-iron coffee table with a glass top.

A slight man in jeans, a navy-blue wool sweater and matching moccasins gets up as we walk in.

'My husband and lawyer,' Mrs Lelanger says, unwinding her scarf and tossing it on the sofa.

'Pleased to meet you,' he replies, shaking hands with us. You're out in force, I see.'

'Lieutenant Grant. This is Sergeant Demers and Professor Montminy, who is leading the interviews with Pauline Caron,' I reply, simply.

'Please have a seat,' our hostess says, gesturing to a sofa. Have you found any more ... bodies?' I notice a subtle shaking of her head when she pronounces the word.

'We're looking at ten victims, for now,' I explain, getting straight to the point.

She pales. 'Ten ... victims? But I thought...'

'We've only found three bodies on your property. But we have ten victims in all,' I reply curtly. 'Ten nameless victims, seven of whom will be very difficult to identify. We have to learn more about Pauline Caron, Mrs Lelanger, so that we can persuade her to cooperate with us, to give ten grieving families closure.'

I mark a pause, hoping the last thing I've said will have a humanising effect on the matter and get our hosts to drop their guard.

'We've found out that in the 1950s, Pauline Caron developed a friendship with your great-aunt, Lucienne Lelanger.'

Yvonne Lelanger stiffens. She flashes her husband a glance.

'I believe your great-aunt was sectioned at Clarence Manor, wasn't she?'

'She remained a resident to her death, yes,' she replies in a clipped voice.

It seems I've touched a nerve. Naturally, I persist. 'The home was shut down after she died, wasn't it?'

'Yes.'

'When was she sectioned?'

Yvonne Lelanger rests and inspects her hands on her thighs. 'At the turn of the century.'

Jules and I exchange a glance. Gina keeps her eyes trained on our hostess.

'When exactly, Mrs Lelanger?' I continue.

'In 1899.'

She swallows audibly. Releases a long sigh.

'What happened to her?' Gina asks.

Yvonne Lelanger crosses her fingers, so hard the joints turn red.

'We heard about the death of her two daughters. Was it this tragedy that prompted her breakdown?' Gina's tone is suave and patient, almost gentle.

The walls are coming down, I think, seeing Yvonne Lelanger open her lips a little. Until now, she's kept them sealed.

'My great-aunt left Quebec when she was eighteen years old to build a life in Paris, where her future husband was waiting. An arranged marriage, as I'm sure you'd suspect. She had two daughters, who died at a young age. They perished in...'

She hesitates and traces a thumb and index finger down her throat, like she's giving her trachea a massage.

'What you're about to say seems painful, Mrs Lelanger,' Gina says, ending her sentence with a smile. 'But this affair is going to bring lots of things to the surface. Lots of terrible, unsettling and perhaps shameful things. I'm sure it's best for the information to come from you than for us to dig it up.'

The suggestion is a sugar-coated threat. It's make-or-break time, I think, casting a glance at the lawyer, who doesn't seem at all ruffled.

'My great-aunt lost her reason after the death of her children in a fire at her house in Paris. She came back here to live with her parents, who were fearful for her health – and her life; she had expressed some suicidal urges. Her father had her sectioned at Clarence Manor, where she was a privileged patient, given all the care and expertise she needed.'

She marks a pause, then looks up at us.

'That's the official version,' she adds, her focus on Gina. 'The version my family made known at the time. But Lucienne, my great-aunt, was a monster. An abomination of nature.'

'Yvonne,' her husband intervenes.

Mrs Lelanger doesn't seem to hear him.

'Aided by her cousin and lady-in-waiting, who was also her mistress, my great-aunt drugged her two young daughters, then locked them in a trunk and set fire to it.'

My body is racked with chills. I close my eyes for a moment.

'The cousin was arrested, after a maid saw her writing a ransom demand. When Lucienne was sent back to Quebec by her husband, her mistress confessed that they had planned and executed the double murder together, so they could love one another in peace.'

Yvonne Lelanger shakes her head.

'She confessed to her crimes and ended up on the guillotine. My great-grandfather greased the palm of the chief of police to buy his silence, and he bribed the manager of Clarence Manor to keep her locked up. Under no circumstance did he want the truth to get out. Imagine the repercussions on the family's business and reputation.' She winces. 'He insisted there be no psychiatric diagnosis whatsoever. A devastated woman mourning her lost children until her death was far less shameful to have in the family than a crazy witch. To keep up appearances, Lucienne was never placed under legal guardianship. She was just forcibly kept in this institution by her family, who deemed her unfit to make her own decisions. *My* family. That was how she was able to bequeath the land at the edge of our property to Pauline Caron. I only found that out after your warrant came through, when my husband's firm searched the titles. At first I thought that was what you were here about. We meant to let you know, and the discovery of those three bodies caught us quite by surprise.'

She blinks, shakes her head once more.

'My God ... ten, I can't believe it. You say my great-aunt and Pauline Caron struck up a friendship in the 1950s? That makes it easier for me to understand why she left her that land. Pauline must have been a teenager at the time, then?'

'That's right.'

'How horrible...'

She irons out the creases on her forehead with her fingertips.

'When my parents had the work done on the manor house in 1971, 1972, or thereabouts, my father showed me Lucienne's apartment here. She had a Goya. A Rembrandt. Sketches. And trinkets. All on the theme of witchcraft. The Devil.'

Gina reaches for her bag on the floor beside the sofa, lifts it into her lap, and pulls out and switches on her camera. Then she stands up and hands it to Yvonne Lelanger, who automatically leans in to look at the screen.

'Are these the—'

'Yes!' she cuts in, 'those are my great-aunt's paintings. Well, reproductions. The Rembrandt, the Goya ... Where were those photos taken?'

'At the Carons' place,' Gina says.

Yvonne Lelanger slowly nods, as if the extent of what her family is mixed up in is now sinking in.

'You know, there's only one memory I have of my great-aunt, from when I was a child. We had come to pay her a birthday visit, here, when it was still Clarence Manor. She was absolutely adorable with me, giving me her slice of cake, plying me with sweet treats. When the grown-ups went down some boring rabbit-hole of a conversation, I went to the window to watch two old women who were kicking a ball around as if they were my age. I remember it made me laugh a lot. On the side table, by the window, there was a big, black, leather book. With a black feather sticking out from between the pages. I opened it and started leafing through, looking at the drawings. I remember seeing the names of the planets and the seasons. Then suddenly, I felt a hand in my hair. It was my great-aunt. I was so absorbed in the drawings, some of which made no sense to me at all, that I hadn't seen or heard her coming. She stroked my hair, leaned forwards in her wheelchair and whispered in my ear, "Take your filthy little sausages off my book before I turn them into mincemeat." Then she leaned back in her chair with a smile on her lips, as if she had just told me the most innocent of secrets.'

53
Lucienne
1899

'Madame, your father is calling.'

'Thank you, Michelle. Tell him I'll be down in a few minutes.'

I didn't want to come back here, to Lac-Clarence. I wanted to stay close to Mary, visit her in prison, perhaps even help her avoid the guillotine. But I was forbidden from all visits and nothing could save her skin, her lawyer told me. Nothing, not even Papa's fortune.

Living with Henri and his mother was wearing me down. I could no longer stand the weight of his body on mine, nor the insistent looks of my mother-in-law, as if it were up to me alone to write the next chapters of our lives. Violette was a source of fresh air, but not enough for me to properly catch my breath. I needed my homeland, my family.

I tuck Mary's scarf beneath my pillow. I've never missed anything or anyone more than her. I find myself looking everywhere for her. Her silent presence, her hand, her lips, her body always far warmer than mine. I talk to her every hour of every day, and when sleep is slow to come. I write to her, even though I know my letters will remain here with her scarf and our memories.

Mary knew that it would do no good to ruin my life along with hers. That the repercussions for me would be far more dramatic and painful. So she kept her mouth shut. She made our guilt her own.

I leave my room to join my parents on the veranda.

'I'm taking you into town to buy you some things,' my father announces, ready to get going.

'Now?'

'Yes, your Parisian coats are too light for our winter,' my mother chimes in, without looking up from her embroidery.

'Very well. You're not coming, Maman?'

A silence precedes her reply.

'No.'

'Your mother must wait for your brother and your sisters. They shall soon be arriving from Montreal.'

'Yes, of course, Papa.'

I approach my mother to give her the *bise* and she tends an absent cheek. Still she doesn't look up from her cross-stitch.

We get into the carriage, Papa sitting across from me, his face turned to the window.

I don't try and engage him in conversation. I can see his mind is elsewhere, surely preoccupied with his business. I sink into my own thoughts. They're all connected to the past. I'm yet to find a way to build the after. I think about Paris. About its carriages, far filthier than ours, here. I never loved that city of gossip. I only loved Violette's Paris, the city I discovered through her, the city that changed me, and I fully intend to cultivate the seeds she sowed in me. Violette, who gave me a trunk full of reading material to take with me when I left France – for my education. She writes to me every week, sending me news of her world and ours.

The carriage lurches to a sudden halt in front of Clarence Manor. I was so absorbed in my thoughts, I hadn't noticed we were going down the driveway through the park. We must be stopping by to drop off some accounting ledgers, or handkerchiefs my mother has embroidered.

'Get out,' my father barks, his gaze not straying from the window.

I look at him, not comprehending.

'But, weren't we supposed to be—'

'Get out, Lucienne,' he orders through tight lips, his voice loaded with aggression.

I don't know what's got into him.

I'm reaching for the door to step outside, as he's told me, when I see two orderlies waiting at the foot of the steps.

I turn to my father.

He sneers at me in disgust.

'You're an aberration of nature, Lucienne,' he whispers, hissing every word, his face a contortion of suppressed anger.

He knows. My mother knows.

'You killed your two daughters. Our granddaughters. You're a monster.'

I suck in a short breath, as if I've just been punched in the stomach. *Mary. Mary has said something.*

I shake my head.

'No, Papa ... no ... I don't want—'

He cuts me off: 'Stop calling me Papa. Just stop it.'

The carriage door opens.

I grab hold of the seat, the backrest, the handles, trying to hang on to anything I can so they won't take me away. I know that once I go through the doors of Clarence Manor, I'll never leave. I can't end up at the madhouse. My life is only just beginning.

My father gives the orderlies a nod.

'It's for your own good, Lucienne,' he says, more for their benefit than mine, keeping up what scrap of appearances he still can.

'Papa ... no ... no!' I beg him, in tears, as four hefty hands grasp me by the forearms.

I'm putting up a fight, more by instinct than in hope, since I know resistance is futile. In a matter of minutes, I will be locked up with a colony of crazies no one will ever come and save me from. I can't even save myself, since I have nowhere to escape to.

Still, until they close the gate behind the carriage driving my father home, I claw in fury at everything that's already slipped through my fingers.

54
Maxine
2002

I pull on a pair of gloves and open the glass case in the Carons' study. I ignore the literary prizes on the top two shelves and remove Sir Arthur Conan Doyle's large sketchbook from its lectern.

Yvonne Lelanger recognised it among the photos taken by Gina the last time we were here. Not only has Pauline kept this artefact belonging to Lucienne Lelanger, she has sourced copies of the paintings that decorated her mentor's apartment at Clarence Manor. Her bond with this woman is beyond obsessive.

'So, it's fair to assume the murders were committed as part of some kind of ritual ... some kind of ... magic,' Jules declares, picking up the old copy of *Macbeth*.

'With the vials of blood in the freezer at the folly and the collection of hands, which were preserved with peppers, verdigris and saltpetre, that does seem to be the case,' I reply, sitting down at Pauline's desk.

'A first edition – unbelievable!' he exclaims, turning the pages of the precious book very carefully.

Standing beside me, Gina leans over my shoulder as I gently place the sketchbook in front of me. It's open to a double page. On the left is a series of notes in French, English and Latin, that have to be written by the same hand in the same ink, as there is no difference in style or colour, at least not to the naked eye:

Bibliothèque de l'Arsenal in Paris, manuscript no 3009
Girardius (Alberti?) Parvi Lucii Libellus
de mirabilibus naturae arcanis
Anno Domini 1730

Albertus Magnus? // Girardius' Bell?
Dr John Dee and Edward Kelly?
(English cemetery, Mathieu Giraldo 1846)

A sketch occupies the whole right-hand page: two concentric circles and, inside those, a series of symbols. At the centre of them is a bell. And there's a word written next to each symbol: *Och, Hagith, Ophiel, Phvel, Aratron, Bethor, Phaleg.*

'There's nothing in *Macbeth*,' says Jules as he closes the book and slips it into an evidence bag. 'No annotations, no notes, no slips of paper between the pages.'

I close the sketchbook and begin to examine the leather binding. It sits flush with the pages and is flat and smooth, so nothing could have been slipped inside.

'We've already been through that document,' says Jules. 'Do you really think the Carons could have written something in there about their victims? If they have, it would almost be quicker to wait for Pauline Caron to open up, don't you think? Just imagine everything there is to decipher in there, what with the Latin, the French, the English and that spidery handwriting. It'll take weeks, if not months.'

Jules does have a point. There is something extremely complex and labyrinthine about Conan Doyle's sketches and scrawls.

'The Carons have been exceedingly cautious,' he goes on. 'They've done what it took to keep up their public image for decades. I doubt they would take the risk of writing in something they keep on display – in a glass case, no less.'

'But there's also a certain arrogance to them showcasing who they truly are and what they set out to do,' Gina replies. 'A paper chase made up of riddles and clues only those in the know can work out. They're thumbing their noses at lay people like us. These paintings that scream witchcraft, but not at first glance; these hands on plinths – we can't say for sure whether they really were hidden; this sketchbook, which belonged to Lucienne Lelanger and overtly establishes the connection between her and Pauline; not to mention the little bottles of sand, which may, as Maxine suggests, contain their victims' ashes. It's behaviour not unlike that of serial killers who like to see their entourage wearing trophies they've swiped from their victims. There's an exhibitionist side to the Carons, and I wouldn't be surprised if they've left some sort of clues in this sketchbook that was—'

Gina stops mid-sentence. She turns her gaze to the paintings on the wall. She stretches out the silence, leaves her words hanging.

'You wouldn't happen to know a priest, would you, Maxine?' she asks me, all of a sudden. 'Here, in Lac-Clarence?'

'Er, yes ... Father Tremblay. He officiated at our wedding, and he did the same for my parents. He even baptised Charlotte. He's been retired for some years, but he still lives here.'

'It's a question of magic. Black magic. And wherever there's black magic, there's Satanism. And maybe a black mass. I think we should show him the sketchbook. I'd also like to ask him about the paintings. Maybe he can fill us in with something I can use to get Pauline to talk. Do you think he might agree to see us?'

The practice comes to an end without Tamara giving me a single look or snide comment. I can't believe it.

However, I must not cry victory yet. She still has time to stick something in my hair or on my coat, or steal my shoes. But, but, but ... I have to concede, I got to sing in peace this afternoon. I kept an eye out, in case she bared her claws. I still don't feel I can let my guard down, though.

Tamara has never been so withdrawn. It's as if all that's left of her is a carcass, and she's dragging it around. An empty shell. Literally, given the circumstances.

She's pale, a shadow of herself in every sense. That's quite fortunate. For her, I mean, because she can say she's not well. That's not so far from the truth, I'm sure.

When Mother came home from her night shift the next morning, we drank our coffee in silence, as usual. She said her first words of the day to me as she was washing the dishes.

She waited until her back was turned before she spoke to me. 'Don't say a word in the village, Lina. To anyone,' she insisted, having to raise her voice over the sound of the water pouring into the sink. 'If anyone were to find out that Tamara was pregnant and came to me for an abortion, all three of us would be in very hot water. Do you understand, Lina?'

'Why did you do it, then?'

She stopped what she was doing, put down the bowl she was rinsing.

'Because no one deserves to have their life ruined at fourteen years old.'

I wondered if she could hear herself.

I waited a few minutes for my temper to cool.

'And what about my life, eh?' I said, finally. 'If you go to prison, what will I have left? It's not like I have a father to look after me.'

'If you don't say anything, I won't go to prison.' Then she finished the dishes in silence.

I got up without a word, wondering what kind of mother chooses another's child over her own.

At the same time, if Mother hadn't helped Tamara get rid of her baby, as monstrous an act as that was, I would never have got my hands on her blood. The blood that enabled me to perform my ritual successfully. And I wouldn't be taking advantage of this divine peace. It's like a ceasefire. Now I can leave the house, go to choir, go to church, walk around the village in freedom. I still feel some apprehension when I run into Tamara, but it goes away and doesn't turn into fear. Still, it's unbelievable. Tamara is an empty shell and I can live my life to the full. Things somehow seem more even between us now.

'Lina?'

I stiffen. It's Tamara's voice.

I've spoken too soon.

I'm not sure whether to ignore her and quicken my step, or answer without turning around.

I go with the second option. 'What?'

'Do you mind if we walk together?'

I stop and turn.

There's no hint of irony on her face. I don't know what she makes of the look I'm giving her, but she lowers her eyes.

'I'd just like to ... talk to you,' she explains.

I keep walking. She falls into step beside me.

She lets a few minutes of silence go by as if she's trying to find her words. Maybe she is. Or maybe she's going to laugh at me. Start cackling. Shove me to the ground, spit in my face or do some other cruel thing to me, like she always does.

'I'd like to say thank you,' she suddenly murmurs.

I slow my stride. There's no double meaning in her voice. Only sincerity.

'For saying nothing. For keeping my secret.'

She gives a jerky sigh.

'I did it for my mother,' I reply, resisting the urge to bark.

'I know. But still, you could have used it against me. You didn't do that. Thank you. Truly.'

She sniffs. Gives her cheeks a quick wipe with the back of her hand.

'You haven't even asked me who ... who ... did that to me. I can tell you, if you like?'

I shake my head. 'I'm not interested.'

I can't be any more honest with her. I really don't care who got her pregnant.

All that matters is what's happening, right now, in this moment. Not only because this *mea culpa* is my greatest victory and my life, my every day is about to change, now the power has changed hands, but also, because my tormentor can no longer victimise me. Because now, she's the victim. What matters, is that black magic really works. Like Lucienne promised me it would.

I haven't seen Father Tremblay since Dad's funeral.

His beard is whiter, but still just as full and bushy.

'Thanks for seeing us, Manuel.'

'My dear Maxine, how are you?' he asks me, drawing me into a strong, warm embrace, his beard tickling my ear.

'I'm well,' I lie, through a thin smile. 'This is Professor Montminy. I mentioned her on the phone. And my partner, Sergeant Jules Demers.'

Father Tremblay gives them both a vigorous handshake. 'Please, have a seat. I've made some coffee. The cups and sugar are there, I'll let you help yourselves. I'm curious, very curious, to tell you the truth. I read the papers and I can't believe it – you know me,' he says to me, twisting the coarse ends of his moustache.

I unscrew the flask and pour the coffees all round.

'You know, I arrived in the parish when Pauline Caron must have been about ten years old. Just after the war. At that time, I was officiating with Father Dion. Pauline has always been a pillar of the community in Lac-Clarence. What I've read, it's...'

He mimics the sound of an explosion, opening his hand like a sun beside his face.

I look down at my cup. The smell of the coffee makes me feel nauseous.

'I suppose you can't tell me much. Any of you, I mean.' He gives the three of us a broad smile and gets up from his chair with the energy of a young man. He crosses the room, opens the refrigerator and pulls out a bottle of milk, which he places beside my cup, touching a brief hand to my shoulder.

'I'm all ears,' he says, sitting back down.

'I'm in the process of questioning Pauline Caron,' Gina replies. 'But many parts of this case remain a mystery. We need you to enlighten us.'

Manuel nods.

'Jules, would you switch places with me?' Gina asks, getting up.

He obliges, gallantly holding the chair for her while she sits down beside Father Tremblay.

'I have a series of paintings to show you,' Gina says, reaching into her handbag for a document holder. 'You might not recognise the painting or the artist, but that doesn't matter. I'd like you to describe what you see. These paintings have something to do with witchcraft.'

Manuel slowly lifts his gaze to Gina, who hands him the pages she printed off at the incident room earlier. He glances at me before turning his attention to the papers.

'You're taking me right back to my years as a seminarian. You have no idea how much time we had to spend studying the forces that work against our Church.'

His fingers venture into the pocket of his shirt for a pair of glasses, which he perches on the end of his flat nose.

One at a time, he peers carefully at the paintings, glossing over the Rembrandt and the two Goyas before examining the other three more closely. Then he selects a few pages: the Maleuvre engraving depicting a naked young girl, an Aliamet of an old woman in a hovel, the party or orgy painted by Gillot, as well as the Goya depicting three men and a wolf, or a wolfdog, standing on its hind legs.

'These paintings illustrate a very important moment for anyone who calls themselves a sorcerer or a Satanist, not to lump the two together,' he begins. 'This is the myth of the witches' sabbath, more specifically the departure for the sabbath. A pagan ceremony, a secret rendezvous with Satan in the night, at midnight, apparently, followed by an orgiastic celebration, with all the feasting and sexual debauchery that entails. The departure for the sabbath is a thing of fascination. Sorcerers and witches are said to change appearance after preparing themselves with a special anointment that also allows them to fly on a broom, to which they may sometimes attach a piece of cloth that fills like a sail. They generally go up the chimney, but this naked young woman here seems to be preparing to depart through the window. In this representation, we've got the full works,' he goes on, pointing to the Aliamet painting. 'Cat, toad, owl and broom, plus a magic circle on the floor, human skulls, candles and a demon with wings. Same for Goya's *La cocina de las brujas*,' he booms proudly. 'The witches' kitchen. A much darker representation of witchcraft. If you look closely at this animal, you'll see its front right paw is a human arm. Goya was fascinated by the witch trials led by the Spanish Inquisition in the early seventeenth century – more than seven thousand cases, if my memory's right.'

He pauses for a swig of coffee.

'Look at the second Goya, this one,' he says, sliding the paper forwards. 'If I may say so, I believe the master called it *Witches' Sabbath*. Here, on the left, you can see dolls hanging from a pole and a body on the ground. And on the right, there's a child with an outstretched arm, so skeletal he looks like he's decaying, as well as a chubby baby being offered in sacrifice. The creature with twisted horns and a crown of leaves in the middle looks a bit like the Greek god Dionysus, or Bacchus as the Romans called him, but make no mistake, that beast is none other than Satan.'

I pour us all a refill of coffee. Father Tremblay takes a careful sip and places the printout of the Rembrandt at the centre of the table.

'This is Rembrandt's famous *Dr Faustus*, an etching the experts have never quite managed to interpret. Some say it represents an alchemist, but any Satanist will tell you this glowing disc is a pentacle used for conjuring the infernal spirits.'

Father Tremblay gathers all the papers and stacks them together like a pack of cards, then slides them back to Gina. He gets up, opens a cupboard and returns with four glasses, which he places on the table. Then he opens an oak pantry cupboard beside the refrigerator and extracts a bottle.

'I have something else to ask you, Father,' Gina says.

'Yes, I imagine you do. Let's carry on with an Armagnac, for those who wish to partake.'

He pours a finger of the *eau-de-vie* into each glass, takes a gulp of his and sits back down, stretching his alcohol-burned lips.

'I'm all ears, Professor.'

Gina reaches into her bag for her camera.

'I'm sorry, these won't be as clear as the printouts,' she says, switching on the device. 'When you mentioned Bacchus, it made me think of something. Does this mean anything to you?' she asks, handing him the camera.

Jules and I move closer, scraping our chairs over the kitchen tiles. She's showing him the picture of the two centaurs perched on the Carons' mantelpiece.

'This reminds me of the satanic rites said to be perpetrated by Catherine de Médici and her son Henri III at the Château de Vincennes,' the priest says. 'Word is, they found the skin of a child and two statues of satyrs turning their backs on the cross.'

Father Tremblay looks up to Gina, then to me.

'Maxine, whatever is going on here? This whole thing reeks of a black mass. And those call for the blood of a virgin – or a child, preferably. I can't believe Pauline would...' He clamps his lips tight and shakes his head, refusing to say another word.

'Thank you, Father.' Gina pockets her camera. 'There's another thing I'd like to show you, if you feel up to it.'

'Yes, yes, of course,' he replies, making a gesture to clear the air in front of his face. 'I'm sorry. Please indulge me.'

Gina opens the sketchbook to the pages that were on display in the Carons' glass case.

Manuel reads the notes on the left-hand page out loud.

'"Bibliothèque de l'Arsenal in Paris, manuscript no 3009. Girardius (Alberti?) Parvi Lucii Libellus de mirabilibus naturae arcanis. Anno Domini 1730" ... "marvellous secrets of natural and cabalistic magic",' he translates. 'Whoever wrote that was hesitant about the author being Albert or Girardius, I think. "Albertus Magnus? // Girardius' Bell? Dr John Dee and Edward Kelly? (English cemetery, Mathieu Giraldo 1846)" ... I have no idea who this Dr John Dee and that Edward Kelly are, but Albertus Magnus, that's Albert the Great. And the term "Girardius' Bell", that refers to the necromancer's bell of Girardius, the bell represented on this drawing here.' He taps his index finger on the sketch on the right-hand page. 'When that bell tolls, it wakes the dead.'

Jules rubs his eyes as if he's trying to get a clearer picture.

'Every inscription you see there corresponds to a planet or a star.' Father Tremblay starts reading from the first inscription at the top of the bell. '"Och", the Sun...' He traces the symbols clockwise with his finger. '"Hagith", Venus; "Ophiel", Mercury; "Phvel", the Moon; "Aratron", Saturn; "Bethor", Jupiter and "Phaleg", Mars. Or is it the other way around? Er, no, no, that's it. "Phaleg", that's Mars.'

Suddenly, Gina grabs one of the printouts of the Carons' lithographs and turns it over, then reaches into her bag for a pen. She draws a rectangle, and divides it into three columns. The one on the left she then divides into three new rectangles, and the one on the right, she splits in two, making the top rectangle twice the size of the bottom.

In the top left rectangle, she writes the word 'study'.

'Are you mapping out the ground floor of the Caron house?' I ask her, feeling a bit lost.

She nods and carries on, adding 'dining room' and 'kitchen' on the left, 'hallway' at the top of the middle column, then 'living room' and 'laundry room' on the right. Then she starts to draw crosses. That's when it dawns on me.

'"*Och*", the Sun,' she announces, tracing the first in the middle column. 'Venus and Mercury,' she continues, adding two more crosses in the living room. 'The Moon,' she adds, marking a cross in the laundry room, another one for Jupiter in the dining room, and then one final cross for Mars in the office. 'Seven planets. Seven hands,' she declares, with a jubilant look in her eye.

57
Maxine
2002

I open the book we've borrowed from Father Tremblay. Two sketches share the page we're interested in. The first represents a closed hand, mounted upright on a plinth, with a lighted candle perched atop the folded middle finger. The second shows another hand, this one open, with each finger ending in a candle, which makes it look like the nails are on fire.

'What's that?' Marceau asks with a frown.

'A hand of glory.'

'Sexy Patrice was right, then,' says Jules, in all seriousness.

Marceau turns to him with a look of puzzlement more than exasperation.

'Patrice Lemay, the forensic anthropologist,' he explains. 'He told us he'd seen a hand like that in the last Potter film at the cinema not long ago.'

'A hand on a plinth being used as a candlestick?'

'I don't know about the candlestick part, but a hand on a plinth, yes.'

'A hand of glory isn't just any old chopped-off hand turned into a candle holder, it's far more elaborate, prepared using a very precise process,' I explain. 'Listen to this: "Cut off the right or left hand of a criminal on the gibbet beside a highway; wrap it in part of a funeral pall and squeeze it well."'

'Is that a joke?'

'Far from it. The instructions come from a book first published in Germany in the eighteenth century: *The Marvellous Secrets of Natural & Cabalistic Magic of Le Petit Albert.*'

'Is that the book you're reading to me from?'

'No, that's an illustrated encyclopedia of witchcraft published in the 1930s. But wait a sec, the instructions go on to explain how to pickle the hand in saltpetre, verdigris and peppers, then how to dry it in the heat of the summer sun.'

Marceau leans over the desk with a sigh.

'Those are the very same things we found traces of on the seven hands at the Carons' place,' says Jules.

I keep on reading. '"The purpose of the hand of glory is to stun those exposed to it and render them as motionless as if they were dead."' I close the book. 'So, the seven hands we found at the Carons' place are all "hands of glory".'

'But what would they have been used for? Why seven of them?' Marceau asks. She seems more confused than ever.

'They were arranged in the house in a rather special way, to observe the form of a magic pentacle of sorts,' Gina explains. 'A canvas in celebration of the Sun, the Moon, Venus, Mars, Saturn, Jupiter and Mercury. This arrangement is based on the necromancer's bell of Girardius, which was used to wake and summon the dead for black-magic rituals.'

Marceau sits down, plants her elbows on the desk and closes her eyes, massaging her temples with her fingertips.

'It seems the Carons wanted to create a protective circle around their crimes to act in all impunity, by invoking the diabolical forces and demons they believed in.'

'Which seems to have worked pretty well for them,' Jules comments.

'They wanted to protect themselves and protect their anonymity and their quest, to obtain some sort of immunity,' Gina continues. 'Don't be expecting to unearth a logical reason for their barbaric acts. This quest sheds light on just one aspect of their psychopathy. Let me elaborate. Richard Chase, the Vampire of Sacramento, an American serial killer who struck in the late 1970s, explained that he had killed and drunk the blood of his victims to keep himself alive and protect himself from Nazi UFOs. What I'm saying is that a psychopath's logic is theirs and theirs alone. And it defies all other logic.'

I throw my leg over my bicycle with a burst of laughter.

'No, no, no!' I cry, pedalling my heart out to avoid the bucket of water the boys are chasing us with.

The back wheel of Tamara's bike can't escape it. Still laughing, she turns around and protests before righting her wobbly handlebars. Julie's a fair way ahead of us; I can only hear the distant melody of her laughter, muffled by the crunching of the gravel under our tires.

I catch my breath and my chest fills with air, around a heart that's lighter than ever. My mouth still tastes of my first sip of beer, the one I savoured in Paul's embrace. I can still feel his warm hand sweeping the hair aside on my neck so he could slip his arm around me, draw me close and claim me as his. My skin, tingling with pleasure at the briefest touch of his fingers. His lips, his lips that tasted like mine after another sip of beer, and his tongue searching for mine. His saliva mixing with mine. My first kiss carried me much further off than any book.

Ahead of us, Julie is dancing more than riding her bike, zig-zagging like a buzzing insect and singing a tune I don't recognise at the top of her lungs, to our general hilarity. Her svelte shadow stretches off the side of the road, floating atop the river and the long grass.

I've never known an afternoon sweeter than this. Never. Not a minute's gone by without laughter erupting. It's like we've put summer in a bottle, with its every carefree, sunny caress, and spent the last few hours lapping it up thirstily.

As we approach a series of bends in the road, I slow down and lose sight of Julie; she's still leading the way, in spite of the beers she's downed. Tamara hiccoughs with laughter as she brakes and I do the same, only just managing to keep my wheels straight.

Suddenly, a screeching tears through the air as if the sky has split in two. Followed by a dull, heavy, thundering thud that only lasts a second. Then another skidding sound and the roaring of an engine.

My first reflex is to brake, and I skid on the gravel. Then, instinctively, I pedal harder, since over there, where the earth-shattering sound came from, is Julie. Behind me, Tamara's screaming the name of our friend. I'm just pedalling, and a bit too fast into the first bend.

I can see her bicycle lying in the middle of the road. The front wheel is buckled practically in two. Then I see her. Julie. Or rather, her arm sticking out from behind a mound.

Not bothering to stop, I jump off my bike, throw it to one side and run towards her, with Tamara right on my heels. The sound of our sandals on the ground, crunching over twigs and stones, is all we can hear. That, and our gasps.

We skirt around the side of the mound.

Julie is lying on her back, one arm over her head, the other by her side, hand turned at a right angle in towards her hip.

I kneel beside her. Tamara screams and stands there, sobbing.

Julie's eyes are fixed on the sky. She blinks them closed every few seconds but can't move her head. Her lips are making inaudible sounds. I lower an ear to her mouth, but hear only her breath.

'It's going to be all right,' I murmur. 'We're here, Julie, it's going to be all right.' My voice is so calm.

I touch a hand to the back of her neck. My fingers sink into a viscous liquid.

'Give me your cardigan,' I order Tamara, turning to her.

She does as I say with a trembling hand.

I slide it under Julie's head and remove my hand.

Suddenly, a shadow crosses her gaze, stealthily, like a veil, before surprise sneaks in. Her eyes widen for a second, as if she's just been told it's time for her to go and that has come as a shock – because it's too early, far too early, for her to say her goodbyes.

And at that moment, I understand. I understand that they didn't want me to perish under the wheels of that car: those for whom I dance have saved *me*, since I am the chosen one. I am one of them. I have become their voice and their eyes. Their flesh and their blood.

Then in an instant, as if to echo my thoughts, the life drains from Julie's eyes, quick as a snap of the fingers.

Behind me, Tamara is in hysterics as I stay kneeling there, thinking about Lucienne's words and encouragement. My Lucienne. Since the beginning, she has seen in me what I'm only just starting to grasp.

59
Maxine
2002

Gina walks into the interview room holding a sheet of A4 paper.

She places it on the table and turns it so it's facing Pauline. It's a photo of the glass display case in their study.

Pauline leans forwards slightly to look at the enlargement of the photo, then sits back again in her chair.

'Here, we have Philippe's literary prizes, in order,' Gina says, pointing to the first two shelves of the case. 'There, on the third shelf, is Lucienne's sketchbook. And on the last of the shelves, an old edition of *Macbeth*.'

Gina pauses.

'This was the order of priority in your life with Philippe, Pauline: first and foremost, his career and his glory – at your expense, I might add – and only then came your black masses, again, to serve his career.'

Pauline is staring at her hands. Gina steps forwards to rest her forearms on the table between them and tries to catch her eye.

'You told me before: "It's like in *Macbeth*. Everything begins with an encounter, a prophetic encounter with a witch."'

Gina touches her middle finger to the book in her photo, then she slides it across to the image of the bound leather sketchbook.

'You met Lucienne, the witch, who initiated you into black magic and its various rituals, enabling you to make demands and have your wishes granted. She was your mentor. She taught you how to use a hand of glory to prevent any intrusion. Protected by Satan and his diabolical forces, you killed to harvest the blood of your victims. On the spring equinox and the winter solstice. That's why you wrote "SEQ" and "WS" on your vials of blood. Those are among the most favoured dates in the Satanist calendar for sacrifices. The figures 67, 68 and 70 represent years, we hope, and not victim numbers.' Gina beams a broad smile, as if she's making light of the remark. Pauline mirrors her expression in amusement. 'Which ultimately led you to kill the king – *your* king. Except, unlike Macbeth, you didn't act out of ambition. So, why did you do it?'

Pauline's fiddling with a corner of the paper.

'If I may say so, Professor, I find your degree of ignorance surprising,' she replies, without looking up. 'What do you think Goya was trying to convey to the Spanish inquisitors who were hunting witches?'

Gina doesn't reply at first, allowing a silence to stretch between them. 'That killing in the name of God was no better than killing in the name of Satan,' she eventually says.

Satisfied with her answer, Pauline gently nods her head. 'And who were those witches, Professor, in your opinion?'

Gina gives her a look that invites Pauline to enlighten her.

'They were women who did not agree to pledge allegiance to a religion that considered them impure and sinful,' Pauline calmly explains. 'A religion that refused their presence in its ranks and especially – most importantly – reduced them to nothing, to a void, in the strictest sense of the term. In a carnal sense, women were considered as empty shells. "Do women have souls?" the Council of Mâcon once debated, can you imagine? Yet we are the bearers of life. We are the soil, the water and the vessel. With the cult of Satan, women could take revenge; they were no longer silenced and made to feel cumbersome, but were necessary and essential. Pleasures of the flesh were no longer condemnable or condemned by a confessor who himself was frustrated and tormented by what the Church denied him. I shall refrain from commenting on the paedophilic horrors of the Catholic Church.'

'Pauline,' Gina interjects. 'What did those lives you took give you, or enable you to acquire?'

'It seems you understand only part of the picture, Professor,' she rigidly replies, still staring at her hands. 'It's like you keep collapsing just before you get to the finish line. That's something I've noticed with you: you're lacking application. Or endurance. I don't know which.'

At last, she looks up at Gina. Now I can see the life – and, curiously, the tenderness – in my former teacher's eyes again. It makes me so uncomfortable, I feel nauseous.

'Indeed, Professor, those lives I took, as you so crudely put it, gave me nothing. But enabled me to acquire a lot. What? An existence of my own. A life that was stimulating intellectually, mystically and sexually. A life of success and satisfaction. And of completeness. The seven lowlifes whose hands we severed were barely surviving from one street corner and one overdose to the next. We had no trouble finding them in Montreal. Even though seven, in a short space of time, was a lot.'

'You didn't bury them. You preferred to dismember them at the folly so you'd be taking fewer risks. Then you wrapped them up and carried them away in ... backpacks, perhaps?'

Gina leaves a long space after her question mark. Pauline sits up and shifts back in her seat, before looking down again at her hands, clasping and resting them on her thighs.

'Then you burned them in the fireplace at the hunting cabin. You kept a bit of their ashes in those little bottles you used to make sunsets out of sand.'

'Do you have one of them with you?'

'I'm sorry, I don't. And the three victims whose blood you kept in the folly, Pauline. Three young girls, weren't they?'

Pauline rolls her eyes. 'Oh, the hypocrisy. "Young girls", you're calling them? Those "young girls" came to see my mother for an abortion. Young girls who spread their legs, I'd call them women, wouldn't you?'

I would have said they were children. Children of my daughter's age. Children who might have been rape victims. I can feel a lump in my throat.

'But isn't the blood of a virgin preferable for a black mass?' Gina enquires.

'For what I had to do, there was nothing better than the blood of an expectant mother. Even if those ... even if they would have rather got rid of their baby. Just because of that, they didn't deserve to live. They deserved nothing. A child chooses us. And when we bear that child, we welcome it.'

'Were you trying to get pregnant, Pauline?'

The corners of Pauline's lips curve downwards. Her chin puckers.

'But your sacrifices didn't work: you've never had a child. You've never been chosen.'

Pauline tilts her head to the side.

'Philippe was expecting a child with another woman, wasn't he?'

She releases her neck muscles, and her chin hangs down towards her chest.

'Your rituals always worked for Philippe. But never for you. Even this wish, your greatest desire, was granted to him – not you.'

Gina pauses. She presses her bosom to the table and turns her head to one side to meet Pauline's downcast eyes.

'He was going to leave you.'

'Once again, Professor, you're stumbling before the finish line: Philippe couldn't leave me.'

She lets the tears flow, and catches one with her tongue.

'I couldn't let him leave with that child. I just couldn't believe he ever thought he could. That child belongs to me.' She pounds at her chest with her fist. 'I summoned him and he came to me. *Me*. I'm his mother, even though I didn't carry him. And *he* was going to take him away from me?'

Her voice is faltering as she tries to stop crying.

'There we were, at last, getting the child we wanted so badly, and he was going to snatch him away from me? With another woman?' Her hair starts to dance as she shakes her head. 'No, no, no. Not that.'

She sniffs, then sighs.

'Lucienne and I have that in common: the children we've had taken away.'

Gina sits up straight. 'No one took Lucienne's children away, Pauline.'

'What are you on about? You don't know Lucienne's story.'

'Oh yes, I do. Of course I know it. Lucienne Lelanger's two daughters died at an early age while the family was living in Paris.'

'Exactly. In a fire.'

'No. Not in a fire.'

Gina waits for a second.

Pauline gives her an avid, anxious look.

'Lucienne killed her two little girls, Pauline. She drugged them, then locked them in a trunk and set fire to it. The fire razed their townhouse to the ground.'

A stain is spreading between Pauline's legs, darkening her inner thighs, trickling down her calves. Urine pools at her feet, spreading out beyond the legs of her chair.

'Lucienne Lelanger killed her two daughters so she could be free to live in love with her cousin Mary. That's why she was locked up at Clarence Manor. To avoid the guillotine in Paris.'

Pauline's face creases with silent tears. The way her mouth is contorted, she looks like a sad clown.

'Lucienne cheated you, Pauline. She cheated you, lied to you and manipulated you. Your transgressions were her victories. Her domination of you and your life was her wicked pleasure.'

60
Lina
1951

I let go of Mother's clammy hand, then get up and cross the nave. The shuffling of my sandals barely breaks the silence. My heart is pounding as I walk up to the lectern. Not because I'm nervous, but because I'm buzzing with impatience: in a few seconds' time, I'll know if God will fear me or punish me.

I place my hands where Father Dion and Father Tremblay usually open their Bible to lecture us on the importance of forgiveness or about repentance and the divine forces at work in the world.

Just a few days ago, I was standing at the centre of the magic circle, dressed only in Tamara's cardigan stained with Julie's blood – the blood of a virgin with a pure heart. I stood facing Och, the Sun, and felt its power shining bright on me.

I look up at the weeping mourners. At their sad faces. Those of Julie's parents and brothers, torn apart by the pain.

I wait for a moment. They'll grant me these few seconds; they'll think grief is getting the better of me, giving me a lump in my throat and muting my voice. I'm waiting for a sign from God, to tell me He won't let me speak. Not in His house. But His objection doesn't come.

My skin bristles with goosebumps in spite of the stifling heat in the church.

I think about the wave of heat that surged through my body when I invoked Och. As if I was suddenly standing in front of a raging fire or beneath the blazing sun. I raised my arms overhead, marking Hagith and Phaleg, Venus and Mars. I summoned the demons, chanting the words to make them come, one more time: 'Bagabi laca bachabé, Lamac cahi achababé, Karrelyos, Lamac lamec Bachalyas, Cabahagy sabalyos, Baryolos, Lagoz atha cabyolas, Samahac et famyolas, Harrahya.'

I draw in some air before I begin to recite my poem. Then I breathe it all out and declaim, in a strong, clear voice:
"'Do not stand at my grave and weep.
I am not there.
I do not sleep.
I am a thousand winds that blow.
I am the diamond glints on snow.'"

Then I extended my arms out to my sides, towards Bethor and Ophiel, Mercury and Jupiter. 'Bagabi laca bachabé, Lamac cahi achababé, Karrelyos, Lamac lamec Bachalyas, Cabahagy sabalyos, Baryolos, Lagoz atha cabyolas, Samahac et famyolas, Harrahya.'

"'I am the sunlight on ripened grain.
I am the gentle autumn rain.'"

I held my hands out behind me, pointing them to the ground, to Phuel and Aratron, to the Moon and Saturn, chanting 'Harrahya', my head swaying from left to right, my feet tapping a beat at the centre of the circle, stomping the beads of my sweat into the droplets of Julie's blood. They were there. They heard me. They were listening to me. I could sense them. And I was dancing, dancing, dancing for them, for them to come and stay with me. Then a quiver of pleasure suddenly seized my lower abdomen; it rose up into my chest, then burst like a bubble in my heart. Like one of Paul's kisses. Except, it wasn't just one soul kissing me, touching me, sliding inside me.

"'When you awaken in the morning's hush;
I am the swift uplifting rush of quiet birds in circled flight.
I am the soft stars that shine at night.'"
That's where I stop.

Lucienne advised me to cut the last verse; for that I must apologise to the poem's author. 'Do not stand at my grave and cry; I am not there; I did not die' seemed a bit too spiritual to blurt out to parents grieving the loss of their fifteen-year-old daughter.

'There are no words, no thoughts, no wisdom, not even of a divine order, to console you,' I continue, with a sorrowful yet dignified look to Julie's family sitting in the front pew. 'Nothing can ease your pain or your grief. But it may comfort you to know that our beloved friend and classmate Julie, with her kindness, her generosity, her laughter and her grace, will forever mark our memory. Dear, sweet, Julie, may you rest in peace.'

As I lower my eyes and see my hands gripping the lectern, I think about the sticky sweat that coated my palms that night.

I release my grip and step down from the lectern to acknowledge the appreciative smiles of Father Tremblay and Father Dion, as well as those streaked with tears of Julie's parents and brothers. I see Mrs Morin's satisfied smile, and my mother's proud grin. I greet the tears and the sniffles of the mourners with gratitude.

God has opened his house to me. And I have made myself at home.

Harrahya
Harrahya
Harrahya

61
Maxine
2002

The only thing I want to pull on is a comfy sweater. I know the occasion calls for a tailored blouse or a fitted top more than some shapeless knitwear, but I just don't have it in me to endure the sight of a body I no longer recognise, or to squeeze myself into something that's going to be uncomfortable all evening.

Pauline has been transferred to Montreal; the incident room in Lac-Clarence has been shut down.

Soon we'll know the identity of the three young women whose bodies were buried near the folly. It'll be a longer process for the victims whose hands the Carons severed, but they shall not remain nameless. We don't know if there are more than these ten victims. Marceau has instigated a huge operation to search the entire Caron and Lelanger properties with sniffer dogs. And Pauline will end up talking, Gina is sure she will.

Settling for a black sweatshirt with a tiny gold logo embroidered over the breast, I glance at my watch. Gina will be here soon to pick me up. We're celebrating the end of the investigation at Jules's place.

The timing's not ideal, but I have to tell my Chickadee I'm resigning to give my family a better life. What that life will look like, I don't know yet. We're going to get away from it all for a few months. Charlotte's doing much worse than I thought. We need to reconnect and lay the foundation for our new family.

The muffled vibrations of my phone echo down the hallway. I must have left it on the table by the front door. I make a dash for it, sliding in my socks, and see the phone on top of the pile of mail. I grab it and answer the call. It's Marceau.

'Pauline Caron has taken her own life.'

My cry sounds like someone gasping for breath before their head is forced underwater.

'But ... wasn't she put on suicide watch?'

'She was, yes. Somehow she managed to get her hands on the shoulder strap from her lawyer's handbag and hang herself with it. But she left us a list of her victims. We have the names and the dates.'

'Does she mention any more victims than the ten we know about?'

'No. Case closed, Lieutenant Grant.'

I let the silence stretch out. Marceau waits patiently. Or maybe she's just doing something else in the background. Then she hangs up.

My heart feels like it's going to beat out of my chest.

'Case closed.' That's what Marceau said.

I'm trying to wrap my head around the news as I make my way back down the hallway. When I get to my room, I find Charlotte standing in front of my wardrobe.

'Shasha, what are you doing there?'

She's rooted to the spot, head bowed forwards. I wonder if she's heard me come in.

'Charlotte?' I persist, moving closer to her.

'Mum, what's...' Slowly, she turns around. She's holding a zip-lock bag. And in that bag is a phone.

I take a step backwards.

'Why do you have Philippe's phone?'

'What? What are you talking about, Charlotte?'

'This! It was hidden in there.' She steps aside and points to my travel bag, which is lying wide open on the floor.

'Why are you going through my things?'

'You're the one asking *me*?'

Her head is bobbing quickly up and down, like she's got the shakes. Suddenly, there's nothing childlike about her.

'Do you really want to know? I've got my period, Mum. And I'm out of tampons. I looked everywhere for some. Then I thought about your travel bag. Up there, on the top shelf.'

She moves towards me, holding the zip-lock bag out for me to see.

'This is Philippe Caron's phone, Mum,' she says, shaking the bag beside her face. 'It's the pay-as-you go phone he bought so the two of us could talk to one another. See the little sticker here? I was the one who put it there.'

Her eyes are filled with horror.

'Why do you have this phone, Mum?'

Now my heart is in my mouth. It's pounding.

'You told me the police hadn't found it. That's what you said, Mum. When I said I was scared the police would trace the phone to me, you told me not to worry, that everything would be all right. You said it hadn't been found. You said *you* hadn't found it!'

That was what I told her, yes.

She's clinging to me with those horrified eyes.

'Mum? Mu-um!'

62
Lina
2002

It's only the second time I've come to the folly alone since I've known Philippe. The first time was the day we met, decades ago. That almost seems like it was in another life.

For some weeks now, he's been distant, and that worries me. Or rather, it makes me feel insecure. These last few months, I've had the feeling he's been somewhere else. He's not preoccupied, no. I know when he's worried about something. This is something deeper. Any woman's thoughts would turn to an extramarital affair, a mistress. But such things, unworthy of what unites us, have never crossed my mind. We have an ancestral bond. Our roots have woven and tangled themselves together over many lives, like the brambles growing over the graves of Tristan and Iseult.

I undress, gripping the vial of blood in one hand. It hasn't completely thawed, and it slides between my fingers like a slippery fish.

I lie down on the table, shivering with cold. The music is floating around me without flowing into me. I turn to my left, foolishly searching for Philippe. His voice, his words, his body. He moves with a wizard's grace and sings with a fierce passion the names of those we worship and for whom we dance. I lift my neck from the table, neglecting to begin the incantation, as if I've forgotten how to do this without him. I miss his hands so much. Their warmth, their caress. His gaze saturated with desire, admiration and love for me, for our life, our vision, even my ageing curves.

I smile. And as I'm about to uncork the vial of blood, I straighten almost bolt upright to sit on the edge of the table. The word 'ageing' is grating on my nerves. Ageing.

My thoughts turn to his frequent trips to Montreal these last few weeks. His sallow tone. His restless nights.

I can feel a ball of anxiety rising in my throat.

Philippe is ill. Gravely ill.

I put the vial back in the freezer, get dressed and leave the folly. I almost forget about the biting cold and finish buttoning up my coat outside in the snow.

I'm the one they chose, not Philippe. I can only protect him if I keep him under my wing.

I quicken my step, wondering why he hasn't said anything, why he would rather spare me the details. We've always worked together, so why keep me in the dark now? There are so many ways to fight sickness, to make it go away; he knows that. Or is it already too late?

I forge ahead in the night, my every question more terrifying than the last. When I reach the house, I see our car parked out front, as well as another I don't recognise. I scale the porch steps with my heart in my mouth, wondering who could be paying us a visit: a doctor, perhaps? I hope I won't have long to wait before I can talk to Philippe face to face. I open the door, wonder what he might be suffering from, and how much time we have to reverse the course of things. But the voice I hear is high-pitched and screaming, and it's not his. It's a woman's voice: I know it, but I can't quite place it.

I hurry into the living room, not bothering to even take off my boots.

63
Maxine
2002

'Mum? Mu-um!'

Charlotte's yelling. Then she starts to cry. I hold my arms open for her automatically. I'm her mother; she's supposed to cry on my shoulder.

Then I lower my arms. She won't come to me.

'I just wanted to protect you,' I say.

'Protect me from what? What are you talking about, Mum?'

If I lose her, I lose everything.

'Mum!'

'From him.'

'From Philippe?'

I nod.

Her teeth are chattering so hard, her lips are trembling too.

My little pearl. My daughter. My child.

'Mum, did you see Philippe, the night he died?'

I lower my eyes. I can't stand her looking at me anymore.

'It was you who ... no, no, no, no, no...'

Now all I can see are her feet, the chipped glittery varnish on her toenails. She's curling her toes like a cat. Then suddenly, she stops.

'Maxine?'

It's Gina's voice, behind me.

I turn around.

'Sorry, but you weren't answering my calls to your mobile. I didn't want to ring the doorbell and wake Hugo up, and the door was unlocked...'

'It was her. She's the one who took my Philippe away from me.' My daughter's in tears; her mouth is twisted in anger. 'She took my Philippe away!'

'Your Philippe was nothing but a monster, Charlotte. He killed, dismembered and drained the blood of I don't know how many victims,' I say.

'That's not true. I know it's not. She's the witch. His wife. She's the crazy one. She's the monster. Philippe told me so. She was the one who forced him to ... to ... do everything. He didn't want to leave her because he was afraid of her. Philippe was the gentlest man I knew. He would never have...'

'Because you've never known another, Charlotte. You don't understand. He's the one who wanted to take you away from me, not the other way around!'

I'm screaming louder than I've ever screamed.

'He stole your life away from you, Charlotte. Can't you see that? Since you met him, you've been nothing but a shadow of yourself. He took everything away from you. He took everything away from *me*!'

'*You're* the one who took it all away from us. Even our child!'

'Your child? You think a pregnancy makes you a mother, do you?'

I press my face to hers.

She's so ungrateful.

'No, it's the eternity that comes after those nine months that makes you a mother. Being a mother, that's what I've done for you – for Hugo and for you. To protect you both. But you, you don't see any of that, through those selfish, irresponsible teenage eyes of yours. I, your mother, I'd just lost the love of my life when you decided to throw yours away.'

There's a hollow sound as my index finger prods at my chest.

I can feel my husband's hand on my shoulder, trying to calm me down.

No, it's Gina's hand.

'And I had to make your mistake my own, Charlotte. Do you realise that? Getting pregnant at sixteen ... for fuck's sake. After all those hours talking to you about contraception, love, pleasure, sexuality and the importance of saying "no". Only realising when it was too late to get an abortion.'

I'm pounding my chest now.

'And I'm the one – me! – who took your life away from you?'

I choke back my tears.

'I was the only one holding your hand while you gave birth to *my* son, at home, because that's what being a mother is all about, Charlotte. It's about putting your child first. Before yourself. All the time. If your son became mine, it was out of my love for *you*, so that you could pick up your life where you left it – your childhood. Because at seventeen, you're still a child.'

I sniff and wipe my sleeve across my face, leaving a trail of snot on my cheek.

'So, when I got home that night, and I found your letter telling me you were leaving...' I release a sob. I'm gasping for breath. 'Telling me you were leaving to be with that man – not the love of your life, like you wrote, but the man who stole that life from you – and you were taking *my* son with you as well, then of course I went to get you back. Both of you. Ask Gina: *she* knows what it's like to be a mother.'

Gina hasn't taken her hand off my shoulder. She tightens her grip. She can feel the anger tensing every one of my muscles.

'You know what he said to me, your Philippe, when I got to his place?'

I'm not saying the words, I'm spewing them. There's nothing but anger leaving my body.

'I begged him to let you live your teenage life. I tried to explain that he was depriving you of your future – your bright future, you being such a bright student. That if you started to raise a child, now, at your age, you'd be left with nothing. And you know what he replied, that Philippe of yours? He said it wasn't just your life anymore, you were a couple, so it was his as well. He was dragging you down with him already. Like Pauline did to him. He told me I was sucking the life out of you – vampirising you, the intellectual shit stain actually said that. He accused me of stealing your life from you.'

I throw my head back and open my mouth wide to draw in a deep breath of air.

'"You're stealing her child," that Philippe of yours said. "You're stifling your daughter and robbing her of her future. You're living by proxy, Maxine." Then you know what he said next?' I sigh, but it comes out as a grunt. '"Maybe you wish I'd put that child in *your* belly, eh, Maxine?" He said that to me right in front of his wife, can you imagine? That monster. And then he picked up that phone,' I point to the zip-lock bag Charlotte's still holding in her clenched fist, 'and he said, "Why don't you call that daughter of yours and tell her that's what you wanted, eh?"'

'That was when my rage sent me across the line; that was when I stopped being rational and my emotions took over. And I succumbed to my urges. Straight away. I tore that fucking phone from his hand and I shut him up. I pushed him, because all I wanted was to see him knocked off his feet. Just to see him knocked to the ground.'

Bracing my hands on my thighs, I bend forwards to catch my breath, but tears are all that come. Because at last, I understand that it all ends here, with Gina's hand on my shoulder.

'Maxine?'

Gina's voice jolts me back, to her and to Charlotte.

'Maxine, where's Hugo?'

He's had a child with another woman.

Not me.

He's the father.

Of a child.

Who did not come from me.

A child whose mother I am not.

A child conceived with a child.

I reach one hand to the back of the sofa to steady myself. My head is spinning. The whole room is spinning. It feels like the ground is opening up beneath my feet. I lean my other hand into the cushion. I look down at my dirty boots, as if to check they're still on solid ground, then I turn my eyes to Philippe. The man I shaped into the man he deserved to be. Truth be told, the man I wanted him to become: a man who would never behave like a man. 'The only loyal, loving and faithful man is a woman, Lina,' Lucienne used to say to me. And she was right, as always: I shaped Philippe to be like a woman.

I see his lips pursed in defiance, his condescending sneer. His delicate hands. But he doesn't even look at me. He's not squirming away from me. He's ignoring me, shutting me out, as if I wasn't even in the room. As if I hadn't walked right in as Maxine was begging him not to ruin her daughter's life.

Suddenly, he turns to me. His arrogance cloaks him like a second skin. He's like a stranger to me.

'I'm the chosen one,' he tells me defiantly. 'And this child of mine is the proof. I'm the chosen one, not you.'

I shake my head, close my eyes.

I open them again and see him still wearing his taunting smirk, as he's accusing Maxine of being a bad mother. A jealous, selfish mother.

Maxine gives me a pleading look. She knows Philippe won't back down. She knows he'll take her daughter and grandson away from her.

But I can't bring myself to step in and intervene. I can barely stay standing. I have no idea what lies ahead for us in the next minute or so.

He keeps pointing the finger at her, as if it wasn't enough to be taking everything from her. He's not himself anymore. That man, standing in front of me, is a bully. A tormentor. Like Tamara. My tormentor, and Maxine's. Her daughter's too. And that child's.

I was right: he's a sick man. His soul is sick.

Maxine is crying. She has understood, this is a battle she won't win.

He moves closer to her. 'Maybe you wish I'd put that child in *your* belly, eh, Maxine?'

All of a sudden, my heart is in my mouth. I take a step backwards.

He puts his hand in his pocket and pulls out a mobile phone I've never seen before.

'Why don't you call that daughter of yours and tell her that's what you wanted, eh?' he says, holding the phone out to her.

I open my mouth, but my cries suffocate in my throat.

Maxine storms towards him, screaming, as if I'd given my voice to her. She snatches the phone out of his hands and shoves him with a rage I feel I am fuelling. It's like she's become a weapon in my hands. Like there are two of us pushing him to the ground. I can see the surprise in Philippe's eyes. He reminds me of Julie, right before she died.

His head hits the mantelpiece so hard it snaps back on itself. He crumples to the floor, like he's a marionette and she's suddenly snipped his strings.

Maxine recoils. She doesn't look at me. It's as if she's forgotten I'm here as well. She backs away, until she bumps into the side table. She seems to hesitate for a moment, turns her horrified eyes to Philippe, to the chimney, the table and the floor, then she turns and runs away, breathless.

The front door creaks open, but I don't hear it closing again.

Philippe isn't moving. He's slumped in that strange, inhuman position. Yes, that's it: like a marionette whose strings have been snipped.

I can't allow him to exist without me, without those strings, those bonds, those roots that define me.

I can't let him leave with that child. The child I summoned and who came to me. I'm the chosen one. That child belongs to me.

'You mark my words, Philippe,' I say out loud. 'You will not have a child without me.'

65
Charlotte
2002

I check the time on my phone.

I've been waiting for Philippe nearly three hours now. It feels like it's been ten times longer, though. The kid just won't shut up. He's been crying the whole time since we got here. I took him out of the baby carrier and put him on the sofa, but as soon as I put him down he started screaming. After a while, I had to put him back in the baby carrier. My shoulders were killing me. I couldn't hold him anymore. It didn't matter what position I sat in, my muscles were frozen stiff and I was scared I'd drop him.

I decided not to bring his pram when I left home. It would have been too complicated to take it on the bus. We'll take care of all that stuff later, me and Philippe. We'll go back and fetch his stuff, and mine. All I brought were some clothes, plus his bag with a pack of nappies, some formula and two bottles. I'll use tap water: the kid's not going to drop dead if I don't put mineral water in the formula for a feed or two. That said, I forgot his dinner. So, I've just put a bit more in his bottle for his bedtime feed, and I'll feed him a bit more if he wakes up tonight. But first, he's going to have to fall asleep. As soon as I take him out of the baby carrier, though, he just screams his head off.

Tomorrow morning, I'll go out and get some baby food. I'll never have Mum's kind of patience to prepare all his meals. Neither will Philippe, I don't think.

I undo the baby carrier.

I'm so done with this kid and his screaming. I can't take it anymore. I really, really need to pee. And there's no way I'm sitting on the toilet with him in my arms.

'For fuck's sake, Hugo, will you just shut up!'

I put him down on the sofa again, on his back, and jam a couple of cushions beside him so he won't fall if he turns over.

He's red in the face, blood red, red with rage.

'Shhhh,' I keep shushing as I back away towards the bathroom.

I pee with one eye on the time on my phone. Hugo's still screaming in the background. I'm going to call Philippe. He should be here. He should have been here a while ago. No ... no ... I'll text him first.

Are you on your way? I type.

He asked me to meet him here, with Hugo. At his apartment on Crescent Street. My Philippe. At last. At last, we're going to be able to see each other without sneaking around.

During the pregnancy, I kept reliving in my mind the moment when he 'tied my heart in knots', as he likes to put it. I was at a literary evening hosted by a bookshop downtown, where a number of authors, including Philippe, had come to talk about their latest book. I had read two of his previous titles before to prepare for a presentation, but I had never met him. When I got up to ask him a question, my legs were shaking like never before. Then he turned his eyes to me. Right then. That very moment. That was the moment that decided all the rest.

It's hell, hearing Hugo's screams. Absolute hell.

I should stay in the bedroom. And leave him in the living room to cry it out. Maybe he'll end up so exhausted he just crashes. At home, I put earplugs in. But he never cries for as long as this. Mum comes running at the slightest sign of tears.

She's always told me how much she wanted me. How happy she was to hear she was expecting me. That wasn't how things were for me, with Hugo.

'Shhhhh, shut up, just stop, shhhh, shut the fuck up,' I whisper in his ear.

I'm rocking from one foot to the other.

No matter what Philippe says, I don't really feel like Hugo's mother. It'll come, I know; that's what Philippe keeps telling me anyway, and I believe him. But it won't happen overnight. It didn't even feel like I was carrying him in my belly, you know. Pregnancy denial is kind of a crazy thing. Even when I saw him come out of me, there was only one thing that struck me, and that was the pain. I keep thinking about that every time I hold him in my arms.

I look at my phone again: still no answer from Philippe.

So I call him.

But it just rings and rings.

I try again.

Fifteen rings.

Why isn't he answering?

'What the hell?' I scream.

Hugo just butted his little head against my breast. I can't believe how much it hurt.

'All you do is torture me. Is there nothing else you can do?' I seethe.

But he just clenches his little fists and does it again.

Just keep on screaming, why don't you!

Mum didn't even clean him up. When he was born. She wrapped him in a bath towel and plonked him right on my chest. And he just started pecking away at me like a freaking woodpecker. Like he's doing now. Except back then, he wasn't as strong, and he didn't have teeth either. He was looking for my breast, that's what Mum said. But I didn't want him sticking his mouth on me. To me, that was ... I don't know ... I mean, of course the primary function of a breast is to feed – or 'nurse' – a baby, but still. Even just the thought of having a kid sucking on me makes me feel like a dairy cow. My breasts have been touched by Philippe's fingers and lips. I just can't see myself sticking that kid's mouth down there.

But what if…?

No, no, I have to get that idea out of my head. Philippe is still coming to meet me, of course he is. If something had come up, he would have called me.

I stick my fingers in my ears. I'm still swaying left to right. Hugo seems surprised. He stops screaming, but only for a second. He's screeching now. I swear he must be losing his voice. But still, he won't stop. It's like he's trying harder. On and on he goes. He's even turning up the volume.

'That's it, knock yourself out. Cry your throat off, see if I care,' I mutter.

When I found out I was pregnant, I felt like I was sinking into a life that wasn't my own. Ah, the lightness of those few secret rendezvous with Philippe, this phone he bought especially for our conversations, this love of ours that didn't care at all about the age difference. All of that fell away, heavy as a stone, as soon as the pregnancy test turned positive.

I'm going to call him again.

Again, it just rings and rings.

What the hell is going on?

I try again.

Fifteen, sixteen rings – and nothing.

I hang up.

'Just stop it, will you Hugo, please! Or else you'll have me crying too. All you have to do is stop crying, can't you see? I can't take any more of this. Do you hear me?'

I've just screamed louder than him. But it's like he's just not hearing me.

I haven't told Mum who Hugo's father is. I just let her believe it was a first-time-gone-wrong kind of thing. I told her I wouldn't hear another word about the father; that actually wasn't so far from the truth, because when I told Philippe the news, he panicked and broke up with me. The ground opened up beneath my feet. It really did. I felt uprooted. Philippe brought some texture, some nuance into my life. I'm not just talking about the pleasures he introduced me to, but also his love, his presence and his company – the way he made me see things through his eyes. The way he took me under his wing. Suddenly, without him, everything seemed flat, empty and dead. There were two hearts beating inside me, but I'd never felt so alone and so empty.

Philippe eventually called me on our phone a few days after Hugo was born, as if he'd sensed our child had been born. He told me I was the love of his life. He said he wanted us to be a family, he wanted us to raise Hugo together. He just needed some time to leave Pauline. To be sure that witch wouldn't have a go at me or Hugo. It just made me love him even more.

'Will you just ... shut ... up! I can't take any more of your crying, Hugo.'

Maybe he's hungry because he hasn't had his dinner. The bottle can't have been enough for him.

I walk over to the kitchenette. I don't know why, but I can't stop swaying left and right. He's really screaming bloody murder now.

'Shhhhh ... I'm going to feed you ... Stop ... just stop, will you?'

I get a bottle ready for him, but I don't bother to heat it up, just so I can get it in him faster. Then I shove the teat in his mouth.

And just like that, he stops crying.

Omigod.

Oh. My. God.

I close my eyes.

Breathe a sigh of relief.

Silence. At last.

That was hell. I've never heard him cry so hard, or so long.

Maybe he misses Mum.

I've been thinking about how to explain things to Mum so she won't worry, so she'll understand I'm grateful for what she did for me, but that now, Philippe and I want to take care of our child and be a family at last. We're going to live here, in his apartment on Crescent Street. She'll always be welcome to visit. Mum knows Philippe. He's a mature, respectable man. He's capable of looking after us.

Hugo spits up his milk and starts crying again.

'Nooooo...' I scream in retaliation. 'Shut up!'

I shove the teat back into his gaping mouth. He coughs and opens his eyes wide, as if he's choking on it. I pull it right out again. He draws a big, wheezing breath, then he starts crying again. He's screaming right in my ear now.

I clamp my hand over his mouth.

'That's enough. Don't you understand what it means to shut up? I'm so done with hearing you scream. Stop it. Just stop it!'

I push my hand down harder, so I won't hear another sound from his mouth.

'Stop it. Stop. Stop stop stop, I said, Hugo!'

There. There...

He's stopped.

Finally.

Silence, at last.

Finally, the sound of silence. Then his head falls forwards. And lands right on my breast.

66
Gina
2002

'Maxine, where's Hugo?' I ask.

She grabs hold of the door frame with one hand, then clamps the other over her mouth and bends forwards. She's sobbing into her palm. Her whole body is shaking.

Charlotte's gaze falls to the floor.

Maxine sniffles and slowly stands up straight.

'I got there too late ... I was on my way back from ... from the Caron place ... when Charlotte called and asked me to come and get her ... them ... and I got there too late...'

I close my eyes. In horror. In pain. Then I take her in my arms and stroke her hair. Her sobs are like spasms, shuddering right through her. I hold her tight so she can let it all out. So she can let go of everything she's been holding in.

'It all happened so fast. I didn't have time to think ... to plan. We'd only just got home when Marceau phoned and asked me to go to the crime scene – at the Caron place.'

She stops herself, shakes her head and then clings to my sweater.

'I thought ... I thought Pauline had turned me in, you know? But no ... no ... she was just asking for me ... because I'm from there, from Lac-Clarence. And then when I got there, I saw she'd stabbed her husband, so I thought that, maybe, I don't know ... it was a sign, you know? That I might be able to get us out of ... all this. Pauline would have killed Philippe, anyway...'

She exhales through a gaping mouth. Her sigh sounds like a death rattle.

'I just kept saying to myself, *Retrace your steps, retrace your steps, Maxine, before forensics get here*. To explain my boot prints, you know?'

She closes her eyes and squeezes her eyelids tight. As if that could rid her of the calculation, the coldness of the acts that disgust and horrify her now.

'Every time she spoke to you, Gina ... I ... I was afraid, I was so afraid...'

She's digging her nails into me.

'I couldn't bury him ... my Hugo ... My child ... my son. The ground is frozen. I couldn't bury him. My little piece of Heaven ... my God. My God...'

She nuzzles her face in my neck. Then she wails in despair. To let it all out. The absence of her son, the pain of her loss, the terror of the aftermath. She screams it all out. The horror of what she did. What her daughter did. She screams out everything she's been holding in.

And then, as I cradle her in my arms, I bring my mouth close to her ear.

'Maxine, will you tell me where Hugo is?'

She coughs, catches her breath.

'Outside ... in his pram...'

I can see it now, the navy-blue pram I've walked past every time I've come to visit. Parked by the front door, out on the porch. With the sun shade pulled up. And the rain cover over the top.

67
Gina
2002

A breeze dances across the lawn. It caresses my face, sends a quiver through my apple tree in blossom and brushes against Jules, who's sitting in a deckchair beside me; then it frolics away towards the children, at the other end of the garden. The well-behaved troupe is working in silence, focusing on every movement. Amélie, the eldest of my grandchildren, is running the show. Tongue sticking out, cheeks puffed in concentration, she's carrying tubes of paint, sponges, brushes and stencils to a wooden table that wears the stripes of our previous experiments.

Jules's youngest suddenly runs over to us, brush in hand. 'Gina, is it true we can paint those planks of wood over there?' she asks, pointing to the fence around the raspberry bushes.

'Yes, that's right.'

'And the pots too? The ones with plants in already? Amélie said we could, but I wanted to make super, duper sure.'

'Yes, and yes.'

Now Jules's daughter parts her lips and looks at me as if I've just given her the moon. She shifts her gaze to him and flashes him a winning smile. Then she runs off again, crying 'Gina's so awesome!', long hair billowing behind her like a superheroine's cape.

'It's like I'm the one she's abandoned, you know?' Jules murmurs, all of a sudden. He hasn't taken his eyes off the kids. 'I keep looking for her everywhere. That's crazy, don't you think?'

I reach an arm out. He takes my hand and holds it in his, then lowers our interlaced fingers to the narrow armrest.

'I didn't see how much she was struggling,' he continues. 'I didn't see a thing. I just put it all down to the kid. All those sleepless nights in the beginning, you know?'

He gives the rosé a swirl in his glass. The wine gets a bit too carried away.

'I get the sense it all started after her parents passed away. It's like she never picked up the pieces.' He shakes her head. 'And then when her husband died. It was so brutal, Gina ... and Hugo, that kid ... can you imagine? The timing when he came along?'

I think back to the navy-blue pram we collapsed and put on top of the suitcases in the back of Maxine's car.

With a shiver, I tug my cardigan across my chest.

It's not what I did that's rattling me. And it's not the lying, either. It's the heap of tragedies Maxine and Charlotte ended up stumbling over. They deserved a different life.

I take a sip of the Bandol in my glass without saying a word.

'Pauline Caron might well have been the straw that broke the camel's back,' Jules continues. 'It's like there was a whole new side of Maxine somehow, and it all came crashing down with that woman. She must have been tearing up her roots one by one, all this time. Do you know what I mean?'

The children's green and yellow shapes are overlapping, all over the fence. Every new splotch of paint triggers a burst of laughter.

'Maybe that's just what she needed to do, you know,' he adds. 'Put down roots somewhere else. Make a fresh start. For the three of them. For her, for Charlotte and for Hugo. In the absence of those who passed. Far away from those who passed.'

I squeeze his hand in my palm. A silent yes. Because our children never leave us. They're the tune we just can't stop humming.

'You know, Gina, I'm not surprised she left without saying goodbye.'

He marks a pause. Drowns his thoughts in the bottom of his glass.

'Still, I wish she had surprised me. It would have been nice for her to give me a kiss goodbye, don't you think?'

He forces a laugh, then washes it down with a sip of wine.

I give his hand another squeeze, and raise my glass.

'To your Sweet Maxine.'

He smiles.

'To Sweet Maxine.'

Acknowledgements

Finally, I feel I've managed to bring a literary baby into this world without it being accompanied by one made out of flesh and blood!

I know what Freud (or Gina, for that matter) would have to say about this story of mine (no comment!). But this story is what connects me, the writer, to you, the reader. Because you and I, we share a desire. We both feed each other, and neither of us can function without the other.

This story was conceived with my friend and research partner Eva, who opened my eyes one day to the secret society known as the Golden Dawn. And so, I plunged first into the depths of nineteenth-century London, then Paris in the Belle-Époque. As one anecdote and one book led to another, I found myself slipping into a cauldron with two, three witches, and ended up deciding to revisit the Golden Dawn in a future story of mine instead (sorry, Mr Crowley).

The Bleeding would never have come to be without my writing fairy godmother, Lilas Seewald, whose hand I'm thrilled to be holding as we embark on this new chapter with the fabulous team at my French publisher, Calmann-Lévy.

Huge thanks to Caroline Lépée and Philippe Robinet for welcoming me so warmly into their home, which I'm so proud to represent here.

Massive thanks to Roxanne Bouchard, my Quebec friend and fellow author, for sharing her words and passion for her homeland that remind me so much of the Catalan fervour. Thank you, my dear Roxanne, for your edits, your suggestions and the time you spent telling me about your home and your people.

Thank you to Caroline 'JM' Vallat, my favourite bookseller, for the passion she puts into promoting books and reading. This last couple of years more than ever, we all needed a dose of her amazing energy!

Thank you to Bruno Lamarque, my brother in the South, for his advice, ideas and casual conversations about Maxine, Lina and Lucienne. My three heroines became stronger and more alive because of you.

Many thanks to David Warriner, my terrific English translator for his invaluable assistance; to forensic researcher Alexandre Beaudoin, for his patient and essential explanations and corrections; and to Delphine Curan, for the incredible information and the amazing roads she led me down – right to the aforementioned witches' cauldron.

Thank you to Karen Sullivan for her confidence, her energy and the passion she puts into promoting her authors. Thank you to West Camel for always bringing a fresh pair of eyes to spiff up my words, and to the whole Orenda crew, especially Anne, Cole and Max, without whom my books would never travel as far.

Thank you to the Lagunas-Langlasse clan for their unfailing support: to my sister Elsa for always being there, day and night, for her precious feedback and her all-seeing psychologist's eye; to my mum for her words of encouragement that always seem to come at just the right time when I'm starting to doubt myself; to my Papou, for his reading patience and our criminal conversations over one dead body or another; and thank you to my clan of Vikings – husband, little dragons and all – whose love and laughter shine a ray of healing sunshine on everything.

And thank YOU, dear readers. Thank you for your support that has kept me going and really helped me through this last couple of years. I'm looking forward to seeing you again and making up for lost time. So much. Let's talk, let's laugh, let's share a glass of wine (or two) and some good cheese, and then let's laugh some more. Maybe we'll even shed a tear or two – of joy, I mean!

London, 2 April 2022

AN EXCLUSIVE EXTRACT FROM

Yule Island

By Johana Gustawsson

Translated by David Warriner

Forthcoming in winter 2023

1
Karl
29 December 2012

This morning I opened my eyes to the nape of my wife's neck and a tangle of strands. My nose fumbled its way to the heart of the messy matter. I parted her curls with my breath to find her skin. And with just the tips of my lips, I kissed her. Again and again, until she quivered. I paused to savour the morning lushness of her mouth, that dewy sound it makes. Then I started all over again.

An hour and twenty minutes later, I'm here on the island of Storholmen, on the other side of the bay. A majestic evergreen towers proudly in front of me, sprinkled with frost like something out of a Christmas story.

The nape of the neck I'm looking at now hangs from the branches.

The icy air burns the back of my throat like a shot of *snaps*.

I free my boots from the grip of the compacted snow with a struggle and move in for a closer look. The rope has lifted her blonde hair up to her cheeks. It looks like there are two clownish tufts sprouting from her ears. She's dangling from a low branch, practically right up against the trunk of the tree, her feet hovering thirty centimetres above the ground.

I place my thumb and index finger on her shoulder. The latex of my gloves sticks to her frozen skin and, for a few dilated seconds, all I see is the mauve of my fingers, a glaring blemish on an immaculate backdrop. Cautiously, I rotate the body towards me. The rope creaks on the branch.

Her eyes are wide open.

I close mine for a moment. She's young. Good God, she's so young. A child. Fourteen, fifteen years old at most. Under the tangle of hair and the rope, there's a leather cord. Attached to it, like an oversized pendant, is a pair of open scissors; one of the tips has nicked her bare breast – the one on the same side as her heart. A great deal of blood has flowed from the gaping cuts on her inner thighs, right at the femoral arteries. The lines are clean and smooth, sliced with seemingly surgical precision.

I crouch down to look at her feet. What I had mistaken earlier for a twig caught between her toes is in fact a black thread, binding her big toes together in a symbol of infinity that twists and turns as the body sways in the wind.

They have to cut her down now. They have to stop this child from hanging there. They have to lay her down on the ground and cover her up.

A crime-scene technician pokes his head out from the skirt of tree branches. He doesn't bother to get up, just motions for me to join him. What else – what worse thing – could be lurking there for us to find beneath this tree?

I nod, gulp, and clear the dry air from my throat with a cough, then I get down on my hands and knees and follow him under the tree's skirt.

It suddenly occurs to me that, since I got here, I've heard nothing around me other than the swishing of our coveralls and the crunching of our boots in the snow. A hushed, ominous soundtrack playing in the background. No one says a word. No one dares to. Something about this island unsettles me deeply. I feel like I have to mute the sound of my movements. And my thoughts. It's like I'm advancing into enemy territory, finger poised on the trigger of my gun.

Storholmen has imposed a silence on the muted crowd that surrounds me. A crowd that stands here listening to that silence, as to the calm before a storm.

2
Emma
22 November 2021

I pull the patchwork shawl I sewed for myself at Christmas over my shoulders and duck through the kitchen window with a steaming mug in my hand. My minuscule balcony – more of an alcove in the building's roof, really – is just big enough for me to sit out on and enjoy my morning coffee or sip a French 75 with a friend.

I barely slept a wink. The fear, trepidation and doubt all kept me awake. But also, I have to admit, the giddiness about these few weeks I'll be spending on Storholmen. I don't know if I'm up to the task I've been given. I honestly don't.

I swaddle my legs in wool and as I take a first scorching sip, I look down at the old city, which didn't get much sleep either. Stortorget Square buzzes day and night, like it's echoing with the steps of the conquerors who've crossed it over the ages. Down there, five centuries ago, eighty-two heads chopped off by a Danish tyrant sparked the Swedish resistance and ultimately heralded our independence. The imprint of time is everywhere, from the vivid heritage facades that were built to be as narrow as possible to outsmart the taxman, to the cobblestones polished by horses' hooves and the blood of the defeated. I revel in this living museum – when I get out of bed in the morning and when I get home from work at night.

Suddenly, my phone sparks to life, its light spoiling my ritual.

I glance at the screen and instinctively close my eyes.

I know I shouldn't pick up. But still, I answer the call.

'It's five in the morning, Mum.'

Silence, then a clucking of her pasty tongue against her palate and a smooching as she parts her lips.

'I have to get going soon, Mum. I—'

A dull thud makes me flinch. She must have had a fall.

Then I hear her mucousy cackle on the other end of the line.

'Swee ... tie,' she drawls drunkenly.

'I've got a hard day ahead of me, Mum.'

'*Ha ... ppy ... bir... thday ... to ... you...*'

She's singing.

I feel sick to my stomach.

'*Ha ... ppy ... bir... thday ... dear ... Em ... ma...*'

I cough to keep my tears at bay.

'You've got the date wrong, Mum,' I mutter.

I hang up and duck back inside the kitchen window, then I dash to the bathroom and give in to the nausea.

*

'Mild out, isn't it?' says the water-taxi driver, sweeping away the white strands the wind keeps blowing across her face.

My reply is drowned out by an infant's cry so shrill it makes me squint, as if my optic nerve were directly connected to my eardrums. On the other side of the cabin, a teenager with headphones in his ears is oblivious to this assault on the senses.

The woman at the helm – Lotta, her badge says – erupts with a hearty laugh that smothers the baby's laments and sets the dad at ease. Any more and he'd be ready to throw the kid overboard.

'It is,' I reply as a matter of course. Making small talk about the weather is our national sport. There's a hint of blue sky amidst the grey. It's warm for November, almost a springlike morning. 'Nine degrees – that's pretty much a summer's day!' my boss at Von Dardel's would smirk, with a soupçon of a French accent. Charlotte von Dardel's directness is refreshing. It makes a change from the convoluted Swedish politeness. Every 'no' is buried beneath so many layers of 'maybe', it takes a lot of digging to get there.

My career owes everything to Charlotte. All the women I've worked for before were so hung up on masculine ideals of success, they wore themselves out trying to prove they had the biggest proverbial you-know-what to swing around. But there's nothing misogynistic at all about the way Charlotte coaxes me up the ladder. There's rarely any parity or sisterhood in the world of work. Always enemies, never allies, the women I've encountered have been the first to pull up the drawbridge to protect whatever little ground they've fought tooth and nail to gain. In Charlotte von Dardel's eyes, sex – the stronger, the weaker or whatever – doesn't matter. Personality and competence are what really count. She judges people on the strength of their work, or how hard they hit, as she puts it, and their 'adaptability'.

A few weeks ago Charlotte offered me a 'fabulous opportunity', the kind you can't refuse at my age. And I don't want to seem ungrateful – it really is fabulous – but this springboard of an assignment is also a test. A personal and a professional one. The Gussman family, whose collection I've been asked to appraise, is the fourth wealthiest in Sweden. From what I've heard, their heirlooms could fill a museum. The thing is, this 'fabulous opportunity' means that I have to go Storholmen. To the manor house. Where the 'hanging girl', as people called her, was found.

'You look like you've seen a ghost,' Lotta exclaims, nipping my ruminations in the bud. 'We're only doing six knots, so it can't be my sporty driving making you feel queasy!'

Her gaze falls to my bag and the laptop case. Her mouth forms an 'o' of surprise.

'Ah ... You must be the expert who's coming to appraise the Gussmans' treasures. I forgot you'd be here this morning. This centennial is quite the event for us, you know. Especially as we're getting loads of grants to update the wharves and make a big celebration of it all.'

She marks a pause, unscrews the cap from a bottle of Ramlösa and takes a sip of the sparkling water.

'Although, I wouldn't be too keen about doing that particular job. Rather you than me,' she goes on, wiping her mouth with the back of her hand. 'Those Gussmans are a piece of work. If that Niklas could have his family coat of arms tattooed on his balls, he would.'

The dad glares at her. As if that kid of his, who's not walking yet and can barely babble, could even understand that kind of language. Honestly, parents these days. They get so hung up about all their standards, rules and restrictions, which they'll only end up dropping when they push out a second kid after giving the whole bloody world grief with the first one.

I laugh to show her whose side I'm on, and Lotta joins in, making me forget for a second about the silhouette of the island that's emerging ahead of us.

'You been here before?' Now we've broken the ice, Lotta's talking to me like we know each other.

I shake my head.

'You must be the only one. Since the murder of the hanging girl, I reckon all of Sweden's come here to see the place for themselves. We even had to bring in a booking system and set opening hours for off-islanders. The hordes of tourists were getting unbearable. People move to Storholmen to get some peace and quiet, not to be invaded. That's why there are no cars on the island. There's not even a corner shop. All we've got is Anneli's café, Ett Glas, and in the summer she only opens in the morning. It's a good thing we don't have a hotel, otherwise it'd be hell on earth. That's put some people off coming, but not enough, if you ask me. Sometimes, we get a few late in the season, before Halloween, but not this last couple of years, thanks to Covid. Honestly, too many people out there are voyeurs. Either that, or they're bloody masochists. If you're that afraid of death, why would you want to be around it?'

I swallow to get rid of the lump that's swelling in my dry throat. Personally, I have no desire to be at the scene of the ... the murder. And even less to be rubbing shoulders, potentially, with a killer who's still on the loose.

Lotta manoeuvres the water taxi up to the dock and pulls a lever with a hand as wrinkled as it is agile. The gangway reaches out to the landing area like a metal tongue.

'I wish you the best of luck, sweetheart. Coming here, you'd better not be afraid of ghosts.'

3
Emma

Twenty or so passengers are waiting on the south dock, in that early-morning kind of silence that extends the sleepy remnants of the night. This stream of islanders is ready to flow to work in Stockholm or on Lidingö – the big island next door that's connected to the capital by a bridge. Some will be picking up their cars in Mor Anna, the small harbour on the north side of Lidingö, where the water taxi docks. What a rigmarole to put yourself through just for a bit of peace and quiet. They must really need it if they're prepared to do all this travel, day in, day out.

The memory of another ferry boat suddenly sparks in my mind, this time in Marseille, aboard the age-old *César*: the short hop between City Hall and Place aux Huiles only took a few minutes, but it always brightened my day. They might have had sleep written all over their faces, but the people down there always had a spring in their step. There's a fire that thrives in the Mediterranean spirit. Up here, we Scandinavians throw a blanket over ours to put it out. That's if it even sparks in the first place. These dark nights will suck the life out of anything. Today, a little bit of that lively French atmosphere would really help me put one foot in front of the other. Literally, I tell myself, raising a hand in response to the old man waiting for me at the end of the gangway.

I give Lotta another smile and step off the boat behind the exhausted dad, whose kid has finally fallen asleep.

'Emma Lindahl,' the old man greets me, as if it's written on my forehead.

He's staring at me. Wild, snowy eyebrows perch like mountain summits atop his grey eyes. His mid-length hair is combed back from a broad face furrowed by wrinkles that lend him the presence of a warrior – which is somehow both reassuring and intimidating.

'Björn Petterson. You ready?' With a quick hand he smooths his beard, the tip of it tickling the collar of his parka.

'Yes, I'm ready,' I assert, thrusting my chin forward, adopting a tone and posture worthy of my title as a representative of the great Von Dardel's auction house.

'Off we go, then. Can I carry that for you?' he offers, pointing to my bag.

'I'm all right, thanks. It's not heavy.'

'As you wish,' he says, clasping his hands behind his back and striding off up the hill towards the manor so briskly, it's a stretch for my legs to keep pace. 'It's not that hard,' he adds a moment later without looking up from the rocky path, 'to get to the manor. From the south dock. Where are you from?'

'I live in Stockholm.'

'Ah,' he replies flatly. 'Lotta must have told you there's nothing on the island besides Ett Glas if you want a bite to eat. I'll let Anneli know you're here, because Gussman's not known for his hospitality, and something tells me you're not the type to cart a Thermos and a lunch box around with you.'

I'm about to protest when my heels and blood-red lipstick draw a smile out of me. If I were him, I'd make the same assumption.

'Thanks, that's very kind of you.'

He mumbles something unintelligible in reply and quickens

his step. I let him go on ahead, figuring we share the same desire for solitude.

A few minutes later, I'm adjusting the strap of my bag on my shoulder when I realise there's not a single sound to be heard on the narrow path that runs alongside these charming, unassuming houses. No engines throbbing, no dogs barking, no children crying, singing, playing or yelling, not even the slightest hint of a hushed conversation. Nothing. Only the clicking of my heels and the clunking of Björn's boots on the rocky surface. The silence makes me want to raise my voice just to breathe some life into the eerie emptiness.

'Here we are,' Björn announces without warning. He points to a little gate to the side of the path.

I stop, and my heart leaps into my mouth. I can feel it pounding.

The lower portion of the grounds, to the rear of the manor house, are home to an English country garden where nature abounds exuberantly, unbridled by human hands. Björn opens the gate and enters the estate. I follow him, reluctant to tear my eyes away from the trees. I'm looking for one in particular. The hanging girl's tree.

Grandiose, yet completely out of place on this understated island, the building towers like the stronghold of a ruler surrounded by the shantytown of his underlings. A double flight of four stone steps leads up to the main entrance, which sits beneath a semi-circular portico flanked by ivy-clad columns. Two lion-shaped knockers adorn the austere wooden front door.

Björn reaches through the vegetation to press a hidden doorbell, and we wait. After a few minutes, the door opens to reveal a man in his early forties.

This must be Niklas Gussman. The very picture of an heir to the family fortune, only too proud to show off his coat of arms, just like Lotta joked. Fair hair slicked back and greying at the temples, subtle wrinkles, white shirt with sleeves rolled up to his elbows to show off his tan and the timepiece that leaves no doubt about the depth of his inherited pockets.

'Splendid,' he purrs, his face devoid of all expression.

Björn gives him a gruff nod and disappears.

'Follow me,' the man says, his voice as gravelly as the stuff crunching beneath Björn's retreating boots, leaving me to shut the door behind myself.

I do as he says. I slip off my shoes, and he leads the way across an entrance hall that's tiled like a chess board.

I'm dying for this man to look at me and introduce himself. I want to ask him not to treat me like his subject. It's like he's in a different century. The inappropriateness of some clients can be shocking. Keeping my mouth shut is what takes the greatest toll on me in my line of work. Managing to bite my tongue and not speak my mind.

Niklas Gussman ushers me into a drawing room that looks out onto a French formal garden punctuated by majestic trees. Two pools, which must be fifty metres long, flanked by tunnels of greenery, draw the eye seaward. My host plucks a cardboard folder from a sleek writing desk and hands it to me without inviting me to sit. I wait politely for him to tell me to open it, but he remains tight-lipped and looks at me inquisitively.

There's nothing intrusive or provocative about his gaze. Rather, Niklas Gussman seems to be examining me, as if he were the appraiser here, and I were one of the objects being appraised.

'So you're the one Christie's has to thank for the 450-million-dollar sale of their *Salvator Mundi* in 2017,' he says abruptly.

'That is correct, sir,' I reply, regaining some composure.

'You were still in your twenties at the time. A stroke of luck, perhaps?'

I smile to keep the sarcasm on the tip of my tongue. 'Like Thomas Jefferson, I'm a great believer in luck, and I too find that the more I work, the more I have of it.'

'Why leave Christie's for Von Dardel's on the heels of such a triumph?'

'Von Dardel's is twice as historic an institution, and by far the

most prestigious auction and appraisal house in the Nordic countries. Not to mention that Ms von Dardel doubled my salary and offered me an obscene signing bonus.'

His eyes are still on me. It's impossible to decipher the message they're sending. For a second I even wonder if Gussman is going to tell me to leave. His next words make me instantly regret my boldness. My arrogance.

'This document sets out the schedule for your visits to the manor and the order in which you are to proceed. You will also find a map showing the layout of the premises.'

Niklas Gussman moves to the doorway, clearly to see me out.

'Your time at work here begins this afternoon at two-thirty. Knock twice to make yourself known before you enter. If you have a question, write it down on a piece of paper and leave it on the dresser in the hall. I shall leave my answer for you the next day.'

The smile I give him is certainly more curt and less amenable than politeness would require, but I'm at my wit's end.

As soon as I'm alone, out by the front steps, I open the folder and glance at its contents. It gives me a sinking feeling: the time slots are six hours at the most, and some are split in two. Bloody hell. I've worked with eccentric clients before, but none as controlling as this. There must be hundreds of heirlooms here for me to appraise. I'm nowhere near even scratching the surface of my assignment. Let alone being able to leave this wretched curse of an island.